HUNTERS OF THE DEEP

The energy in the cables continued to crescendo exponentially until the cable began whipping the DropShip at its end back and forth. The destructive energy bled into the other three cables until all four wove a pattern that could not last.

Horrified, but unable to look away, even most of the scientists stopped working to watch the coming end.

It came quickly and with brutal efficiency, as the sine waves on three of the four cables momentarily matched rhythm and descended to the anchor points at roughly the same moment. Unimaginable kinetic energy tore into the anchors, which were not designed to withstand even a fraction of such stress, buckling and snapping meters-thick composite plates.

The JumpShip's spine snapped in a glittering blizzard of shattered metal and composites, three of the four cables tearing completely away and slithering into the silence of space like snakes escaping their confines; the fourth continued to hammer the mortally wounded ship, jerking as though desperate to join its now-free comrades.

HUNTERS OF THE DEEP

A BATTLETECH® NOVEL

Randall N. Bills

A ROC BOOK

ROC
Published by New American Library, a division of
Penguin Group (USA) Inc., 375 Hudson Street,
New York, New York 10014, USA
Penguin Group (Canada), 10 Alcorn Avenue, Toronto,
Ontario M4V 3B2, Canada (a division of Pearson Penguin Canada Inc.)
Penguin Books Ltd., 80 Strand, London WC2R 0RL, England
Penguin Ireland, 25 St. Stephen's Green, Dublin 2,
Ireland (a division of Penguin Books Ltd.)
Penguin Group (Australia), 250 Camberwell Road, Camberwell, Victoria 3124,
Australia (a division of Pearson Australia Group Pty. Ltd.)
Penguin Books India Pvt. Ltd., 11 Community Centre, Panchsheel Park,
New Delhi - 110 017, India
Penguin Group (NZ), Cnr Airborne and Rosedale Roads, Albany,
Auckland 1310, New Zealand (a division of Pearson New Zealand Ltd.)
Penguin Books (South Africa) (Pty.) Ltd., 24 Sturdee Avenue,
Rosebank, Johannesburg 2196, South Africa

Penguin Books Ltd., Registered Offices:
80 Strand, London WC2R 0RL, England

First published by Roc, an imprint of New American Library,
a division of Penguin Group (USA) Inc.

First Printing, October 2004
10 9 8 7 6 5 4 3 2 1

Copyright © 2004 WizKids, LLC. All rights reserved.

Cover design by Ray Lundgren

 REGISTERED TRADEMARK—MARCA REGISTRADA

Printed in the United States of America

To Loren and Heather Coleman.

In the bleakest times, a friend's true colors are revealed. In one of my family's darkest hours, you both showed the brilliance within: a hand in aid, a shoulder for comfort, an ear to listen. True friendship is a rare and precious gift, and in that circle, you are both counted highly.

Thank you.

Acknowledgments

To my first readers, for catching some great stuff: Herb Beas, David McCulloch, Jeff Morgan, Oystein Tvedten, and especially Jason Hardy.

To Michael Miller, for the help on the spinning DropShips.

To Loren Coleman, who kept tossing additional writing projects at me during this novel and helped to prove I can do it.

To Jim Long and Janna Silverstein, for going to bat for me when they didn't need to; I hope the novel is worth the hassles that may have followed.

To Sharon Mulvihill: eight years and counting; thanks for the friendship and the constant help along the way in improving my writing.

Finally, to my magnificent wife, Tara, and beautiful children, Bryn Kevin, Ryana Nikol, and Kenyon Aleksandr: I simply couldn't write without their love, support and understanding . . . nor, I imagine, would I want to.

Prologue

Clan Sea Fox CargoShip **Voidswimmer**
Zenith Jump Point, Berenson System
Prefecture VI, The Republic
19 June 3134

The data cube fit in the palm of his hand, its sharp-edged, angular realness a harsh contrast to the dark secrets it so jealously guarded.

And the day had dawned with such promise.

"ovKhan." Petr Kalasa pulled his gaze from the inert object that had swallowed his concentration for long minutes and watched Jesup enter his command cabin. Petr never locked the door. He set the cube on the small desktop and leaned back with studied casualness. The creak of his spine betrayed the length of time he'd been hunched over.

Petr almost commented on the ungainly way Jesup moved into the room, but refrained when he realized it might shame his aide. If he moved so awkwardly in the magnetic slips that kept him attached to the deck, then he truly must be in pain. It seemed the man fought innumerable Trials of Grievance; had his latest trial come close to defeat for Jesup?

"What is your report?" Petr tried to conceal his amusement; Jesup's burning ears marked his failure.

"The repairs to the *Behemoth* proceed apace. Senior Technician Pol assured me we will be cleared to make the jump to the Augustine system within the hour."

"What caused the breach? We sealed the *Starmoth* more than three years ago; the other two have been attached far longer with no deterioration in their seals."

Petr stood and walked around the left side of the desk. He refused to glance at the cube, but could almost hear it calling him, a keening siren luring him to return and breathe the flames of life into the banked coals of its contents.

"Pol has initiated an investigation, and assures me any trials required to challenge shoddy maintenance will be dealt with. Personally."

Petr moved with the deliberate grace of one long-accustomed to gravity slips. If he were claustrophobic, the addition of one more person to the command cabin of the *Voidswimmer* would have driven him over the edge of sanity. If that were the case, years of being trapped within the metal skin of a vessel 1,508 meters long, adrift in the unimaginable largeness of the galaxy (not truly adrift, of course—Petr's mind held a laser-lock on the hundreds of coordinates constituting the stellar path Delta Aimag would travel in the next few weeks) would have driven him mad or downside long before now.

"Pol has never lacked in initiative, nor disappointed with performance. I do not doubt by week's end we will know what happened." He shifted slightly, his dark blue one-piece body suit undulating like gentle water in moonlight.

"Still, it has given me time to think." He glanced expectantly at his aide, waiting for the usual acerbic comment, his eyes emerald chips that could cut if he were provoked.

"Beta Aimag?"

"What else?" The man must be seriously hurt if he had abandoned his habitual sarcasm. He must find out who came so close to defeating Jesup in a Circle of Equals.

"Your obsession with ovKhan Sha Clarke will be the death of you."

"Of course it will. But I will kill him first."

"Kill?" scoffed Jesup.

Petr laughed out loud. "You are right. I have always said death is too good for the *surat*. I need only steal from under Sha the deal that would make him a legend, the deal that would guarantee his place in The Remembrance. Then my work will be done and I can pass. My genetic material would be judged superior and used to create a new shiver of Sea Fox."

Jesup's laugh echoed down the corridor. "Your humility never ceases to amaze me."

There is the sarcasm I am used to. Petr pushed away from the wall and stepped back toward the desk. Still he refused to acknowledge the insidious call of the data cube. "Humility is an invention of the weak to salve their egos when they fail."

Jesup held up his hands. "And you, my ovKhan, are anything but weak, *quiaff*?"

Silence was the only appropriate answer. Jesup insulted everyone: there were times when Petr believed his aide insulted those around him for the sole purpose of creating the opportunity to put others in their place with a pile drive of his bony flesh. One day, Petr himself would call his aide to the Circle and Jesup would learn there *are* limits.

This day, like many days before, would not be that day.

"You understand that he will try to beat us to the prize?"

"He will try, my ovKhan. Sha, like you, is simply trying to do what is best for his Aimag. All for the greater good of the Clan, *quiaff*?"

Petr's eyes burned with an inner fire. "*Neg*. You know as well as I that he is a parasite masquerading as ovKhan of Beta Aimag. Spina Khanate would be well rid of him."

"Do I?" replied Jesup. "Has he not brought great glory and honor to his Aimag? To Clan Sea Fox?"

"Are you trying to aggravate me? You appear to be in no condition to accept a challenge." His anger overwhelmed his decision to allow Jesup his self-respect. Petr would no longer ignore the man's pain and the near-defeat it indicated.

Jesup's eyes widened, yet Petr caught a hint of something more behind his aide's expression of surprise. "Far be it from me, ovKhan, to provoke a challenge from your august person. I would be destined to lose, for have you ever lost a challenge?"

Rage burned in his chest; a vortex of emotions battered his iron control. He choked on the memories invoked by Jesup's veiled reference. He took a half step toward Jesup, his hands balled into fists. "I will accept no such reminders of my failures." Each failure was etched on his soul as a searing brand to goad him to greater perfection. Especially one, whose connection to Sha he ignored.

"Reminders of what, magnificent ovKhan? It would seem I cannot even remember how to fight. How can I remember anything but your glorious victories for our Aimag?"

Though Petr could almost taste a strange undercurrent to Jesup's response, the man's tone of voice, his shrug and slightly canted head worked their usual magic, pouring water on the heat of his anger, drowning the flame and leaving only ashes. He permitted a small smile to touch his lips. "One of these days you will not find the words, and I will relish that moment."

" 'Words spill like solar wind from a star, nearly infinite—the *right* words, precious commodities to be hoarded and wielded with laser precision.' "

"You quote our Clan's founder to me?" Petr pretended outrage.

"If I become a small footnote next to Karen Nagasawa, I will be honored indeed."

Petr couldn't help sink a barb, so rarely did the other man offer such an opening. "More so than by a Bloodname? How . . . unClanlike."

Jesup jerked as though kidney-punched, then assumed a contemplative look for several long heart-beats. "I will take both, *quiaff*?"

Petr laughed. "*Aff*, Jesup. Now *that* is what we need in our Aimag. The determination to seize victory."

"If that is what we need, ovKhan, then simply challenge him to a trial and remove him. Be done with this obsession."

Petr grimaced and waited for the flood of anger. It failed to materialize, allowing the memory of his last trial against Sha to rise to the surface. He attempted to distract himself from the memory with a glance at the mysterious data cube, but that further soured his mood. Already he had spent hours trying to pierce the veil of its central riddle, to no avail. One obsession (to himself he would admit that word) was bad enough. Two would be intolerable.

"Jesup, such action could have . . . unintended consequences." He met Jesup's gaze. "The Khanates' loyalty to Khan Hawker could be considered weak; some may even question the Aimags' loyalty to each Khanate." Sha's name echoed loudly, though unspoken.

"And one ovKhan messing in the affairs of another Aimag might cause a cascading effect?" Jesup finished the thought.

Petr smacked his palm against the desktop, venting his frustration. For the first time in many years, multiple Aimags worked in close proximity, with dozens of JumpShips and multiple ArcShips canvassing the same tracks of interstellar space, covering the same worlds. He feared for the consequences. More important, he feared what ovKhan Sha Clarke might do.

The vehemence of his attack on the desk made the data cube jump, and once again it snared his attention.

Could this have something to do with Sha? With the great endeavor saKhan Mikel Sennet marshaled the entire Spina Khanate to achieve?

"Leave me," he said abruptly.

Silence was the only reponse; even Jesup knew when to abandon a line of questioning and leave his superior.

For the first time in memory, Petr closed the hatch and dogged it before returning to his chair; his mind barely registered the squeal of springs that usually jogged a mental note to chastise the labor casteman assigned the task of properly maintaining his equipment (promptly forgotten). Picking up the data cube, he weighed it in his hand, as though to assess its value simply by tactile senses, and then slotted it into the reader.

A holographic image immediately materialized and the head of an astonishingly ugly woman spun into view from nothingness. Her lackluster black hair (shorn off with a dull knife?), pimply skin and swarthy complexion made Petr wrinkle his nose, as if he were preparing for an olfactory assault that could not exist. He wanted to dismiss this woman out of hand, but her smoky gray eyes held an intelligence that could not be denied. And her message, and the means of its delivery, intrigued him.

"Salutations, ovKhan Petr Kalasa. You are no doubt wondering how this data cube appeared on your CargoShip, when no DropShip has made planetfall for more than five weeks. And beyond this mystery, you must wonder why I believe such a powerful man would agree to meet with such a lowly person as myself. The fact remains that I have information you will find

most . . . valuable. Information that affects your entire Khanate, and possibly the whole of Clan Sea Fox.

"Oh, I know this sounds like hyperbole, but that is for you to decide. If you wish a meeting, I will be on Adhafera when you arrive."

The image dissolved into the nothingness from which it came. Petr was intrigued by the appearance, as if by magic, of the cube in his cabin. This accomplishment alone, for such an ugly woman, brought admiration.

But in the brief discussion with Jesup, the idea had blossomed that this somehow tied in with Sha Clarke. Could the *surat* have managed this? Could Sha truly have sunk to such a level that he would use ugly spheroids to accomplish his work?

He stood abruptly, pulled the data cube from its socket and moved to undog the hatch.

It was time to alter their course.

1

The scientists swarmed like microbes, attacking the body of their experiment in their desire (need!) to make their work succeed.

Petr floated just above the deck in the Scientist Quarter of the *Voidswimmer*, observing the almost frantic activity with satisfaction. *They do this for me, for the Clan.*

"We barely deploy the sails and already you have the scientists jumping through hoops? Oh great one, what hoops may *I* jump through?"

Petr turned to find Jesup expertly sliding in next to him, though he engaged his magnetic slips to latch himself to the deck.

"I see you are moving better today, *quiaff*?" Petr said with a tight smile.

"*Aff*, oh my most observant ovKhan. A good night's rest strapped into your bunk will make any bruise disappear as an underarmored vehicle flees before a storm of PPCs."

Petr's smile became real under the deluge of sarcasm and feigned sophistry. Jesup did not possess the seasoning to untangle the tight whorls of current in a negotiation, yet he seemed to delight in hiding his true intelligence behind a facade of obviousness. It made him look stupid at times. A lack that, normally, Petr could not stand.

Good thing he makes me laugh, among his other qualities.

A minor tone insistently pierced their conversation. They both turned.

"So the experiment," Jesup said, more seriously than usual; they both regarded a veritable mountain range of computer terminals, monitors and other objects Petr simply couldn't identify.

"Proceeding apace." Petr tasted the breakfast paste he had swallowed too quickly in his desire to arrive early. Be tasting it all day. He grimaced, then brightened as the tone changed slightly. It would begin soon.

"Hard to believe scientist Kif outbid scientist Jonnic for the right to present first."

Petr shrugged. "Scientist Kif believes he has found the answer that has eluded us."

"Do you not wonder if he might have pushed too hard, too fast? He has a reputation for recklessness. His attempt could be disastrous."

Petr locked his emerald eyes with Jesup's questioning gaze. His aide held up under the stare this time, apparently feeling more himself today. *Do you believe that, Jesup, or is this another of your allusions?*

"We are all meant to seize our futures, *quiaff?*" Petr responded. "I laud scientist Kif for seizing the advantage."

"*Aff*, ovKhan, but if the shortcuts are too short, his conclusions might lead to the deaths of thousands, even tens of thousands. Perhaps not today, or tomorrow, but eventually." Jesup paused. "You have not achieved your goal if you sacrifice those you are trying to help. I simply believe we should make sure scientist Kif did not overstep himself."

Petr found no accusation in Jesup's eyes, but the words rang a little too close to their conversation yesterday. *Recriminations, again? You could never tell with Jesup.*

"ovKhan Kalasa, we are ready," a voice interrupted.

Petr turned to scientist Kif, and the man's gauntness struck him anew. All Sea Fox Clansmen who spent most of their lives in microgravity tended to have slight physical builds and skinny bodies; only the Clan's genetic engineering allowed them to compensate for all the degradations the body encountered in such weightless environs. Yet Kif seemed to embody the extreme; if he turned sideways, he just might disappear.

Petr nodded his head. "Proceed."

Uninvited, Jesup accompanied Petr and Kif as they made their way closer to the milling scientists and their tools.

A phalanx of computer monitors and other machines formed a large bulwark ring around a central holographic table, while multiple large-screen projection monitors showed exterior shots of the depths of space. At least forty white-coated individuals worked at various stations, monitoring and inputting information. Though he found the whole exercise fascinating, Petr knew most of it passed over his head.

To each his own. To each his contribution to the Clan.

They stepped carefully over what seemed like kilometers of twisting, multicolored wires—interconnecting all of the various computers and electronic equipment—around bustling scientists and between tables before breaking into the relative calm at the eye of the storm around the main holographic table.

"As you know, ovKhan," Kif began immediately, "there have been numerous attempts to create a large, mobile, simulated gravity, and until today, all have failed. They tied themselves too firmly to centuries-old technology: drastically increasing the size of a gravity deck, spinning the entire ship, latching the DropShips onto a spinning collar and so on. All failed and will continue to fail because they rely on such outdated methods, rather than changing the paradigm within which we work."

Jesup and Petr shared a brief, hidden smile at the pompous tone and obvious jab at Jonnic's own research.

"Please turn your attention to the central display, and I will provide an explanation of what is about to unfold." Scientist Kif waved his hand at the holographic display, showing an *Invader*-class JumpShip in exquisite detail.

"My epiphany occurred almost three years ago during the *Voidswimmer*'s refit at the Tukayyid orbital yards. There, I watched an extrusion of a carbon polymer composite cable, part of an attempt to make a cable with the strength to create a space elevator. Though those attempts continue to fail, I reasoned the tensile strength, in ratio to the thickness of the cable and required length to create a full standard gravity, would allow for the creation of a series of tethers for DropShips, provided they could be spun within the necessary parameters."

Though Petr fought his mind's impulse to drift, the man's technical jargon made him glassy-eyed; instead, he gave his attention to the display, concentrating on remembering the information gleaned from progress reports.

The initial challenge was to understand the need to create standard gravity. Though literally millions of Fox Clansmen lived most of their lives in microgravity, there was a significant enough number of downsiders who lived on Fox-controlled Inner Sphere worlds that large-scale, movable simulated gravities needed to be built for training these personnel. This goal had proved elusive as a result of technical and structural limitations.

Until today—at least, that was scientist Kif's claim.

The *Invader* hovering in the air before him represented the quintessential JumpShip: bulb at the front end, connected to a five-hundred-meter, relatively narrow length ending in the stationkeeping drive and solar sail array, giving rise to the ubiquitous description "needle thin." Close to the middle of the vessel, a narrow, collarlike structure circled the diameter of the JumpShip, housing cargo holds, docking collars for

DropShips and small-craft launching bays. Nearly four months of in-transit reconstruction had radically modified that section.

The previously flat plane of the collar was now broken in two, a fifteen-meter gap between each overhanging outer section providing a view of the interior section in the middle. Petr knew from the reports that that central, mostly hidden section now spun. Those extensive modifications, however, did not captivate him so much as the four monstrous cables anchored to the central trough that swung out to where four DropShips lay tethered.

Two *Mules*, a *Mammoth* and a *Behemoth* kept station at different distances, the twin *Mules* and their 11,200 tons of empty weight tethered at equal distances of just more than a kilometer. The 52,000-ton *Mammoth* was tethered at less than half that distance, and the gargantuan 100,000-ton *Behemoth* at half again. As the DropShip's cargo weights shifted, their tethers would adjust in length, automatically compensating (that much came through from Kif's endless talking).

The whole thing suddenly reminded him of a child's toy he'd seen on some forgotten downside years ago: a top, with four strings attached, metal beads at the end of each. If spun correctly, the beads created a counterbalance, increasing how long the top would spin, while eliciting oohs and ahhs from the gathered children as the sun glinted off the solid-appearing line of metal spinning in a flat arc around the top's center. Yet if spun poorly, those strings would tangle hopelessly, stopping the top before it could even begin spinning. As he stood arrested for that moment, Petr watched a half dozen children try to spin the top, and only one of them succeed.

Jesup's words filtered through the memory, giving Petr a moment of disquiet. *Is Kif that child to set it spinning correctly, or will it be hopelessly tangled?*

"By your leave, ovKhan?"

For an instant, Kif's voice held the timbre of a small child; then Petr shook himself from his reverie. Concealing his unease, he nodded. "Proceed."

With a smile almost childish in its glee at the coming victory, Kif nodded to his scientists, who fell to their tasks, entering alphanumerical sequences only they could understand into several remote command consoles.

Though he knew what to expect, Petr still felt disappointed as long minutes passed and apparently nothing happened. The grins and nods of the scientists, however, told him they were excited about something he could not see.

Petr decided to focus on the monitor showing the interior of cargo hold 1 of the distant JumpShip. A giant skein of wires spun into view, connecting the control monitors to the bulkhead of the *Invader* and the housing for the mammoth axle. He had a sudden image of a living, breathing machine, the scientists tapping into the mechanical beast with their devices in an attempt to control it. He shook his head at this flight of fancy.

"So exciting," Jesup commented. Kif looked at Jesup as if he had just become aware of his presence, then nodded firmly before returning to his work.

Petr smiled at the scientist's obliviousness to the sarcasm. Another handful of minutes bled away, and finally he could see a change. The holographic display showing the entire vessel and the visual feeds from numerous shuttles arrayed around the ship revealed movement.

The cable's length required the DropShips to spin up at a glacial pace, or his tangling top image would prove all too accurate. The experiment should have bored Petr, but the scientists' ability to be mesmerized by the minute shifting of objects hundreds of kilometers distant kept him enthralled. The minutes ticked into hours as the DropShips showed visible movement. Petr still did not understand the technology, but he did understand the potential of such technology.

A little more than four hours after the experiment began, a terrible Klaxon began to blare, demanding immediate attention. Petr quickly found the monitor displaying the warning, but he could not make sense of the information cascading across the screen.

"Scientist Kif, what has occurred?" Anger began to burn as the scientist ignored his question. As he opened his mouth to demand an answer, Jesup laid a hand on his shoulder.

"They have enough to worry about, ovKhan. Let them work," Jesup advised.

His aide's serious tone jarred him more effectively than harsh words. Petr nodded his understanding. There would be enough time for trials later.

Another handful of minutes passed as the scientists moved at what could have been light speed in their attempt to rectify the problem. In the exterior views, Petr could make out the blazing plumes of attitude jets firing on all four DropShips; they were trying to stop the spin, and quickly.

He clenched his fists, the biting pain of his nails

digging into his flesh keeping his anger at bay. Petr rarely sat on the sidelines, unable to affect unfolding events. The forced inaction scraped his nerves and mashed him flat with suppressed rage.

Finally, even Petr could see the problem: one of the cables was oscillating. Where the movement originated or why it had begun didn't matter at the moment. What mattered was that, as the vibration undulated up and down the cable, one of the *Mule*s began to swing as the energy peaked. The interior view of the *Invader* leaped and the entire ship shuddered as the sine wave slammed into it; the horrific energies built.

Despite firing the attitude jets, they would not stop the experiment in time.

Petr stepped forward and Jesup grasped his arm once more. He wrenched his arm away and spun toward his aide, eyes blazing.

"There is nothing to be done," Jesup stated simply. "Let them salvage what they can. After all, there will be a lot to salvage."

Petr allowed himself to be calmed, and they turned to watch the conclusion, as inevitable and unavoidable as the tides.

The views of the exterior began to shift as the shuttles obeyed orders to remove themselves from near space. Twin shuttles launched from the *Invader*, carrying away the few personnel on ship.

The energy in the cables continued to crescendo exponentially until the cable began whipping the DropShip at its end back and forth, like a frustrated child banging that long-ago-seen top on the ground. The destructive energy bled into the other three cables until all four wove a pattern that could not last.

Horrified, but unable to look away, even most of the scientists stopped working to watch the coming end.

It came quickly and with brutal efficiency, as the sine waves on three of the four cables momentarily matched rhythm and descended to the anchor points at roughly the same moment. Unimaginable kinetic energy tore into the anchors, which were not designed to withstand even a fraction of such stress, buckling and snapping meters-thick composite plates with the ease of a child breaking the wooden top.

The JumpShip's spine snapped in a glittering blizzard of shattered metal and composites, three of the four cables tearing completely away and slithering into the silence of space like snakes escaping their confines; the fourth continued to hammer the mortally wounded ship, jerking as though desperate to join its now-free comrades.

Even after a lifetime in the soundless vacuum of space, witnessing such horror in absolute silence still created a surreal sense of distance: as though events were not real, but unfolded only within a reality created by the digital display unit.

But Petr knew it to be all too real: the cost in the destroyed JumpShip and its expensive KF drive; the failure of hundreds of thousands of man-hours of work. Petr's mind always fell to the bottom line.

For the length of several labored breaths, the room held motionless. Then the scientists dove back to their work, attempting to salvage what they could of the information deluge. Everyone except Kif. The scientists subordinate to Kif would suffer no adverse consequences from the experiment's failure. Kif, however, stood fully responsible.

Like a deer caught in headlamps, Kif turned glassy, stunned eyes toward Petr.

"There will be time for trials later," Petr said, forestalling the man before he could speak, pleased with his lack of anger (it happened so seldom these days). "Now your duty is to determine exactly what occurred and why. You have fourteen days until a Trial of Grievance"—he paused a moment—"to be fought by scientist Jonnic. You will prove to Jonnic's satisfaction that your design can succeed, or you will be reassigned to the technician caste." The man flinched as though struck by a micrometeor. He just might have an answer by then, faced with such an incentive.

"*Quiaff,*" the scientist barely managed.

He turned to Jesup and speared him with a raised finger. "And I have no wish to hear of failures from you."

"I would never speak to you of your failures."

Petr held his gaze, a contest of wills. *No, but you would remind me without a word. Remind me of past failures and my hatred . . . and rage.*

Breaking eye contact, Petr unclamped his magnetic slips and arrowed toward the exit hatch. Tried to forget the look in Jesup's eyes.

You cannot compare scientist Kif to me. When I reach to achieve my vision, it will not end in failure.

2

Clan Sea Fox CargoShip Talismantia
Non-Standard Jump Point, Vindemiatrix System
Prefecture VIII, The Republic
20 June 3134

The infrared signature of an incoming JumpShip spiked into existence, spreading out like waves from a rock dropped in a pond. Generated just less than eight hundred million miles from the inhabited planet, the signature from the emergence point would take seventy minutes or so to reach the planet; by then, of course, it would be indiscernible from the soft roast of background radiation.

In one of the universe's most delicious jokes (it surely laughed uproariously at the frail human minds that strove to comprehend), the infrared spike blossomed in the target system before the Kearny-Fuchida hyperdrive of the imminently arriving ship even initiated the jump sequence some thirty light-years distant.

To detect the IR spike, a monitoring vessel or station needed to be within fifty thousand kilometers of the emergence point. In a backwater system whose star could already feel the oppressive weight of its corona and the coming frost that would extinguish its nuclear fire, imminent arrival should've gone completely unnoticed.

It didn't.

A JumpShip waited in the void, its micron-thin solar sail already spread like angel's wings, greedily gulping solar energy given freely to any willing to seize it. A *Scout*-class, its single DropShip complement bore the same marking as was reflected on the prow of the giant, needle-thin starship: a jade falcon in flight, a katana clutched in rapacious claws. The activity on the bridge crested as fingers flew and instruments probed the darkness in anticipation. They came here in answer to an offer they could not refuse. Now they'd learn if the gypsies were honorable, or if they deserved the Abjurement discussed for so many years by the remaining *true* Clans.

The fabric of existence screamed, its walls shredded by unfathomable energies wielded like a quantum blade. A JumpShip, which moments before floated two hundred and eighty billion kilometers distant, flashed into being in the here and now.

It began.

The small craft clanged as it settled onto the hull of the *Scout*; the snapping of metal grips announced a successful mating. Unbuckling himself, Sha Clarke slowly floated up a few centimeters, as the last vestiges of kinetic energy washed away.

"Prepare for pressure equalization." The toneless, mechanical voice seemed too loud for the small, ten-passenger S-7A Bus. Of course, with an elemental in full battle armor as an honor guard, almost any shuttle would seem small. His ears popped as the pressure thickened for a moment before his body acclimatized. Tucking his legs up toward his chest, he tapped lightly against the armrest and sent himself in a short spinning arc over two rows of seats. In midflight, Sha extended to his full height and spun three revolutions before coming within reach of the bulkhead and the hatch, which would open to a whole new world of possibilities. With languid grace he lifted a thin arm, snagged the edge of the bulkhead buttress, flexed whipcord-strong muscles to straighten his body perpendicular to the floor and brought it to a standing position; his magnetic slips immediately adhered.

"We are doing right, *quiaff*?" Sha glanced over his shoulder at one of his most trusted Star colonels, Coleen Nagasawa. Her overlarge eyes held a doubt mirrored in the wrinkling of her expansive forehead.

"*Aff*," Sha responded softly. "How can bringing glory to Clan Sea Fox not be right?"

"But are we bringing glory to the Clan? Or only to Spina Khanate? Only to Beta Aimag?" She moved down the short aisle and stopped just out of touching distance. Sha entertained an errant thought; her neck appeared too thin to support such a massive cranium, and he wondered if she could only survive in the relatively gravityless environment of space. Her longish hair, having slipped from its coil, floated lazily.

Sha eyed the hair disapprovingly. "Is it the Falcons?

I know your particular . . . distaste . . . for them, but we cannot choose where the next deal may take us, or who may sit across from us at the table."

"I know that as well as you, ovKhan," she responded; her momentary anger did not touch him. "I may wish their genetic material flushed out the nearest airlock, but I will deal with them and take their honor and resources like any other."

"Then what?" The genesis of the goal toward which he had worked so long and hard now lay just behind several centimeters of metal; after all this time, suddenly she became timid, like a first-year trader?

"What we are about to do . . ."

Sha saw the struggle of her thoughts as clearly as if a Star of 'Mechs battled across her face.

"What we are about to do is prove, in a way none can deny, that our Khan has become a weak old man whose only desire is to suck the rest of the Khanates dry, while his ilKhanate feasts on the fatted calves of our labor." Though his voice never wavered from its soft, low-pitched cadence, Coleen's jaw snapped shut like the clink of a Gauss rifle cycling its last round into the chamber. Power swam in his words.

He turned away, moved forward and undogged the hatch. Pulling it open, he ducked through before his security detail could protest. Stepping out on the other side, he straightened to see three individuals sheathed in the formal black and jade uniforms of Clan Jade Falcon. The Falconers' almost ostentatious dress made his own deep blue single-suit seem shabby by comparison; their eyes confirmed this impression. He bowed low in the tradition of all Sea Fox Clansmen in the opening salvos of negotiations and his lips twitched in a smile his adversaries could not see; their arrogance would be their undoing.

Blood in the water.

3

Clan Sea Fox CargoShip **Voidswimmer**
Nadir Jump Point, Savannah System
Prefecture VII, The Republic
4 July 3134

Petr once again entered the Scientist Quarter, this
time wearing his ceremonial leathers. The detailed sea
fox stitched across the torso of his suit conveyed dig-
nity and power; he'd need both in officiating this trial.

Moving through the corridors of the scientists'
berths, he could feel the wash of babbling voices eddy-
ing around him as he drew near the main conference
room. Grasping the handhold at the entryway, he
tucked his knees up, spun himself through the opening
and performed a half twist to plant his legs against
the bulkhead on the inside; he paused a moment to
make sure his path lay clear, then pushed, shooting
toward the central dais at the top of the inverted
half-sphere.

With practiced ease, he grasped the pole set into the armrest of the ovKhan's chair (only used for such occasions), spun around once to slough off extra inertia and expertly settled himself into the seat; nodules across the surface felt his presence and turned on their static charge, lightly but insistently pulling at his suit, keeping him stationary.

The half-bowl held a panoply of scientists, all adhered to their seats by static charges, each wearing the single-suit of a Sea Fox Clansman. The shoulders of their suits were colored to match their subcastes: yellow for teachers, green for doctors, red for the eugenics specialists and so on—a flowering bed of the Clan's brightest minds, filled with equal parts genius, their own kind of arrogance and naiveté.

That last quality, of course, was the reason Petr found himself here.

At times Petr thought perhaps all castes should undergo the same rigorous training the warriors endured. Naiveté did not last long under the grueling physical and mental exercises begun at the age of seven, or the ruthless pummeling of a shiv-trainer molding a new warrior to suit his ultimate calling.

Jesup flowed into the room. The man arrowed toward him, grabbed the same pole Petr used, then spun around to the back of the chair, coming to rest with his magnetic slips adhering to the deck.

"Are you ever *not* early, oh precipitous one?" Jesup mocked.

Petr smiled. "Someday I might be late, but hopefully you will not see it." They both chuckled, then grew somber as scientist Kif entered. The man appeared to have aged a decade in the fourteen days since the disastrous results of his experiment.

"I do believe he is ready for a solahma unit," Jesup said, his own tone warring between humor and horror.

"I have never heard of a scientific solahma unit. Age does not inhibit them as it does us. After all, unlike a warrior, they cannot die in one last attempt at glory and honor for the Clan they failed."

"Oh, but they could. For example, Kif could have been on the ship he destroyed," Jesup responded, deadpan.

Petr turned so quickly that he nearly broke the static charge and floated free. He saw humor dancing in the other man's eyes, though a slight crease in Jesup's forehead made Petr think his aide believed Kif (or any person, perhaps—another dig?) should be put directly in the path of his choices, to suffer the consequences immediately and not allow them to be ignored or to affect others.

Petr slowly shook his head and fought a smile (it was ironic to think of the man going down with his ship). "One of these days you will reach too far, Jesup."

He swept a flourishing bow. "As you say, oh mighty one."

"But until then you will be my court jester, as though I am a spheroid tyrant?" Petr cocked an eyebrow, waiting for the response.

Jesup swallowed, then looked slightly abashed.

"Do I find you tongue-tied?"

"Naturally not, ovKhan, but—we are ready to begin."

Petr looked at the two benches directly in front of him and found scientist Jonnic already present, the waiting throngs silent and peering at him quizzically. He gave Jesup a dirty look before turning to the crowd.

He stood, tapping his feet to the deck to attach his slips, then bowed formally in a mimicry of the sea fox, a mark of respect for those present. "Scientists, we have gathered this day for a Trial of Grievance. Because both individuals hail from the same subcaste, there is no need for a quorum of Bloodnamed from the Clan Council extant in our flotilla. Instead, scientist Kif will be judged by his peers. I, as ovKhan of Delta Aimag, will mete out the final sentence. In this, we shall not deny justice. In this, we shall all prosper."

"Seyla," echoed around the room, the scientists sealing the trial with affirmation.

All bowed formally in return.

"Scientist Jonnic, proceed," he said, then resumed his seat.

A tall woman stood, pale of hair and flesh, with fingers that reminded Petr of spider legs in their length and skeletal appearance, not to mention their almost constant flickering. Disengaging her slips, she used the small pneumatic air pump at the small of her back to smoothly maneuver into the air, then spread her arms to bow once more, and began.

"Scientists, I am present to prove unequivocally that scientist Kif grossly underestimated the challenges involved in this experiment, and wasted precious Clan resources, in the destruction of the JumpShip and in the wasted man-hours of the scientists on his development team and the technician and labor castemen tasked with the construction of the failed prototype," she began, her sonorous voice weaving a cadence that immediately enthralled her audience. Petr wondered how she found the breath for such long sentences in her emaciated-looking body.

"Not because of an unforeseen problem," she continued, "but due simply to his arrogance. His belief that he knew a shortcut the rest of his peers not only could not see, but would never see if he did not show the way."

She tapped the small remote she held, and the lights dimmed as holographic projections filled the room. "Each of these diagrams elucidates the points that Kif failed to take into account, thus leading to the failure of his program, regardless of the promise it held for success."

Petr glanced sideways for a moment at Jesup, startled to hear even a backhanded compliment from Jonnic. Did the rival scientist actually accept Kif's theory? A slight shrug from Jesup reflected Petr's inability to answer that question. Only time would tell.

"Diagram A demonstrates, of course, the most egregious error and yet the simplest correction of all the issues he failed to address. Why did he not use a mock-up JumpShip for this experiment? Rejecting such an obvious choice reveals Kif's arrogance and recklessness. His imminent failure would then not have destroyed such a valuable asset as the *Invader*."

Suspended among the glowing spheres of data, her long hair floating around her head in a halo of slowly undulating waves, her hypnotic voice flowing into the darkness, she captivated her audience like an avenging angel come to serve justice to mere mortals. Though

Petr could not make out Kif in the shadows, he knew the man cowered on his seat, wishing he could avoid the inevitable consequences of his actions.

"Turn your attention to Diagram B, where his second error can be seen. The anchor points have no safety cutout feature. A simple series of explosive bolts would have saved the JumpShip; the DropShips could easily have been retrieved at a later time."

"There were safety measures in place," Kif exploded, surging up from his seat, his head just breaking into the light cast by the holographic images.

Jonnic flinched, then speared the man with an outstretched arm. "Do not interrupt me, *stravag*."

"They malfunctioned," he babbled, tumbling gently, unable to master his own maneuvering pack in his urgency to defend himself. "The vibrations must have disabled them, or—"

"Silence!" Petr spoke softly, but the chill of death in his voice cut off Kif's protests as though he were struck dumb. "You will not speak until your turn in this trial, Scientist Kif. For your outburst, you have forfeited your right to present counterarguments point by point. If you commit a second infraction, I will pass judgment summarily, relegating you to the laborer caste. I will brook no further interference in this trial." No need to ask if he understood.

Silence descended, a viscous entity born of Petr's decree; even Jonnic recoiled from the ruling. Significant failure within a caste required the offending party be ejected from his station and moved to the next lower caste—in this case, scientist to technician. For a scientist of Kif's abilities and preeminence to be relegated to the bottom rung of Clan society meant he would never be able to atone for his mistakes and regain his previous station through hard work and perseverance. Three lifetimes would not be enough to work his way up such a distant ladder.

A soft grunt echoed in the room as Kif reseated himself.

"Proceed," Petr said. Though Jesup made no movement or sound, Petr knew—just knew!—that his aide was at this very moment thinking that those same iron-clad penalties should apply to the ovKhan.

How many times have I erred due to my arrogance? The lost market on Chamdo that led to such deadly conflict; the lost chance to build an enclave on Chesterton; the lost colony around Klathandu IV. Petr suppressed a shiver and shoved those thoughts deep into his mind.

Visibly collecting herself, Jonnic continued. "Diagram C illustrates another lapse in judgment. Though a series of counterweight balances were installed on the tethers to dampen oscillations and to compensate for shifting weight within the DropShips once the system entered standard use, the addition of antioscillation myomer lines to further strengthen against dangerous vibrations spiraling beyond accepted parameters would have prevented this entire affair."

She slowly rotated around, centering attention on the final holographic image. "In this final image we see one more example of Kif's arrogance and unwillingness to follow proscribed and logical steps for safety, which led to failure instead of success. Rather than risking four DropShips on a single collar, scientist Kif could have chosen to balance a pair of DropShips, an appreciably easier task. This would have allowed us to fully test and vet the entire system, measuring peak and trough parameters of each subsystem. Once full success was achieved, then a series of spinning axles could be built across any given JumpShip. Instead of four DropShips anchored to a single collar, a set of four collars—or more—could anchor eight vessels, each within a larger margin of safety, thus limiting the possibility of future mishaps and guaranteeing the Clan's expansion within an acceptable margin of error."

The imagery disappeared as she brought up the lights, then slowly rotated, bowing to the entire assembly. "Thus the primary points have been presented. Each of your compads have now received this data. I thank the assembly for hearing my words." She finished, then smoothly transitioned back to her seat, a predator gone to ground, toying with her prey before launching for the throat.

"You have thirty minutes to review the material," Petr announced, moving to the next phase, "then input any queries for scientist Jonnic in her second cycle of the Trial. At that time, scientist Kif may argue to prove the accusations false."

"ovKhan," Kif said, slowly standing.

Petr's face darkened with rage at his audacity; gasps and startled murmurs swept through the gathering.

"I know I risk your extreme censure for once more breaking the forms of this trial," he began. His voice gained composure as he spoke; his face and body took on the appearance of calm as though imposed by sheer force of will. "And if you deem me fit only for the laborer caste, I accept your judgment. Yet I would voluntarily spare the Clan's expense of any more time and effort on my behalf. Of my own free will and accord, I do not contest the accusations against me. Scientist Jonnic is correct on all accounts. I speak a surkairede to voluntarily accept Abjurement from the scientist caste."

The stunned silence thickened the air, tension drawn to the breaking point. Despite the man's terrible failures and twice interrupting this council, Petr found admiration stirring within him. Staring at a man reborn from his broken state simply by admitting his failure and by his willingness to accept the consequences—when so many others would have fought like cornered diamond sharks to retain their place—Petr was compelled to his feet. "So be it," he intoned, respect coating his words. Then he bowed deeply, holding the position for a long moment.

A ripple of surprise, then a wave of bows swept the assembly. Scientist Jonnic bowed last, stiffly, as though forced to perform the honorific against her will. Then, in a move that sent another shockwave through the assembly, she took two steps and grasped Kif's shoulders, saying something only he could hear. He looked stunned, then pleased, a small smile lighting his face.

Kif bowed in return, then moved toward the entryway. His former colleagues turned away in unison; though the assembled scientists obviously respected Kif's courage in making his choice, he was no longer of their caste, and no longer deserved their full attention.

The assembly began to break up. The abrupt conclusion to the trial, expected to stretch for many more hours, created small groups animated by emphatic nods and gestures.

"Now *that* was unexpected," Jesup said.

Petr nodded. His own feelings exactly.

"I have rarely seen such honorable actions outside the warrior caste. To so freely take on his burdens— would we all have such grace when our time comes, *quiaff?*"

"*Aff*," Petr responded, though he couldn't decide if Jesup meant his comment as a general statement, or a pointed remark directed his way. He stood and launched himself away from his chair, content to accept his aide's words at face value.

4

***Clan Sea Fox CargoShip* Voidswimmer**
Nadir Jump Point, Savannah System
Prefecture VII, The Republic
7 July 3134

"I do not understand why we do not attempt to go downside." Jesup's voice, though powerful, almost failed against the hum and babble of Beta Community.

Petr looked at his aide as they both made their way through Market Square Beta. Of course, it was not square (or round or any other recognizable shape beyond an amorphous line stretching and snaking around to mark an open region), but the human mind, even one as adapted as the Sea Fox mind to the rigors of long-term space travel, latched on to traditions as old as human society.

Jostled, Petr turned to find a kind-faced woman with a thick swatch of dark, almost black hair pulled back in a severe braid. Her uniform bore the double stripes of the laborer caste, and the hurried look on her face made him think the woman late for her duty assignment. When she realized who she had run into, she swallowed convulsively and bowed deeply, the hurried look replaced with one of shame.

"ovKhan," she began in a stammer, "I apologize. This unworthy one did not see you."

Though a warrior born and bred, with centuries of Clan tradition supporting the superiority of the warrior caste (with the possible exception, in Clan Sea Fox, of the merchant caste), he knew the duty of an ovKhan to his Aimag to show respect when necessary. Reaching out, he raised up the woman's head.

"Woman, there is no need to bow to me." He smiled, though the expression did not quite reach his frosty green eyes. "You obviously were intent on reaching your duty assignment on time. What greater honor can you do me and our Aimag than to attend to your duty with such dedication?"

Though a certain wariness remained, she blushed, babbled thanks and nodded once more before vanishing into the throng of several hundred people.

"Ah, such fidelity is so admirable," Jesup said.

"Do you mock?" Petr continued on, weaving between people moving with great purpose; he couldn't completely conceal the distaste in his voice for his aide's words.

"Of course I do not mock, ovKhan. Your humble servant only observes the devotion of your Aimag."

As usual, only silence could answer such a comment. Petr felt the casual conversation almost inappropriate in the communal spaces, the cathedral Sea Fox had built to their new society.

A glance up revealed a massive, bowl-shaped open-air region—with the "market square" at its base—that flared out at the bottom and rose to a dome some one hundred fifty meters above his head. Stair-stepped around the base of the bowl and then climbing one another, like ivy run riot in an ecstasy of verdant growth, square habitats filled his vision.

Perhaps hanging nests for human occupants better described them. In addition to those using magnetic slips who moved around him, the region above held hundreds of individuals casually traversing the open air. Each landed lightly on a heavily padded wall of a given habitat and, grasping a strap, pulled him- or herself to a metal strip that allowed his or her slips to lock on, and began walking the short distance to their destination. Others launched themselves back into the open, creating an immensely complex choreographed dance accomplished without a single mishap. At any given moment, a sea of humanity met his gaze, all standing at innumerable angles, while others darted like fish in heavy currents.

The decades saw the slow transformation of one of the first *Behemoth*-class DropShips to be permanently sealed parallel to the *Voidswimmer* from an interplanetary vessel to the hollowed-out shell of Beta Community: home to more than twelve thousand.

One of four such vessels on his ship, and still small compared with Alpha Community.

Look what we have accomplished, all for the glory of my Clan! The thought resonated within him like a struck bell.

Jesup did not suffer silence well. "You did not answer my question, ovKhan."

"No, I did not." Without a backward glance, he began to make his way toward one of the original loading bays, which under heavy modification became the entryway leading directly into one of the primary corridors of the *Voidswimmer*, with enough room for several abreast.

He'd finished his quarterly review of Beta Community.

"Petr, why will you not answer my question?"

"Because it is not a question worthy of answer." He stopped in midstream of humanity, uncaring of the disruption this created, and focused the full intensity of his emerald eyes on his aide. The moment stretched as Jesup attempted to hold his gaze, his growing agitation plain. He finally lowered his eyes.

A soft murmur of voices reached him, and Petr did not realize that all nonwarriors who came within sight of their ovKhan immediately fell silent, conversation stopping as though shut off like a water spigot; even their careful zero-g walking became more so.

"Why do we not go downside?" Petr repeated the question with an edge to his voice, causing those nearest him to shy away even farther; Petr remained blithely unaware. He had great respect for his aide (why else had he not pulled the man into a Circle of Equals for his arrogance?), but there were times when he simply could not tolerate the man's inability to grasp the obvious. Jesup wished to seize command of a vessel at some point and begin to earn credibility by sealing his own deals. He'd never succeed in this goal if he did not think more quickly on his feet.

"That is what I am asking." The frustration was plain on Jesup's face. "I did not question when we simply passed through Augustine—seven days when we might have made planetfall and begun bringing enlightenment to these darkened worlds. And no, the failed test of the JumpShip did not count as any sort of activity for either of us and you know it. Then another eight in Miaplacidus, once more, inactive."

He has been storing this up, waiting to expel it when the opportunity presented itself. Petr withheld his response, to see where this might lead.

"Now half a week has passed, and though the Trial of Grievance against scientist Kif was a diversion, once more we sit, wasting time." He began to pace and the flow of humanity smoothly bowed around his tight path of agitated walking—a stone the water gave no heed to beyond making room for its presence.

"ovKhan Petr, I do not mean to second-guess your decision, but why else did saKhan Sennet send us here? Are we not tasked with contacting these worlds? They have been in the dark for almost two years. They will be desperate, hungry for outside contact. Their economies will have suffered and we will be their salvation: merchant gods to rain gold upon their heads and bring them news from afar. The potential is enormous. And—yet—we—sit!" Stopping, facing Petr, Jesup held his head up and met his ovKhan's gaze unflinchingly, knowing Petr might challenge him on the spot for such insolence. The man was no coward. If a fight were to come, so be it.

Petr could not help but admire his aide; he knew how upset he must be to have gone through so many words without a single sarcastic comment. He took pity on him. "Think, Jesup. I know my directive. I know the other Aimags are already gathering, like shivers of sharks hunting for the choicest feeding grounds. Why would I pass three worlds, any of which could be the beginning of more glory?"

A long moment passed as Jesup struggled within for the answer he knew to be there; he had been Petr's aide far to long to believe a reason did not exist. The slow light of understanding began to blossom. "You have information."

"Of course I have information. Of what?"

"That a world ahead of us is the key to this region. You bypass these worlds because they will only become important later. Once the real prize has been taken."

Petr applauded silently, as though rewarding a first-year cadet who'd answered correctly. "Now you begin to understand. And as much as I believe only I hold this information, I cannot discount the possibility others may have obtained it and are already on their way. I curse this ship for not having a lithium-fusion battery to double our speed. We make good time, nonetheless."

He turned and began walking again—the deliberate, careful steps natural to those accustomed to microgravity and magnetic slips—with Jesup close behind. "The feeding ground is near Jesup. Very near."

The river of castemen closed and swallowed them into their current without a ripple.

5

Clan Sea Fox DropShip **Ocean of Stars**
Atmosphere, Adhafera
Prefecture VIII, The Republic
15 July 3134

The demilitarized Clan-built *Overlord-C*-class Drop-Ship shook lightly as it made interface with the upper atmosphere of Adhafera. From this altitude, the blue-green ocean spread below like a living mat—a sponge deceptively beckoning for an incoming DropShip to land on its benevolent surface. Of course, the ship's captain ignored the siren song that would end in death as surely as being ensnared by a randall's rose. Began the long lateral trek across the ocean, toward the continent of Vanderfox, the waiting city of Halifax and the world's only DropPort.

The ship raced the sun as it dropped lower and began to make final preparations for landing. Those up this early on Vanderfox witnessed a false dawn as the drive plume of the *Ocean of Stars* pumped out plasma in a miniature star that kept the 11,550-ton vessel aloft and descending at a manageable velocity.

Star Captain Jotok sat in his command chair as though astride a throne, viewing his miniature kingdom and its industrious citizens: the labor and technician castemen who crewed the vessel and kept it in top operating shape.

OvKhan Petr sat strapped into a jumpseat in a forgotten niche of the bridge as it hummed with the activity necessary for a landing vessel. Incoming transmissions were already verified, the appropriate landing codes transmitted and authorization received. Acknowledged.

Petr was Star Captain Jotok's superior, but even in the rigid hierarchy of the Clans a man did not lightly intrude upon the domain of another's vessel. He waited. The captain would deign to tell him soon enough.

Time bled away like the velocity the ship sloughed off, and finally the captain nodded once, firmly. He turned to Petr and gave him his attention for the first time in almost an hour.

"We will be grounded in fifteen minutes, ovKhan."

"I see that," Petr responded. No impatience shaded his tone—a victory.

The man leaned away slightly, a speculative look in his eyes—perhaps not such a victory after all.

Petr continued. "The local governor will be meeting us at the DropPort, *quiaff*?"

"*Aff*. It would appear that way. I note that they referred to the man as first governor."

Petr shrugged. "We have seen more drastic changes since the collapse of the HPG network. If that is the only change, we will be lucky, *quiaff*?"

"*Aff*, my ovKhan." The man's eyes returned to the activities of his crew and for just a moment Petr lost the battle with his patience, though he managed not to speak aloud. *I granted you your due before, but now your attention needs to be focused on one thing, and one thing alone.*

Jotok looked again at Petr and cleared his throat at his ovKhan's expression. "They also wanted to know why, if the ovKhan of Delta Aimag of Spina Khanate actually orbited their world, he did not accompany the DropShip downside."

Petr smiled. Already it had begun. "They did not ask straight out, *quineg*?"

Jotok laughed, a good-natured sound that filled the bridge. "*Neg*, ovKhan. None have ever been so bold, in my experience. The day they are, is the day I have found a spheroid worthy of my respect. For now, I answered their question as indirectly as they asked it."

Petr nodded. "We have a world as open as a Jade Falcon heart is cruel. It is time to get to work."

Petr unstrapped himself, nodded once to acknowledge the man, moved off of the bridge and began to make his way toward the only remaining 'Mech bay on the vessel.

Yes, time indeed to get to work.

The crowd of nobles stood several hundred meters back from the blast pit as the DropShip made its final thunderous entrance into their lives. The hiss and crack of cooling metal filled the air with its gentle rhythm after the brutal onslaught of the mammoth plasma drives.

Like peacocks come to market, the nobles were decked out in their finest. Silks, heavy clothes brocaded and festooned, capes and feathers and jewel-encrusted hats: a jarring eyesore. They moved among one another, nervous of the new element arrived on Adhafera, yet to take its measure. For more than a year now, not a single vessel had made planetfall; for all they knew, the rest of The Republic had ceased to exist, sucked into an astronomical maelstrom. Many of these nobles, including the first governor who quietly seized power, would just as soon it remained that way.

The abrupt shaking of feathers and tinkling of dangling jewels marked the flocks' increased agitation as the screech of metal and massive whine of hydraulics broke across them like an incoming wave.

A wave that would drown them—they just didn't know it yet.

The group grew even more agitated as the main DropShip ramp descended to clang onto the ferrocrete, looking for all the world like the opening of a mouth into the black maw of some metal beast who'd come down from the stars to tear away at the power base they'd built.

Not a warrior among them, they did not immediately recognize the slow, rhythmic pounding and the whine of servo actuators that echoed out of the ghastly hole. Only once it emerged into the full light did a woman scream and most of the nobles take several steps back, panic written large on their pallid visages.

The *Tiburon*—a Sea Fox–designed BattleMech—stood at the top of the ramp and raised its arms, as though stretching after a long slumber, luxuriating in the warmth of the new dawn sun. The move further terrified the nobles, and only the first governor's steely grip on the situation kept the flock of birds from taking flight.

Of course, the *Tiburon* only weighed thirty-five tons and its mere nine-meter height marked it as a light BattleMech—a good design, but it could not stand up to a heavy or assault BattleMech. To the shivering flock of nobles, however, it might as well have been a metal god, they had so little experience with BattleMechs. Even the legate of this world (who had "accidentally" been left off of the list of those notified of the incoming vessel) did not ride a 'Mech, but instead commanded the local militia from the open hatch of a vehicle.

The 'Mechs began to move down the ramp, its thundering steps echoing across the landing field. Once more, the steel grip of the first governor stayed the flock, though his control became more tenuous as the monstrous machine towered closer and closer: the thudding of the reaper come to claim his due. Unnoticed, a small hoverjeep moved along in the 'Mech's shadow, a puppy at the foot of its master.

Twenty meters from the crowd of terrified nobles, the *Tiburon* stopped. A long moment stretched, and a true silence smothered the DropPort, too early for any other activity. Almost four minutes passed before the nobles realized a single man had already crossed half of those twenty meters. A few elbows unglued eyes and brought them down from the magnificent pinnacle of seven centuries of warfare development . . . to a simple man.

He was of average height, his physique obvious in the deep blue single-suit he wore; his thin, almost emaciated body spoke of years in zero gravity, but the whipcord strength belied such apparent weakness. He had a ready smile (if they'd not been so dazzled by the spectacle of the 'Mech, they likely would've noticed the arrogant cast to the grin), and long hair pulled back into a ponytail. As the man strode up to the first governor, several of the attendant women admired the deep jade eyes; their glances lingered and knowing looks ignited.

The men, of course, saw only a man—a pale shadow of the giant at his back. The verdict? Instantly and thoroughly dismissed.

It wasn't really their fault. After all, they simply were outclassed.

Petr sized up the gaudy group of nobles and dismissed them. He'd already won. He just had to show them.

He came to a stop only a meter from the man who obviously held power on this world, and bowed deeply. The first governor appeared to be in his late fifties, with a distinguished goatee and short hair beginning to gray at the temples. His dark brown eyes and sharp nose spoke of intelligence, but the effect was spoiled by the sycophants even now surrounding him with useless service and petty needs. The blue satin jerkin the man wore, coupled with the white trousers and the flowing carmine robe, made the governor appear to be the jester of the court, not the king.

"First Governor Jeffries, I greet you and bid you

thanks from Spina Khanate of Clan Sea Fox. We thank you for the hospitality of your world. More, we thank you for your august presence at our first meeting." Enough flattering filled Petr's voice for ten men.

The man stared at Petr, determined to dismiss the messenger as quickly as possible and speak with the real power just grounded; his gaze kept sliding impatiently toward the 'Mech. He finally inclined his head.

"On behalf of the people of Adhafera, I greet you and bid you welcome to my world. It has been long since any have made planetfall here and never in my memory has the vaunted Clan Sea Fox set foot on our shores. I hope your stay will be beneficial to us all."

Petr almost laughed out loud. The governor's voice might have been filled with utmost respect, but Petr could tell it was pitched to reach the 'Mech, not his ears.

Just then a clang rang out as the cockpit hatch of the *Tiburon* spun open on the back of the head. The collective breaths of the nobles were indrawn—several in outrage, most in admiration—as the MechWarrior climbed out onto the back of the 'Mech and made her way around the shoulder to a steel ladder that had just dropped to the ground.

MechWarrior Jesica—in the standard MechWarrior outfit of short boots, skin-tight briefs, a small, thin T-shirt and a cooling vest—began to make her way down the ladder; she displayed more bare skin than most of these men and women likely ever had seen in public. Her hair ruffled in the slight wind that picked up in the brightening morning, and Petr felt a smile pull at his face as several of the waiting men subconsciously swayed to the movement of her narrow hips.

"First Governor," Petr began. The collective group of nobles almost jumped at the interruption; they pulled their eyes away from the approaching female and gave them contemptuously back to Petr. He gloried in their dismissal. "As you no doubt know, Clan Sea Fox prides itself on helping worlds to achieve their potential. With the loss of so much due to the collapsed HPG network, we have redoubled our efforts to find those worlds that need our aid. To find those worlds that can benefit from our expertise, that can prosper with our guidance. There are many markets and much to be gained in this new darkness. Though it saddens us to see what the darkness has wrought, there will also be a silver lining. We wish to help you find that lining."

Their eyes said it all.

He continued. "I could not help but notice your local merchants do not appear to be in attendance. Would it not be wise to have their advice at this, our first of what will surely be many, many beneficial meetings?"

If possible, their collective eyes became more frigid. Why did this errand boy continue to annoy them, when the obvious power of the Sea Fox Clan on their world strode toward them? Several of the men began ogling her once more. He could also read the further disdain on their faces at the mention of the local merchants. The nobles, of course, did not need factors, the Clan equivalent of business agents, to negotiate for them. *They* were the power on this world, after all.

The governor replied almost absently. "Though Clan Sea Fox has not previously touched our world, word of your preeminence had spread far and wide, long before the current troubles. *I* look forward to speaking more on the subject." The emphasis was almost painful.

With that, the man turned to face Jesica, who'd crossed almost the entire distance. As usual, her timing was impeccable.

The first governor stepped forward, a warm smile blossoming on his face. He opened his mouth to speak just as Jesica stepped slightly past him and thumped fist against chest, with a slight forward lean. "At your command, ovKhan."

The angry look that began to form on the first governor's face slammed hard against confusion and the two warred as Jesica's words fell among the flock of birds like a grenade. Realization dawned cold and brutal.

The first governor struggled to regain his composure, stiffened and turned back to Petr, a false smile pasted on his face.

"ovKhan, we are honored by your presence. Please accept my hospitality. We can relax, dine and discuss matters at our leisure." His voice sounded as if a mule had just caved in his manhood.

With a smile that revealed the predator within, Petr replied, "First Governor, I have named already the people I want to see. The merchants of Halifax will just be rising for the day. I would speak with them in a location of their choosing."

The governor flinched as though struck in the face, and quickly turned to a lackey to hide his expression. After giving a brief order, the man glanced once more in Petr's direction; hate flashed in his eyes.

It was the expected reaction. It was of no significance. Petr did not need this one's approval. He sniffed the air and reveled in the aromas flooding his senses. The smell of alien flora and fauna. Of a world untouched by Clan Sea Fox. Of new possibilities.

The new deal had begun well.

6

Snow hugged the shadows like a lover desperate for the warmth of an embrace. Yet the shadows betrayed as easily as they saved; danger came.

Moving down Fourth Street of the lower Eastside, Snow found a moment in the desperation to chuckle. The Earl of Stewart tried so hard to ignore this part of his beloved city and yet it sat like a canker sore, irritating and infectious. If he didn't do something about it soon, he'd find it a lot more than just irritating, especially now that the local economy was going bad. Then again, it made her life easier, so she shouldn't look a gift branth in the mouth.

Coming to the intersection of Fourth and Harold, she paused with her back against the wall, waiting.

The blare of a far-off horn sliced through the night; a baby's cry drifted from a nearby apartment complex; machinery hummed (the ever-present vibrations every city created but that citizens failed to notice); a night trawl screeched close by, almost causing Snow cardiac arrest. But her pursuers had not discovered her latest backtrack.

They'd be on her trail soon enough.

Moving onto Harold, she passed Fifth and then crossed the street in the dim light of an equidistant point between two streetlights; if she held one wish in the world, it would be that whoever created streetlights burned a long time in Hell.

Passing an alley entrance, she froze as a sound caught her attention. She flattened against the wall. Her black clothing—thick wool to mask her heat signature without announcing the depth of her resources by the blatant use of a sneak suit—blended well into the depths of the alley's blackness.

Closing her eyes, she marshaled her will and centered herself as she'd been taught. Choosing one distraction after another, like a master weaver whose nimble fingers pick apart the skein of a complex weave, Snow pulled herself loose until only the twin threads of her hearing and the sound remained. In practice, such trancelike concentration would allow a person to strike her and she'd not immediately feel it. As such, she played a dangerous game in an alley where any wino might come looking for a dime and find easy prey, leaving her beaten . . . or worse.

The thumping of her heartbeat came from a remote location, but served as a metronome for the passing of time. No other sounds intruded, but she knew; she'd dealt too often with these particular people to not know they hunted her as surely as a Sea Fox who smelled blood in the water when a good deal materialized. She'd tried flight before and that failed. Only made her sloppy. For just a moment her concentration shifted and a third strand tugged: the caress of the plastic-coated verigraph scraped against the taut skin of her belly.

After another long pause, during which a minute or five might have passed, when no sound vibrated along the thread Snow held, she slowly began to reweave the skein of herself, gradually retwining existence. In another few moments she breathed deeply and released a small, pent-up sigh of frustration. She snorted, moved to the entrance of the street and began making her way once more down Harold, to the waiting DropShip several kilometers distant and her future meeting; by her calculations, her invitee should already have made planetfall and might be just a little agitated if he could not find her.

A fiery fist of pain hammered into her shoulder from behind; she lurched forward and dropped to one knee as her concentration momentarily splintered into a prismatic stream of a thousand points of light. Damn! Sloppy again.

No need to be on your guard one hundred percent where SAFE is concerned. The intelligence branch of House Marik is a joke, a cakewalk. There might have been some truth in that myth at the upper levels. But on the mean streets of the back end of a dark hole, those agents were every bit as dangerous as any she'd dealt with. More, they seemed almost desperate to prove themselves. As though they felt responsible for the splintering of their realm and were out to prove they could match any agency, any individual, that might cross their path.

Snow thought she'd learned her lesson. Obviously more, and painful, lessons were yet to come.

She tugged hard once and regained her concentration, leaving out the thread of pulsing pain that sent lances of agony down her arm, numbing it into uselessness. She immediately dropped to the ground, rolled toward the alley mouth and heard the cough of a well-made silencer, the *tang* of ricocheting rounds bouncing off pavement; a hot chip of the street sliced her cheek.

Once in the alley, she rolled, pushed against the wall with her good shoulder and levered herself quickly to a standing position. She looked down the alley and muttered a curse that would've curdled her mother's ears—blocked. They would know they'd hit her and more than likely they knew the alley offered no outlet. After all, she'd discovered quickly enough the world of Stewart might be part of The Republic of the Sphere in a geographical sense, but in every other sense it belonged to the Marik-Stewart Commonwealth. SAFE agents roamed freely on-planet, and they would know this city, know this street, *know* this exact alley. The unexpected. She needed to do the unexpected.

If they knew they'd hit her, they'd be expecting a strike from the alley floor. Attempt to hide behind a Dumpster, or break into an alley door and try to slink away. The sound of the silencer had come from some distance, so she still had a few precious seconds.

Unbuckling her belt, Snow pulled it loose and then

swung it around her chest, catching it between herself and the wall. As though she'd practiced the move a hundred times, she quickly bound her now-useless arm to her side. She ran to the large drainage pipe mounted against the wall, where she squeezed between the wall and the pipe. She began to make her way up the pipe. Her fear it might rattle or creak with her movement proved unfounded. Six meters up, she found a ledge and dismounted from the pipe, latching on to a windowsill and edging farther out toward the mouth of the alley.

Sweat dripped down her face and began to plaster the wool clothing to her stocky body. The thread of pain could not be refocused and it became a hot pincer grinding against her concentration as she made her way along the ledge. She began to pant from the effort and tears slowly leaked from the corners of her eyes. Almost at the edge of the alley, she stopped. Listened. The inferno of her shoulder threatened to flare out all other considerations and black spots swam in front of her eyes as oblivion opened its embrace to accept her surrender.

The verigraph crackled against her skin.

Her eyes narrowed and the indomitable spirit that had dragged her from the ugliness of Talitha, which made this slum look like the lap of luxury, blossomed in her smoky gray eyes.

Irregular sounds intruded. The slow steps of a cautious man. The steps of a man who wished not to be seen or heard.

They drew closer. With a wrenching twist, she realized she could not reach the needler snugged up against her left breast, the handle positioned for a cross-body draw. She cursed silently; it had been a mistake to immobilize her arm. Still, no going back now. Flow with the blow. How to take him? The information she held could not be lost.

The man's head appeared and disappeared like the flicking tongue of a lizard around the corner. Once again, appear-disappear, this time at a different level. With a large-bore handgun (she couldn't make it out clearly from this distance in the dark, but it looked like a Sternsnatcht Python; leave it to a SAFE agent to try and silence such a monster) held out in classic shooter style, the man edged around the corner. He moved to the other side of the alley, eyes, body and gun covering every angle.

Her arm began to tremble with the strain of supporting her body, and the flame of pain began to reach critical levels. She could just make out the silhouette of his head as he slowly scanned up the walls. It was only a matter of time before he saw an anomaly on the wall—an anomaly that would then feel the force of several large-grain soft-tip bullets splattering her tissue messily against uncaring bricks.

Her mind racing, she quickly came to a decision. Made her choice.

From six meters up, with a lame arm strapped to her chest and a body aching with the strain of the climb, she pushed hard away, somersaulted with a half twist and dropped into the darkness.

7

The Merchant House was not a house in any conventional sense, unless a building as big as a large DropShip fit the bill. At a hundred fifty meters on a side and half that in height, the mammoth structure seemed a monument to commerce. And though Petr could certainly respect that, he had no previous experience brokering in the commodity his own merchant castemen were attempting to secure. The odor was . . . overpowering. Born and raised on a ship, where he breathed air scrubbed clean with almost religious regularity, he became unnaturally attuned to discerning scents. It was a strength he enjoyed and used to his advantage—in most situations. Not even the close confines of Alpha Community following the breakdown of one of the primary air scrubbers, however, could compare with the smell of the Merchant House.

Now it was a weakness. . . .

"ovKhan." He turned to see Merchant saFactor Tia striding toward him from the small door he had exited a short while earlier. Though he stood almost fifteen meters from the door, the stench managed to escape during the brief opening and oozed across the ground like a living creature bent on assaulting the man who tried to flee its grasp. His nose tingled and scrunched, remembered tears almost began to flow once more. How the other merchants could talk so long and not vomit with the stench of so much bovine flesh and feces stuck in the back of their throats, he did not understand.

"Tia," he acknowledged. Though she was young for her station, her quick mind matched her flashing blue eyes. Her overlarge features—particularly her hatchetlike nose and jutting chin—allowed her to look foolish (throwing off the unwary) or commanding with equal ease; she used both qualities well and seized her position with a savagery barely contained within her petite body. A shame her abilities did not allow her to participate equally in the glories of the negotiation table and the battlefield.

"ovKhan, I thought I might find you here. The stench is too much, *quiaff*?"

Blunt as ever. He stiffened for a moment and then relaxed. He looked away and gazed down the hill toward the city of Halifax, and could just make out the egg-shaped form of the *Ocean of Stars* at the far-distant DropPort. The Merchant House, on a hill overlooking the entire area, held a commanding view. He breathed in the blissfully sweet-smelling air; it calmed him.

"What have we accomplished this day?"

Tia smiled, though the humor did not lighten her eyes. "I believe we have them on the run. I am looking for one more concession today, before going for the throat tomorrow and closing the deal." Her raised eyebrows were blunt question marks. He should know this, after all. But the distractions seemed too much. He'd been off his game. Weakness.

"They have managed an excellent defense," Petr said, hating himself for deflecting the unasked questions.

"They have indeed. If this is any indication of what this Prefecture will be like, I relish the coming months."

"At this rate, it will be years, *quiaff*?"

"*Aff*, ovKhan. *Aff.*" Her eyes became brighter, if that was possible.

"I assume the first DropShips are already on their way?"

"Of course. I laid my trap almost a week ago and on my own authority I ordered four DropShips to begin a high-speed burn to planet. The slaughter will commence within the week and we want the meat fresh as it is packed and we prepare to move it."

"A week ago? You must be slipping, Tia. Your traps inevitably spring mere days after they are positioned."

She shook her head and waved her delicate hand. "All the more glory when it is finished, ovKhan. You, of all people, should know that."

The double meaning once more. Again, twin question marks stabbed upward on her forehead and he turned away. If he could not answer the questions himself, how could he answer her? Was she turning into Jesup now? Constantly probing?

"Keep me apprised of the situation. I will join you tomorrow to seal the victory."

Like all his Aimag, they knew when they were dismissed. "Yes, ovKhan." The sound of feet displacing gravel chewed into the morning. The door opening and closing—releasing another wave of odor—caused him to hitch his shoulders against it and he felt disgust at himself. Such weakness!

Petr turned sharply and stalked through the gravel toward the wall of the Merchant House, his eyes seeing the path his own feet had trod numerous times around the circumference of the building. His anger pulsed brighter at this blatant sign of his own inability to confront the situation. Inability to confront, because the *surat* could not be found! The sweet air was forgotten as his mind raced.

For almost a week he had attempted to contact this Snow. At first, he assumed she would contact him. Several days passed unnoticed as he immersed himself in negotiations with Adhafera's local merchants, but the slow realization that she had not made an appearance began to distract him. To disrupt his thoughts. He even began to make mistakes, which cost them days of negotiation.

Five days ago he began to walk through the streets of Halifax. Ostensibly to garner more information on the inhabitants, which might be used against them across the negotiation table. In reality, he moved to let his whereabouts be known. Perhaps she simply didn't know the Sea Fox were on planet.

He rounded the corner of the building and came to one of the mammoth doors towering almost twenty meters above him and twice as wide; the cattle were driven to and from the building through this main artery, with secondary arteries on the other side of the building only used when the flow of flesh grew too great. The stench wafted out of the structure like heat eddies, almost visible. He began to gag slightly and tears once more slicked the back of his eyes. His rage grew until it engulfed him. Though his nostrils tried to close against the assault and his feet to move away of their own accord, his iron will kept his nose open and his feet firmly planted while he drew in a huge lungfull of vileness.

She managed to have a data cube deposited on my ship. She could not possibly be so clueless as to not know we are here. The echo of his own thoughts from three days ago now rang in his head and pushed out the sensory torment he put himself through. With new determination, he began canvassing the town at night, showing himself in every filthy dive and out-of-the-way bar he could find. All to no avail.

He began to wonder if she existed.

He thumbed the data cube in a small side pocket of his single-suit—a talisman to keep his anger, his frustration, at bay. He willed his body back under his control, taking in another lungfull of air, forcing himself to glory in it.

She did exist, and when he found her, he'd snap her neck. He strode forward, marching back into the battle.

8

Clan Sea Fox CargoShip **Talismantia**
Zenith Jump Point, Remulac System
Prefecture VII, The Republic
28 July 3134

OvKhan Sha Clarke stood on the observation deck
and gazed back along the eight-hundred-meter length
of his ship. The command CargoShip for Beta Aimag
of the Spina Khanate.

He was wrapped in quiet contentment.

In another life, another age, this vessel bore the
name *Nagasawa*. During the dark night of the Jihad,
it was gutted at the final naval battle of Tukayyid.
With the molting of the Diamond Sharks to their original name and a new form, so this vessel gained a new
lease on life: transformed into a CargoShip he used
to great effect in reaping glory for his Clan.

Through the ferroglass of the main observation window, he watched as the black flower of the *Talismantia* furled its petals. On the world of Breukelen in the Lyran Commonwealth, Sha encountered a local flower that closed its petals to a bud by noontime; the life-energy it needed drunk in the early-morning hours, it sealed itself from the killing glare of the system's blue-white supergiant for the rest of the day. Now Sha watched with fascination as the solar sail (most referred to it as a jump sail, but Sha found more depth and meaning in the word "solar") slowly furled, the molecules-thin, high-strength polymer material folding like that exotic flower; it too had drunk its fill and within the hour the CargoShip would jump from this system. Light flared around the sail like a corona and began to brighten the entire ship as its shadow extinguished, letting Remulac's star bathe the *Talismantia* in pumpkin-bright light.

"Magnificent, is it not?" Sha said, his soft voice loud in the dead calm of the room.

"It is a jump sail, *quiaff*?" Star Colonel Ryn Faulk's tone said it all.

"*Aff.* Of course it is."

Her silence actually *felt* confused. Sha smiled. "What do you see?"

"I see the array furling the jump sail. We jump to Savannah within the hour."

"Is that all?"

"*Aff?*"

His smile grew until mocking laughter threatened. He held it, refusing, as always, to give in. This, after all, was exactly why he brought Ryn here. One of the last significant holdouts in his Aimag. She would see.

"*Neg*, Star Colonel."

"I do not understand, ovKhan. Is it the K1IV star beyond? The *Talismantia* itself?"

"*Neg*, Ryn. It is the solar sail and yet it is not." He raised his right hand and placed the palm flat against the ice-cold pane. Strange how cold burned just like fire; his fingers would quickly grow deadened, but the sensation always fascinated him. Though it mimicked fire, it ultimately lulled you into a false sense of numbness. A numbness that led to a lowering of your guard, to mistakes. To death and, worst of all, failure.

Cold would always beat fire. Always.

He turned to look at his companion. Shockingly, for the second time, used her first name. "Ryn, this vessel is three hundred and eighty-four years old. It has unfurled and furled its solar sail untold thousands of times, the act becoming completely mundane. An exercise in mechanical technology that has dropped below the notice of all save the man whose job it is to operate the jump sail array. Even that technician, I would wager, finds the work dull and repetitious—a task to be accomplished and forgotten."

"But ovKhan, you describe reality. The truth."

"Yet truth is subjective, is it not? A BattleMech is the supreme military vehicle of the thirty-second century. Has held that place undisputed for nearly seven hundred years. And yet any MechWarrior can tell tales of almost losing their mount to the battle armor squad they ignored, *quiaff*?"

"*Aff*. What does this have to do with the jump sail?"

He once more fought the smile at the quizzical look painting her features. He shifted, felt the distant machinery sending tiny vibrations through his slips.

"What it represents. It is so fragile, so delicate, it takes well over an hour to unfurl it and twice that long to furl it. If it is damaged, it is almost impossible to repair. Yet upon such a foundation is interstellar travel possible. Such a little thing, yet magnificence is achieved through its careful and methodical use. Each time I see a sail furl, I see the sweep of humanity's victories before me." He pulled away his hand, knowing almost to the second when to do so before leaving a layer of skin adhered to the surface, and moved to stand directly in front of Ryn. His pale blue eyes stood out unnaturally large in his scarecrow-thin face and blazed with the cool fire that drenched his hand in pain. Nothing showed on his face.

"Star Colonel, all that humanity has accomplished in the centuries since the *Pathfinder* made that first jump to Alpha Centauri can be tied to the Kearny-Fuchida drive, and that drive is almost entirely dependent upon the solar sail. The colonization of thousands of planets. The foundation of the true Star League. Even the greatness of the Clans, of *our* Clan, is intrinsically tied to the solar sail, and yet most hardly acknowledge its existence."

"But, ovKhan"—the slight hitch in her voice repulsed him—"there are other ways to charge the drive, *quiaff*? The reactor. A recharge station?"

Pity clouded his vision. Must it always be so difficult for others? "*Aff*, Star Colonel. But they are dangerous, expensive and require support, *quiaff*?" He continued before she could respond. "The solar sail, in its simplicity and beauty, is completely self-sufficient. It need depend on nothing but what the universe gives of its own free will. Shouldn't we be the same?" He saw the revulsion in her eyes at his use of a contraction; he hoped the emphasis had been worth the vulgarity.

"Clan Sea Fox is independent. What are you saying?"

"Many things, Star Colonel, many things." The flaming pain devolved into the tiny pinpricks of an almost awakened hand, the last breath of a dying beast he defeated. Once more.

"Why did you ask me here, ovKhan?"

"To show you the beauty of the solar sail."

"Is that all?"

Sha looked carefully at Ryn. Watching the play of muscles across her face, the hint of saliva on her lips and the heave of her chest, he came to a decision. She would not, or could not see.

Discard.

"Yes, Star Colonel, you may go." She saluted smartly and turned to leave. In her haste to depart, she unstuck herself from her magnetic slips and vaulted toward the hatch and the waiting corridor beyond.

He turned back to contemplate the simplicity of the solar sail. She had been useful in the past, despite the need to cast her aside. Her genes, of course, would be useful again in a future generation.

"ovKhan." The electronic voice echoed through the room. He moved toward the comm station at the side of the observation window and touched the flashing button.

"ovKhan here."

"*Farstar III* has just materialized in-system, ovKhan. She sends word Delta Aimag has been located in the

Adhafera system, in deep negotiations for the last week and more."

"Thank you." Sha smiled slowly and casually rested his forehead against the ferroglass; the cold immediately sank teeth deep into his forehead. *The time is coming, ovKhan Petr. We have swum the same currents for too long, too much wounding of flanks and butting of snouts in indecisive displays. Finally, the time has come to meet your fire with ice.*

It felt as though the cold was tearing chunks of flesh right from his skin, but Sha's smile broadened.

Cold always wins.

9

Marik Quarter, Halifax
Vanderfox, Adhafera
Prefecture VII, The Republic
7 July 3134

Even close to dusk, the yellow-white light beat down like the hand of an unmerciful god that would see Adhafera's inhabitants dead before the blessed rains came. Staring up at the cobalt sky totally devoid of even a wispy hint of white, Petr found it hard to believe the locals were already preparing for the savage rainfalls they said would be arriving any day.

Moving into the shade of an eave—he felt sure the hammer of light targeted his head with brutal and malicious efficiency—he watched an elderly woman across the street for a moment. She stooped to grasp an apparently light, yet unwieldy sheet, which she then heaved into place with a snap across the front window of her store; he'd heard it mentioned several times the wind could drive raindrops so hard they would break glass. The rainy season threatened, which is why the cattle slaughtering normally occurred at this time.

Petr stepped away from the curb and began walking briskly down the street, still hoping to find Snow. And to bleed off anger; his temper flared again as he thought of the local merchants' most recent behavior. *Stupid spheroids.* Didn't matter that he moved among their worlds. He was trueborn bred and trained, and the spheroids' ways might as well be alien intelligences for all he could understand them at times.

They had a deal. How dared they back away at the last minute!

He felt the lightest of brushes against his right elbow and immediately spun to the left, down and around into a defense crouch. He'd been downside on worlds that made him feel as though he moved in powered-down battle armor, their crushing gravities making even walking arduous. But on Adhafera, with its .77 standard Terran gravity, he could move almost as lithely as though still on the grav deck of his ship.

The old lady he'd watched for a moment screeched and took several quick, mincing steps backward. Sha knew many Clansmen, especially those still confined within their occupation zones, who would be revolted by the skein of wrinkles that mapped her life in relief across her bronzed skin; Petr didn't bat an eye, too accustomed to seeing this and worse in ports of call.

Still, he couldn't believe the audacity of this hag to touch his person, and the familiar warmth raced along his blood, setting off the dull thump that would soon soar to a roaring beat, the soft, tickling sensation on his skin that would eventually set him afire.

"You got no right to frighten me so," the hag scolded, speaking to him before he could begin to chastise her properly; her face wore the look of a sibko trainer about to berate an errant shiv. The beat in his ears grew by increments.

"She tells me to tell you, that's all. She gives me good C-bills, so I don't mind. But I got work to do. With Pappy gone, I'm all the store's got. So I didn't see ya gawking and suddenly you're walking like hell's on your tail."

The internal heat grew as the brazen woman stepped a little closer and the musk of fresh soil and age, mixed with good clean sweat, sailed up his nostrils as he breathed deep to keep it under control. She began to shake a finger at him.

"Then I come near to knocking myself off—ticker not so strong anymore—and then you leap about like some weasel and look like you gonna hit ol' Timma." She gummed her mouth several times; his lips curled at the dentures.

"Don't matter what that ugly women say to me, taking a message to you offworlders not worth the time to spit."

Frigid waters cascaded across his temper, sublimating it in a flash that almost stunned him; without conscious thought he stepped toward the woman and assumed his most disarming look, casually slouching his body to appear less threatening. "My good Timma, I must apologize for my actions. Where I hail from, we simply do not have the great spaces you enjoy in which to live. To work. As such, we are accustomed to not touching one another." He broadened his smile, added a twinkle to his eye. "It's a way to create artificial space where none really exists. You simply startled me." Contractions were always a nice touch with spheroids.

She cocked her head at him and gummed her upper lip several times; this close, he could see the fine dirt that filled most of her wrinkles; he suddenly felt she was a soil etching in need of a good dousing to reveal the true sculpture beneath. "You got no right, still, to be surprising me like that. Bang, could've been dead. Then how sorry *you* be?"

Petr added a hint of sorrow to his features. A warrior on the field needed no such subterfuge, but this was a battlefield, if of a different sort, and like a heavy medium laser from his *Tiburon*, he would use whatever resources he found at hand. "Then I would hold your spirit on my conscience for all the days of my life. A specter to haunt my CargoShip." A touch of a smile.

She wrinkled her forehead even more—if that were possible—then burst into loud laughter. "That's exactly what I be doing to you. You be careful, offworlder, or you have a flock of old women haunting your spaceship."

Petr bowed low to accept the rebuke; his eyes flashed once as they were hidden, returned to their charade by the time he finished the flourish. "Timma, you spoke of a message a woman gave you to pass on to a Sea Fox Clansman, *quiaff*?"

"Don't be knowing nothing about no *kiaf*, but this wasn't for just any offworlder."

She stabbed a finger at him and almost touched his chest. Glad she didn't; he would hate to slip and ruin what he had wrought.

"She describe you down to the tip of those fancy space boot thingies you got. No doubt you the man."

"And this message? What is it?"

"Just be glad Timma the forgiving type, or I be walking away. Can still feel the ticker a racing."

Please do not walk away. Had to keep this clean, especially after the negotiations became blocked; the coolness began to thaw.

"She tell me to say to this offworlder—you, o' course—to meet this woman (ugly!) at Dipson's Five and Dime Diner."

Petr simply strode away, knowing exactly where to find the eating establishment—calling it such brought a sardonic smile. He didn't look back once to see the gaping mouth of Timma, flabbergasted out of speech by the way Petr simply dropped her presence and sped away like demons from Hell snapped at his heels.

It took him most of an hour to cross this portion of Halifax. They called it the Marik Quarter, but he could find no distinguishing characteristics—neither architecture, nor smell—to tell it apart from any other portion of the city. By the time he reached the diner, full dark quenched the light and cast up its own pale imitations; without the streetlights, he would have found the going difficult.

Opening the door, he stepped in and for a moment wondered if the stench he sought to escape so many times at the Merchant House had found its way into this building as well, waiting to pounce upon him once more.

Dim and dirty. Few occupants. It fit the image he

had carefully crafted of Snow over the last few weeks. A cockroach would revel here and so would she.

He moved away from the door, weaving in and out of aisles of chairs sitting askew, his boots conveying the squelch and smack of every puddle of liquid—the aroma told him some of them were not just spilled alcohol—and morsels of soggy food. Though several people raised their heads, most were too drunk to give him more than a passing glance. The one or two whose eyes actually quickened at the realization a Sea Fox strode among them quickly resumed their previous postures as his blazing eyes swept the room and turned any interest to ash. The anger stirred, roared; he should be glowing, his skin an incandescent covering to the blazing furnace within.

Toward the back, he spotted her and stopped dead. She sat unconcernedly, a stoop to her posture, as she gazed at a wilted and wrinkled menu. Her left hand strayed to her mouth and she bit absentmindedly at a nail and casually spit it out the side of her mouth. Her swarthy skin blended into her short, hacked-off hair, and with a side profile, her bulbous nose appeared to swell out like the snout of an ice hellion; would she be as whiny and backbiting as that dead Clan? Her stocky body and shabby clothing (a mix of several shapes and colors Petr felt sure she stripped off some street itinerate) plunged a spike of physical loathing through his rage.

Such an abomination would've been terminated by the scientist caste overseeing the birth before the mother carried it to term. He didn't even think of the trueborn possibilities, confident such a creature could never have flowed from the Clan's iron womb program. On the verge of turning away, he remembered the data cube tucked into his pocket. The image of those smoky eyes. She managed to place it on his ship; he must give her credit for such a feat. He could stomach her presence long enough to find out if her message held merit, or whether he could give in to his desire to wrap that stump of a neck with his hands.

He moved to the booth and slid in.

"Took you long enough. Get lost?" Her voice came out deep and husky, not completely unattractive. "Haven't had somebody staring that hard at me since Jack Rilley used to peek in at me when I took a shower." She casually chewed off another nail, spit it out and then glanced up; the merriment they held almost redded out Petr's vision and he gripped his thighs to keep from reaching across the table. " 'Course, I looked a whole lot better back then, so don't know why you're staring. But hey, if you're in to me, you are. Nothing I can do about it. Right?"

She is trying to provoke me. The voice came as though stretched and thinned by an endless haze of gore and shimmering heat. He breathed in deeply, hunting for scents, trying to regain his focus. He expected a foul miasma to match the reek of this place and instead detected the scent of flowers. A soft, herbal scent totally incongruous with her appearance. *She is playing with you.* The voice gained strength and his vision began to clear. *It is a facade. If she is good enough to seed a message on your ship, she is good enough to play you like a harp.*

"Waiter," he abruptly called in a loud voice.

She quirked her mouth and leaned back.

His eyes began to pick out details he missed the first time, and the rage began to return, but this time directed inward. *She may have been on-world this entire time and simply waited in order to throw you off balance. The first move perhaps went her way, but no more.* She slouched against the back of her chair, but did so a little too carefully. As though to keep her right shoulder at just the right angle—for what? Was she carrying? Did it matter? She did not bring him all this way to kill him.

"So, with those steaming eyes of yours, I think I'll call you sweetness. Practically got engaged." She smiled, and her almost-too-white teeth gleamed in the dim light like the dials of his 'Mech's cockpit console glowed at night.

His normal response to any such advances would have been vehement revulsion, but he could not afford that luxury here. It put him off balance. Off guard. He gripped his thighs hard as he tried to roll with it.

"Got something going on under the table, do you?" she said, her voice dropping to a sultry timbre; she leaned forward and tapped her hand on the table several times, her index finger pointing toward his arms. "Those biceps are filling your suit real nice and, well, can't help but wonder if we shouldn't be moving right to the wedding day." The smoky gray eyes almost gleamed in the darkness, her soft voice and words at total contrast with her repellent physicality. He couldn't seem to pull himself together.

The waiter arrived. A scrawny teenage boy with a runny nose, peach fuzz on his lip that he no doubt doted over, and a greasy apron. "What ya ordering?" He didn't look up; he'd learned to not get involved.

Snow leaned back again, still with the stiffness around her shoulders, and waved a hand in his direction. "You're the one who thinks we're on a date, so you can order for me."

"I am not hungry," he responded gracelessly and berated himself again. How did she manage to keep him off his guard? He was surprised in the street by the hag and yet responded instantly with his usual zeal and effectiveness in negotiations. This encounter was quickly shaping up to be a disaster.

"Oh, straight to bed, then?"

He couldn't help but stare. Was she actually coming on to him? The silence stretched and he could see the skinny brat actually glance up and begin to turn away.

"Twin beers. Anything." He looked a question at her.

"Fine. Sure. If you want to get me drunk, I'm all for it." She laughed out loud and several people from two and three tables away glanced in their direction.

He spoke immediately once the waiter departed. "You should not be so loud. Do you wish to draw others' attention?"

"Why not? Only if we skulk and hide in the corner could we possibly be doing something we shouldn't. Even if it is exceptionally strange for an offworlder— much less a Sea Fox—to come, at night, to such a seedy bar in his uniform [*no doubt of the sarcasm there*], if she's loudmouthed and it looks like he's simply got strange taste on local women, why should they care?" She smiled, and for the first time, he caught a glimpse of her real smile; the warmth surprised him, but the wariness remained.

He savagely dug his fingers into his thighs one last

time, for the final point he gave up, and moved his hands to the tabletop.

"That's better," she said immediately and chewed on another nail. "This may be a little seedy, but it's a family establishment after all."

"Must you always speak with sarcasm?"

"Are you kidding?" She laughed. "I'm not sure I could complete a sentence without it."

"Perhaps you should try. Explain why you brought me here."

"Did I bring you here?" The laughing tone of voice fired his ire once more.

The skinny waiter thumped down two beers and Petr gaped as, before the waiter took five steps, Snow slammed back the beer, draining the bottle quicker than the collapse of a compartment to decompression.

"Keep 'em coming!" she bellowed, and the waiter partially raised a hand, but continued away.

"Hey, I'm a thirsty gal. Work's been hard of late," she said when she noticed Petr's surprise.

"You *did* bring me here." He took out the data cube and carefully placed it on the table. He almost winced when he saw how much his constant rubbing, the nervous tick of his anger, had worn it down.

"My, my, my," she said, looking at the cube and then turning those searchlight eyes on him once more. "Seems I should've brought a bouquet. You were anxious, weren't you?"

Petr ignored the comment. "Why?"

"Ah, left at the altar again. Well, I've come to expect it. You've got some pretty Foxer you're bedding, right? No place in your life for little ol' Snow."

He slapped his hand on the table and ignored the

curious looks from around the room at the gunshot sound. "Snow," he ground out, trying to keep a rein on his temper, "I do not have time for this. You managed to get this cube on my ship, which I am sure you know is the only reason I'm here."

She placed her hand gently on the table, as though to mock his own brutal impact, and laughed quietly. "Ah, now you're starting to use vulgarity with me. If you're going to leave me at the altar, the least you could do is not argue with me. That's for married folks."

Petr trembled and his eyes flashed red. He closed them; he would not react. Would not!

"Okay, okay," she said.

He opened his eyes to find her face slightly altered. He could not put a finger on it, but something had changed.

"Yeah, I brought you here. I've got some news I know you'll find interesting."

"How?"

"Because you're Sea Fox. You keep your fingers in every pot you can." Her right hand dipped below the table and reappeared with a new data cube, which she placed on the table and lightly flicked with her index finger. It sailed smoothly across the surface—a testament to the permanent grease ingrained in the fake-wood top—and Petr closed his hand over it.

He gritted his teeth. "I hope this one provides more information than the last."

"Hey, I couldn't tell you everything right off the bat, sweetness. And I did get you here."

He could only nod his head. Too many points to her this round. *This* round.

"What will I find on this?"

For once she did lower her voice and casually lift the new beer the waiter had dropped off only moments before. "Information about the imminent invasion of this part of The Republic of the Sphere by the Marik-Stewart Commonwealth."

Petr stared at her, incredulous. *This* was her vital message? He'd be angry if he didn't find the situation so ludicrous. He laughed out loud. "This is your urgent news? Please!" Petr slid across the bench to stand.

Snow quickly leaned forward and something flashed through her eyes. "Listen, I know why you've come to this Prefecture. And an invasion could either ruin it, or for those who know it's coming, they might just make huge profits off events to come."

He settled back down, not from her urging, but more from her knowledge of why he'd come to Prefecture VII. Could she know it all? How? He saw pain in her eyes. His gaze caressed her shoulder and returned to find her eyes boring into his. She was wounded. And she knew that he knew. Not that he knew what to do with that information, but he filed it away for possible future use. It did, however, show her in a new light. More information for him to use.

"And how could I possibly find it worthwhile?"

"You've a good-sized force at your command. The Republic can be generous to those who help them. *Very* generous."

Was she asking for aide? Mutual defense? "The Republic and Clan Sea Fox already have a mutual nonaggression treaty. Why not have your precious exarch try to negotiate a further treaty? You obviously are Republic. Why all this backroom dealing?"

She leaned back in the too-casual way that confirmed his find; her right shoulder was wounded.

"Maybe I do work for The Republic, probably not in the way you think, though. But this doesn't have to be something dragged through the light of day. Just a friendly agreement between betrothed. Right?"

He finally began to get the mettle of her and smiled in his own, easy fashion; she had scored enough easy marks. No more. "Yes, but I have isorla to take from this wedding and it will not be *you*, I wager. You did not answer my question."

"You're right. I didn't."

Her gray eyes filled his vision. Though he began to function once more with his usual grace, he found those eyes still pulled him off balance.

Such amazing eyes.

"You look over the information, then tell me you're not interested. Like I said, The Republic knows its friends and can be very generous."

The meeting had reached its end. He slowly stood, pocketed both data cubes and looked down at Snow. Not once did he ask for her real name; he knew she'd not likely divulge it. Though she still could be called nothing but ugly, the complete revulsion of his first impression was gone. As with the data cube on his ship, he couldn't help a begrudging admiration for the way she'd manhandled him. Not often did he meet someone his equal at the table. But he would take her in the long run.

"I will think upon it. How will I contact you?"

"Oh, I'll contact you." She laughed. "I know us girls are supposed to wait for your call, but I just won't be able to."

He grimaced despite himself. "I had a feeling you would say that," he replied; he accepted that she had scored the final point, and walked out.

Her sultry laugh followed him into the night, a companion for many nights to come.

=10=

Clan Sea Fox DropShip **Ocean of Stars,** *Halifax
Vanderfox, Adhafera*
Prefecture VII, The Republic
7 July 3134

"**T**his is what they waited for?" Petr raged at Jesup.
"We had the deal ready to ink and they pulled back
because they somehow found out Beta Aimag jumped
in-system?"

"It would appear that way."

Immediately upon returning from the unpleasant
encounter with Snow, Petr learned the reason for the
sudden "troubles" preventing the local merchants
from signing the agreement. Could the day get worse?
He moved along the corridor of the DropShip toward
the bridge, and realized it could. He would have to
speak directly with Sha. The arrogant *surat*.

The record of wins and losses between them was

nearly even . . . except for his last, most humiliating defeat at Sha's hands. Still unsettled by his encounter with Snow, he could not stop the memories that flooded his mind.

By the Founder, why did I not explore that asteroid belt in the Lungdo system further? Can I truly claim it was an honest mistake that my people did not discover the small germanium ore deposit there? Controlling a supply of the rare core component for building K-F drives would have brought Delta Aimag so much honor and wealth. . . .

Sha pursued the advantage in the Trial of Possession so aggressively that he must have known of the ore going into the negotiations—and I should have realized there was a prize worth any price at stake. Did my hatred for Sha keep me from recognizing the significance of his extravagant offers? If only I had been willing to concede access to our orbital repair facility in the Castor system. . . .

Even after two years, the questions still haunted him. As he did every time they surfaced, Petr pushed them down and shut them away.

Petr reached a ladder and began to shimmy up when the voice of Jesup floated up around him; for an instant he thought of the hag Timma and her haunting spirit, and actually smiled despite himself. Anything to distract him from the coming confrontation.

"So what are the odds he would come to the very world where we first make planetfall? Twenty-six worlds to choose from, and he comes downside here first?"

"You mean twenty-five. After all, our enclave on Castor does not really count, *quiaff*?"

"You know what I mean, oh great one of infinite wit. Did he throw a dart at a board? I do not think so. We arrived before Beta Aimag in this Prefecture and, considering how long we have been here, he must have come directly to this planet."

Petr climbed the last rung and entered a new passage; this one terminated at the main bridge. He knew Star Captain Jotok would already be at his station. He once joked that the man slept there, and Jotok's blank stare in reply actually alarmed Petr slightly, before he acknowledged the man could command his ship how he saw fit.

"Could he have encountered the same information that required us to come here?" Jesup jabbed with his voice once more, hoping to open a crack. Petr ignored it.

"I doubt that very much, Jesup. I doubt it very much." Yet the idea stuck in his mind. According to what she said (no time to verify her story, beyond a cursory look at the data cube), her plan involved "bribing" a Sea Fox Aimag into stopping an invasion of The Republic of the Sphere by the Marik-Stewart Commonwealth. If one Aimag worked well, wouldn't two work even better? Not to mention she seemed to know so much about him. Did she know of his animosity toward Sha? Could she have somehow managed the same trick on the *Talismantia*, causing Sha to come running with the same urgency? Perhaps she believed using two such adversaries would improve the chances that one would follow her call, if not both—both afraid the other would reap benefits that would carry him above and beyond the other.

Petr almost stumbled with the myriad questions

somersaulting through his mind, a terrible riptide threatening his concentration. Only moments remained before he faced Sha, and this was how he would present himself? Incoherent? Frothing at the mouth? Sha would win before he ever set foot on Adhafera soil.

"Your silence is very edifying, oh great and powerful ovKhan. If he did not come running in response to the same source of information as you, then, considering your own personal *fascination* with the leader of Beta Aimag, perhaps he has a similar fascination?" Petr halted mere steps from the bridge and turned to find Jesup practically on his heels. "And when I say 'fascination,' what I mean to say is 'obsession.'"

Petr hardened his gaze and Jesup immediately brought his hands up in a mock-defensive measure.

"I meant no disrespect, ovKhan, but the mind simply boggles at the possibility that he would come directly to the same backwater world. Yes, the meat garnered here will allow us to make inroads into other worlds, but this deal will hardly be profitable in itself. So the information that sent us skipping across the length of Prefecture VII obviously had little to do with commerce. If Sha doesn't have that information, then he comes for you."

Once more Petr ignored his aide's fishing for information. "Jesup, I do not need your banter at this moment. You know I must confront Sha and open up the official trials between our Aimags. I do not look forward to it."

"But why? You could confront him, ask about the information that led him here." The crooked smile only served to further darken Petr's mood. Asking such a question outright would only prove his own ignorance. Sometimes Petr did not know if Jesup's sarcasm was real or feigned to cover ignorance. He hoped the former, but thought the latter on numerous occasions.

Turning his back on Jesup, he stepped onto the bridge. Jotok was not there. Surprise actually stopped Petr in his tracks for several long seconds as he looked again. He saw only four crewmen on the bridge, two of whom were in the process of putting the holographic display through its annual servicing.

"Where is Star Captain Jotok?" he asked, raising his voice to be heard above the din. He moved toward the communications bank and its crewman without waiting for an answer.

"Star Commander Alisa on watch, ovKhan. We have called repeatedly for Star Captain Jotok, but he has yet to respond to our hails. He actually took shore leave, sir."

"Really?" Did wonders never cease?

"Coms, you have the incoming DropShips?"

The technician looked as though he had just graduated from a shiv to active duty; he couldn't be more than eighteen, possibly nineteen years old. He moved with grace and confidence, however, that spoke well of his bloodline. "Yes, ovKhan. The flotilla of DropShips will interface with the atmosphere in three hours and twenty-two minutes at its current velocity. Their trajectories will place them directly into Halifax."

No surprise there. Petr shook his head and felt the weight of his hair swing against his shoulders. He could continue to wait, to delay, but to what end? It would reflect poorly on him among his subordinates—

and an hour or two longer would not change his discomfort at the conversation.

"Coms, patch me through to the lead DropShip. OvKhan Clarke is aboard that vessel and I wish to speak with him."

"Yes, sir," the boy responded, and immediately began transmitting the appropriate codes for opening communication.

A few seconds passed and the front viewscreen materialized into the bridge on the command vessel of the incoming flotilla. A short-haired, scarecrowlike man stared coldly across several thousand kilometers. Those dead eyes almost sent a shiver up Petr's spine, caused his anger to pile up in a flash.

Sha Clarke.

A thorn in his side for years, and now he intended to be one again. This time, however, it would be different. There would be no going back. No stopping.

"Ah, Petr, I see you have begun to develop what I will take."

He gritted his teeth. Having a complete unknown like Snow clip his fins and rattle him might be tolerated, but he would not allow Sha the same enjoyment. Too much of that before.

"Is that a challenge?"

"Why, no." That surprised him. He expected Sha immediately to challenge for a Trial of Possession. "We have more important issues."

"Fighting a Trial of Possession for the right to negotiate this planet would not stop our traditional trials."

Even digitally reproduced, the knowing look in Sha's eyes felt like a slap in the face. Those too-cool eyes in a face that never seemed to show more than a spark of animation. "Oh, I am well aware of that. My news is that Star Captain Tal Sennet has died. As a quorum of those warriors who will be nominated to fight for his name is within our two Aimags, Khan Hawker has given permission for the initiation of a Trial of Bloodright."

That abruptly stopped the activity on the bridge and even brought Petr's chin up. A Trial of Bloodright had not been fought within the jurisdiction of his Aimag in more than five years, and the thrill of the honor to come sang in his veins. Even so, a dark note tempered his excitement.

"When shall we initiate the trial?" he said, infusing an enthusiasm and respect into his voice that he never felt in dealing with Sha.

"No time like the present, *quiaff*?"

"*Aff*, Sha."

"I have already transferred the appropriate personnel for the ritual; my *Breaker of Waves* has adjusted her trajectory to enter a standard orbit; the rest will make planetfall. Gather your personnel and boost to intercept. Out."

The screen went blank. Petr felt almost let down by the encounter. None of the normal stabs and jabs, beyond the obligatory opening parry. It was as though Sha simply had too much to deal with to indulge in their old rivalry.

Though the Trial of Bloodright would indeed require great resources, it would not completely occupy either of them, and certainly offered no barrier to fighting a Trial of Possession for negotiation rights with the planet's merchants.

The other DropShips. He became aware of Jesup

standing almost at his shoulder, understanding written on his face. *He actually might have picked up on it before me.*

"Why would he use the distraction of the Trial of Bloodright to allow his merchant castemen to try to gain an edge on our efforts here?" asked Jesup. "Why not simply declare the Trial of Possession and be done with it?"

"I cannot say, Jesup, but it worries me. It worries me a great deal." He considered the too-knowing look in those blank eyes, the way Sha simply dismissed him. As though he moved in deeper waters, currents Petr simply could not compete in.

A shiver ran down his spine.

11

Overlord-C *DropShip* Breaker of Waves
Near Orbit, Adhafera
Prefecture VII, The Republic
8 July 3134

Petr floated gracefully into the Trial Chamber.

Shaped like a perfect sphere sliced in half—flat side the deck—the chamber spanned twenty meters across, half that high. Though not the largest Ritual Chamber in Petr's experience, it was a respectable size—larger than his own and likely the reason Sha arranged for the Trial of Bloodright ceremony to occur here.

A slow, steady stream of warriors flowed in with him, each grabbing the bar that ran waist high around the circumference of the room. Thirty-two individuals in all, they spaced themselves equidistant from one another, stopping in front of an equal number of Clan Sea Fox symbols on the chamber bulkhead; each warrior tucked his or her feet under a small bar on the deck in order to remain stationary. Each wore the ritual garb of Clan Sea Fox.

Though many Clans' ritual clothing included extravagances from headdresses to long flowing capes of fur, twisting ropes of beads and diaphanous robes, the current Sea Fox ceremonial clothing was Spartan. A one-piece suit—fitted neck to ankle to wrist—of a rubbery gray material turned every warrior into an aquatic predator: a shark, ready to seize destiny by the teeth. To complete its effortless elegance, an embroidered fox-head pattern adorned the front.

The simplicity—a sharp contrast to the Diamond Shark ritual attire, which matched any Clan for finery and lushness—followed a dual mind-set: the merchant mentality, always strong with the Clan but grown to paramount importance, spoke of the waste of such finery—more practically, because all rituals occurred in microgravity, such extraneous clothing was problematic, even dangerous.

After a pause to review the chamber, Petr pushed off from the ground at an oblique angle to the entry hatch, sailed with ease toward the domed ceiling, grabbed the bar and settled his feet onto his assigned pedestal mounted six meters off the floor. With casual grace he turned, felt the stretch and flow of his suit, could almost taste the energy and power in the room. The elite of the elite stepping forward to risk all and obtain a sacred Bloodname—the highest honor a Clan warrior could receive.

Surveying the chamber, Petr watched the final participants arrive and move to their assigned positions. Several small platforms dotted the dome as it rose above the deck; metal mushrooms festooned the bulkhead. In addition to himself, two others were present on the dome: ovKhan Sha a quarter way round the dome and positioned slightly higher as the host, and Jet Sennet, leader of Blood House Sennet, whose platform rested directly across from and above Petr. Because his age eclipsed any present, Jet Sennet would officiate as Oathmaster, traditionally the oldest member of a Blood House, for this Trial of Bloodright.

The older man—he looked to be in his mid-forties—raised both his arms and spoke. "Trothkin." His voice held a note of firm command. "We have gathered within the black waters of the void. For all present the currents have been strong and treacherous. Yet you have never lost the scent of blood in the water. None can gainsay the honor you have earned by your presence this day. Still, a deal is not done, a victory not achieved, until it is sealed. The honor currently bestowed is a pale imitation of what will come with a Bloodname. Warriors, swim the void, seize your name and carry your glory to the Clan!"

"Seyla," echoed from thirty-four voices; all eyes turned to gaze at the deck.

A star map of the Inner Sphere filled most of the deck of the Ritual Chamber, leaving very little room around the circumference. The map did not lie flat in a mural, nor balloon on the silent electrons of a holo. Instead, the star map consisted of solid, three-dimensional objects: 2,141, to be precise. Each hand-made sphere a world in miniature, reflecting the correct size, color, standard atmospheric conditions and axis tilt as of January first Terran Standard; a map of every inhabited world within the Inner Sphere and near Periphery. The worlds recessed into holes in the deck, where small pneumatic clamps held them stationary during transit and grounding. At the ritual statement of acceptance from the gathered throng, the clamps loosened and several thousand magnets—one above and below each world—slowly lifted them in perfect synchronicity, positioning them horizontally and vertically to represent their spatial X, Y and Z coordinates.

Though he'd been present for several such rituals, Petr held his breath, enthralled by the simple majesty. Each time he saw it, especially when viewed from the height of the dome, he experienced momentary delusions of godhood, as though he watched an accelerated (if abbreviated) holovid unraveling a view from the Big Bang until the present.

It never ceased to awe him. To excite him.

The possibilities in the universe were endless, the currents to hunt unending. He automatically began to draw on the jump paths, trade routes and jump points—a skein of undeveloped deals and glory, honor and combat to be unraveled and traveled. The universe held in the palm of his hand, waiting for his ambitions to unfurl and engulf it like a giant's hands.

A god's hands.

"First warriors, advance." Jet's voice filled the room with a new tone and power. Perhaps he too felt the grandeur of the vision before him—likely the reason for such extravagance, to impart to those present the universe of possibilities for a Bloodnamed warrior and the honor it ultimately would bring to Clan Sea Fox.

Though Petr did not see the movement, he knew

Jet had a small remote control attached to his belt, which he thumbed. An algorithm ran for a microsecond, then fired a microburst transmission, causing the Sea Fox insignia behind two randomly chosen warriors to light and chime. As with any combat, whether on the battlefield or across the negotiation table, fate and the luck of the draw held sway every step of the way.

The gathered warriors looked to the top center of the dome, where a clear polymer platform descended three meters. On the platform rested an opaque block of polymer; out of its flat top a length of clear tubing rose a meter and half before bending sharply and descending back into the block.

The two chosen warriors let go of their toe bars and thrust toward the ceiling. Though there existed the possibility of a warrior striking a planet, knocking it out of alignment, he'd never heard of such a thing occurring; the dishonor that would accrue to such clumsiness ensured that it never happened.

As the warriors drew close to the podium, Jet kicked off from his position and arrived just after they did, each grabbing one of three rods that held the podium to the overhead, pulling themselves to their positions on the podium, tucking feet under three identical bars.

"Trothkin," Jet began once more, hands raised to encompass the assembly, "these warriors present themselves as worthy of obtaining a Bloodname. Should we not know of their deeds?"

"Seyla." The individuals coalesced into a mob of one.

Jet pointed his right arm at one warrior. "By what right do you present yourself before this skate?"

"I am Heb, warrior of Blood House Sennet," the tall, muscular warrior spoke boisterously; unusual for Beta Aimag, he had shoulder-length hair, which floated around his head like a frond of seaweed in a slow ocean current. "Many are my exploits, great my victories. However, for one thing alone am I sponsored for this Bloodright: I defeated a Knight of the Sphere in single combat."

Even the warrior facing Heb was visibly impressed at this pronouncement. Though Petr could not care one way or another about The Republic, their Knights were warriors to be respected; for a non-Blood to defeat such an opponent in ritual combat spoke volumes about his battle acumen.

Petr shifted slightly, stretched his neck. *Would be very interesting to hear the full tale; he is one to watch.*

With his right arm still elevated, Jet raised his left arm, pointed to the other warrior. "By what right do you present yourself before this skate?"

The smaller female warrior drew herself up and projected a quiet, but firm voice—no hint of reservations over her foe. "I am Sanda of Blood House Sennet. I am sponsored for my Star's victory against a far superior number of Oriente Protectorate raiders. Also, for the concessions into the markets of three new worlds I seized across the table following the combat."

Petr almost laughed out loud. He'd been mistaken. Though she might lose this battle—Heb's battlefield prowess would be formidable—he would be watching Sanda for the glory she would eventually reap. If she failed at this Trial of Bloodright, no doubt another opportunity would present itself. Someone who could fight equally well across the battlefield and negotiation table, worth a Star of 'Mechs. Though the Clan tried hard to instill such abilities within its warriors, few truly rose to the occasion; few held the versatility and mental agility to excel in both fields.

"You have both been found worthy before this skate. Present your tokens," Jet said, opening up his hands, palms up. Both warriors reached to their waists to an unseen pouch, withdrew polymer coins the size of their palms, passed them to the Oathmaster.

Jet raised his hands, presented the tokens to the assembly and spoke. "As with the random selection of your opponents, any battlefield, any negotiation table can turn to savage you with the sharpest teeth. Who will be your opponent cannot be known. Where your conflicts will occur cannot be foreseen. Any warrior worthy of a Clan Sea Fox Bloodname must overcome any odds, any situation, any circumstance."

He raised one coin. Though at too much of a distance to see clearly, Petr knew it showed the image of a sea fox with bared teeth, as though ready for the kill; the warrior's name was engraved across the bottom. "The hunter lands on top and chooses the form of combat: unaugmented or augmented."

He raised the other coin, which Petr knew displayed a sea fox with bowed head, protecting itself, ready to turn a setback into victory. "The hunted lands on bottom and chooses the venue for the combat. In this way, each warrior fights in a form not of his choosing."

"Seyla," filled the chamber, as though spoken by a single voice. A god's voice, proclaiming the nature of blood and whose genetic material would be used to create another generation of warriors. Almost the definition of deity.

Jet moved to the mechanism on the podium. Used almost universally by the Clans, the funnel in standard gravity couldn't be simpler. The coins were inserted; then gravity dragged them spinning down, chasing each other until one fell on top of the other.

In microgravity, this system could not work. In its place (and appropriate for the Sea Fox and their aquatic namesake) a water-fed tube system served. A continuous tube ran in a squished donut shape: two straight pieces approximately a meter and a half long, joined with two elbow pieces. The bottom third of the pipes sank into the funnel-shaped opaque base that gave a nod to the funnel used for centuries and hid the pneumatic pump tied into the system. The upper portions of the pipe were a clear polymer, which revealed a dizzying array of rods connected to the walls of the pipe, creating a maze through which the coins would fight.

Within this closed system ran freshwater taken from the oceans of Itabiana (one of the few worlds wholly owned by Clan Sea Fox), where the sea fox, transplanted on the brink of extinction in the last decades of the previous century, now thrived.

Jet moved to the base of one of the tube sections and inserted both coins through rubber seals, tapped a button. The surge of water as the pump created circulation sent the coins on their desperate bid to be the hunter. Almost hypnotic in their motion, the coins bounced, jittered and skated over and under the obstacle rods, inexorably dragged forward by the current. Up a meter, flattening along the top and pushed back down to brave another terrifying jumble.

A coin sank into the first suction trap, cutting off

flow there and sending the other coin to the second suction trap; the pump cut off immediately and both coins cycled out through double-walled seals, dried on the way: the hunter on top, the hunted on bottom.

Jet reached forward, grasped both coins firmly and raised them for all to see: hunter in right hand, hunted in left.

"Heb, you are the hunter. How say you?"

Drawing himself up to his full 2.2 meters, he practically shouted, "I shall fight augmented."

That surprised Petr. Heb towered over the diminutive Sanda; an unaugmented fight would be difficult for Sanda to overcome. Perhaps he knew something about her zero-g fighting skills Petr did not.

Jet held up the other coin and turned toward Sanda. "Sanda, you are the hunted. How say you?"

Without a moment's hesitation, she spoke with a demure confidence Petr instantly took a liking to. "The moon of Coma."

Jet nodded firmly, raised coins until he joined both in clasped hands directly above his head. "And so it begins."

"Seyla."

Petr watched as both warriors launched themselves back to their assigned positions; all would traverse this cycle of the ritual before any departed for their coming battles. Jet thumbed the remote at his belt and the sequence began again.

Though he fiercely loved the traditions of his Clan, at times they warred with the merchant within. Was this all worth it?

The extravagance of Trials of Bloodright were legendary. A DropShip would spend precious time and fuel reserves to burn to the moon of Coma, simply for the purpose of the fight, simply because Sanda requested it. Other such requirements would unfold this day as well. The battles would repeat themselves, as would this ceremony: the sixteen victors returning to be paired once more, the eight subsequent and so on until only one victor emerged. Until only one stepped forward—one warrior proving worthy to hold a sacred Bloodname.

Petr slowly shook his head. There were times to be a merchant (plenty of times), but today held room only for warriors, and traditions stretching back almost three centuries to the Founder himself. There could only be one answer to such a question.

Aff.

12

Tumbled Heights, Near Halifax
Vanderfox, Adhafera
Prefecture VII, The Republic
14 July 3134

The bivouac bustled with energy.

Technician castemen scrambled across mud-slicked ground, uncomplaining of the same conditions that elicited moans of protest only yesterday. Laborer castemen worked hard to clean up the mess the monstrous, gale-strength storm (whose claws tried to drag even the multiton 'Mechs across the ground) wreaked across a half week. Hauling away logs, righting tents, cleaning off vehicles, making small repairs where needed: a veritable labor of Hercules.

They bounced with anticipation.

An ancient J-27 ammo truck procured from the locals churned through the mud in a vain attempt to bring its metal food to the hungry bins of a waiting *Thor*. Spinning, slipping tracks kicked up a rooster's tail of goop and slop that shot four meters into the air and a good ten meters back, splattering vehicles, 'Mech legs and personnel alike.

Nothing could dampen the mood.

Though the Trial of Bloodright began several days ago (an honor for all, whether one participated or not), today would be different—a different honor altogether. An honor—unlike the Trial of Bloodright— that allowed nearly every Sea Fox warrior, along with a significant percentage of the laborer and technician castemen, to directly participate.

Today began the Rituals of Combat, live-fire training exercises pitting everything from battle armor to 'Mechs to aerospace fighters against one another. Because they were so often in the depths of space for long months, if not years, Aimags took any opportunity to test their warriors' edge, ensuring they did not become dull from lack of use. The Rituals of Combat were so much more than mere exercises—imbued with mysticism and invested in tradition; points won and lost in the Rituals impacted an Aimag's honor and glory within a Khanate and even the rest of the Clan

Petr walked gingerly, trying not to splatter mud onto his calf-high 'Mech boots. Though the temperature had dipped precipitously during the storm, it now sat at a balmy 35 degrees and almost 100 percent humidity. Petr breathed deeply.

He stepped around a particularly large puddle and into shadow, recognized the dark embrace of his own 'Mech. Petr walked another half dozen paces toward the metal trunks towering before him and stopped.

Slowly ran his eyes over the metal giant he called his own.

The *Tiburon* stood nine meters tall, the sun baking away the last of the moisture; Petr smiled at the idea of the 'Mech stepping from a fresh bath, air drying and priming for the coming show. A show far too long in coming.

"She looks ready. Strong." Jesup stomped up through the muck. Petr watched him approach the last few meters to his side, obviously unconcerned about the droplets of mud flung onto his legs or caked on his boots.

"You are going to drag that into your ride?"

"Uh?" he responded, looked down, back up. Smiled.

"Unlike your prissy 'Mech, oh fastidious one, my *Thor* does not mind a little mud on the floor mat."

Petr shook his head and felt the still-wet strands of his hair slap his bare shoulders, almost stick in the webbing of his coolant vest.

"It is not about prissy, my slob of a friend. It is about respect. I respect her and she respects me."

"My *Thor* respects me because I control it."

"You think you control it, but as in combat or negotiations, such control is fluid at best. In such situations you work within the confines of the circumstances to achieve victory. Never truly controlling them, only planting your strengths of will and knowledge in such a way as to create an outcome to your liking, *quiaff*?"

"*Aff.*"

"There is no difference with a 'Mech. You work with it to achieve victory. *Quiaff?*"

"*Neg.* I do not see it."

"Perhaps that is why you have yet to defeat me, though your ride outweighs mine two to one." Petr spoke without even turning toward his aide, and so missed the bitter look that transformed Jesup's features at his words.

"Are you prepared for today? I would hate for Beta Aimag to defeat my aide. It would look bad," Petr continued, turning his head and smiling.

"Me, defeated! Never! Only you, great ovKhan, can defeat me. A defeat I bask in."

"I am serious."

"And so am I. You have no need of fear from this quarter. Do you fear defeat in yours, oh omnipotent one?"

Petr waited for the normal irritation, but found none; nothing could bother him this day. "Why should I fear a loss?" Of course, he knew why.

Jesup returned the look, no emotion on his face.

Petr attempted to hold that gaze, but for once pulled away first, felt his breakfast sitting heavy for a moment, tasted the tang of bile before swallowing it away. "It will not happen again."

"Of course it will not, oh mighty one."

Petr's anger sparked momentarily and he brought his jade eyes back online with Jesup, no evidence of sarcasm in voice or face. But always the hint of it, despite the apparent innocence. Always the stab into his sore spot. "Do you doubt your ovKhan?"

"I never doubt my ovKhan's abilities."

"That is not the same thing," Petr ground out, trying to hold on to his good mood.

"Is it not?" Jesup responded, raising a quizzical eyebrow, though something danced in his eyes.

Petr drew in a harsh breath to respond, then bit it off; he would not let his aide's propensity for pestering ruin this day. Of course Jesup did not doubt his abilities . . . or him.

"Then let us be about shaming Beta Aimag."

Jesup hesitated for a moment, then nodded and moved away toward his *Thor*. Petr turned back to his own magnificent ride, the cooling balm of the moment washing away any vestiges of ire.

As ovKhan, he could choose to pilot literally any 'Mech within his Aimag. Yet he fell in love with the *Tiburon* in his first Trial of Position, and only death would separate the two of them.

Approaching the back of the 'Mech, he grasped the aluminum chain-link ladder dangling from above and began the ascent; the cool metal caused goose bumps to sprout along his bare arms and legs. Reaching the top of the ladder, he stepped onto the back of the shoulder, right where the head met the neck. Spinning open the dogged hatch, Petr swung it out with practiced ease; the sunlight splashed playfully into the dark interior, partially illuminating the metal cave where Petr lived more often than not (not enough now!).

Stepping through the hatch, he swung it back, sealing out the sunlight and fresh air, dogged it closed. Sidling around the command couch, he eased himself over the side of the chair, careful of the throttle mounted there. He closed his eyes and breathed deeply.

Stale odor of his own dried sweat; acerbic tang of spilled chemicals from a torn coolant vest; slight musk from the synthetic material in the seat; slick whiff of lubricants; dull, flat aroma of metal and polymers;

something (there!), barest hint of his own blood, spilt and forever wedded to her: home.

Opening his eyes, he reached up behind and pulled down the neurohelmet from where it rested, placing the light helmet upon his head, adjusting the fit until the neural receptors found their accustomed positions. Leaning to the right, he grasped a large yellow lever and pulled it firmly down, locked it into position; the growl of an awakening beast echoed up beneath his feet, as the first sequences of the fusion reactor initiated in preparation for startup. The aluminum ladder slapped the *Tiburon*'s rear armor plating as it automatically reeled in; it sounded like gnashing metal teeth.

A hunger needed to be satiated: the 'Mech's, his . . . the same.

Opening a small hatch in the right arm of the command couch, he pulled out several wires and a small bag. The first cord he plugged into the bottom of his coolant vest. Next, he took several medical monitors out of the bag, stowed it, then stripped off their covering and adhered them to the insides of his upper arms and thighs, smoothly attached alligator clips, then ran them through a pinch loop on his vest to keep them from tearing out during combat, ran the ends to a central plug. Finally, he jacked in the neurohelmet.

Stretching, he felt the weight of the helmet and the slickness of the seat under him, sensations that increased his regret for being gone too long. One of the great joys of his life sacrificed for the glory and honor of his Aimag.

Within the 'Mech's bowels, the initiation sequence

terminated and the reactor spun online; power surged in abundance, yet still lay trapped for the moment. Leaning slightly forward, he keyed the identification sequence. Her warm voice filled the cockpit with its embrace.

"Voice Identification, initiated."

"Petr Kalasa, ovKhan of Delta Aimag, Spina Khanate, Clan Sea Fox."

"Voice authorization confirmed."

Petr knew most warriors did not even notice the mechanical voice as they went through the motions of unlocking their 'Mechs. For Petr, however, the voice was part and parcel of his *Tiburon*. The first sign of the power about to be given into his hands: power to destroy, to kill . . . yet the power to create and build.

He bathed in the sound, luxuriated in it.

"Code Identification, initiated."

"There is always a price to be paid." Despite the constant prodding by his aide, Petr knew well the price to be paid for any action. Any warrior held such knowledge, or he did not live long; any merchant courted the knowledge, or he failed. As both, and leader of an Aimag, he was doubly aware of it. Confusion swirled within for a moment at the doubt that surfaced in his mind; he wrenched it about with the force of his will. *Of course, I do.*

"Code authorization confirmed. Command is yours." The voice went silent and power poured into the cockpit, igniting a rainbow of colors across the control panel. Leaning slightly forward once more, he brought the various 'Mech systems online. A quick glance through several screens showed weapons fully loaded and charged, while the armor schematic portrayed a pristine picture, ready to protect against the hellish energies about to be unleashed.

Almost squirming with glee, Petr settled back into the command couch, grasped the throttle in his left hand and moved it partially forward while using the foot pedals to direct the movement. The vibrations welling up from the first footfall spread a savage grin across his face.

Too long since he sat in this seat. Too long since his own Aimag encountered another, thus initiating the Rituals of Combat. Too long had this warrior been gone from his home port.

Petr returned to his true calling.

Petr waited impatiently for his turn. Staring out the forward viewscreen at the one-on-one duel unfolding a half kilometer distant, he could almost taste the tang in the air from discharged particle projector cannons and the cordite from exploded missiles and spent autocannon shell casings.

"I see Beta Aimag has improved since our last meeting." Jesup's voice exploded in the neurohelmet, dislodging Petr's thoughts.

"And I see your sarcasm is improving as well."

"Of course, oh great ovKhan."

"Regardless of my distaste for Sha, they are Sea Fox Clansmen. Of course they would improve. It has been almost three years since our last chance to test our mettle against them, of—"

"There," Jesup interrupted, as the arm of Torrin's *Mad Cat III* tore away under the horrific assault of twin hypersonic Gauss rounds from the Beta *Sun Cobra*. The fight ended immediately, the Beta warrior victorious.

Petr gripped his joysticks, infuriated by the loss. *"Stravag."*

"Torrin or the Beta MechWarrior? After all, the other warrior clearly held the upper hand."

"You, Jesup."

As usual, Jesup's loud laughter actually managed to loosen the tight knots across his shoulders and neck, to cool his temper rather than boil it.

"Come now, oh magnificent ovKhan, surely Torrin will learn from this exercise. He will not be so quick to confront a superior foe next time without using the terrain to his advantage, *quiaff*?"

"Aff," Petr managed to growl out. A smile even peeked out momentarily from the thundercloud of his face following another merry burst of Jesup's laughter.

How does he manage not to be killed by my own hand?

"It would seem to be my turn," Jesup said casually.

Petr once more gripped the joysticks, wanting, needing to take his place.

"Seize the day, Jesup."

"Aff, ovKhan," the response came back, for a wonder free of its usual embellishments.

The *Thor* next to Petr's *Tiburon* lumbered forward and quickly picked up momentum; it could not match his 'Mech for mobility, but considering its seventy tons, Jesup's *Thor* held respectable speed.

Almost a kilometer and a half distant, a Beta *Warhammer IIC* began to make its way forward. Though

Jesup's opponent was considerably outside his weapon range, Petr couldn't help but bring up the targeting reticule on the forward screen; centering on the enemy, he zoomed in, waiting, hoping for it to flash the golden tone of a lock. After a moment, he pulled the reticule off target, lifted away his hand. Jesup would claim this victory, not him.

His would be waiting, as he knew it would from the beginning, against Sha Clarke.

Strange.

The difference between watching combat and finding yourself in the thick of it was like reading about an interstellar jump and experiencing the heart-stopping, wrenching reality of having the fabric of your existence torn asunder, then to be pummeled and prodded until you reappeared light-years distant. The two could not compare.

For Petr, combat consisted of a series of time dilations that spun down and back in jerking scenes that could be disorienting, to say the least. Fifteen minutes could pass between one eyeblink and another.

Now, as he watched the fight between Jesup and his Beta opponent unfold in the distance, the time dilation gyrated in the opposite direction, the minutes elongating until each second felt like a life's age, each minute a living, breathing epoch, ready to devour him with his own impatience. His own need to fight.

Two cerulean beams of man-made lightning cut only swaths of air, as Jesup used the *Thor*'s superior mobility to keep just a microsecond ahead of the Beta's gross firepower. Even while jumping, Jesup managed to land several laser shots and half a barrage of missiles into the lower flanks of the *Warhammer*, burning and blasting away armor.

A game of armor and firepower versus mobility. A game requiring the utmost from a warrior. A game he desperately hoped Jesup would win, tipping the balance of wins and losses firmly into Delta's camp.

A game he did not believe Jesup could finish.

Another flurry of fire drew his eye once more. Azures, crimsons and flickering oranges filled the sky as the battle unfolded. Another leap with its jump jets launched the *Thor* across a rocky ravine, dropping it down desperately close to the *Warhammer*, but on its flank, where it would take precious seconds for the Beta 'Mech to turn in order to bring both PPCs to bear. The *Thor* unleashed everything at its disposal. Terrible energies washed over the *Warhammer*, stripping armor and shaking the behemoth as though it still stood in the storm only recently petered out.

Though he appreciated the gutsy move, Petr winced at the oven he knew the *Thor*'s cockpit became with such weapons fire.

Jump. Petr leaned forward. *Jump.* Tried to will it. "Jump," he said out loud.

Whether because, in his arrogance, he believed he had sufficiently damaged the *Warhammer*, or a moment's hesitation brought on by the crippling heat, the reason did not matter; the *Warhammer* made the torso twist in almost superhuman time and unleashed cobalt fury before the *Thor* could escape. Both PPCs' cascading energy converged on the already damaged right leg.

Armor sublimated, liquefied, ran in sluggish rivulets,

bared the internal structure to the sun-hot energies that destroyed the right leg bone with equal ease: the upper leg simply ceased to be. For a moment the *Thor* stood—a tree that had lost its battle against the logger but for a moment refused to yield, desperate and ashamed to give in to gravity.

Petr imaged he could feel the impact of it slamming into the ground even at this distance.

Petr's fists slowly tightened until tendons creaked and the blood pounded in his forehead like the thundering of the *Tiburon*'s feet sprinting across the tundra. Now it would be up to him to tie. An overall win was no longer possible.

Pushing at the rage, unclenching his fists, he slowly brought it back under control. As any good Sea Fox merchant could tell you, at times a win was not possible. In such circumstances, a tie would have to do.

And since defeating Sha would be a win in Petr's book, it would more than do.

13

Tumbled Heights, Near Halifax
Vanderfox, Adhafera
Prefecture VII, The Republic
14 July 3134

"What other outcome did you expect?" Sha said, his voice a winter breeze wafting through the desert wastes of Petr's heated cockpit.

"Come now, ovKhan, we both know where this will lead. Accept it. Give in to the inevitable."

The almost imperceptible whiff of blood he previously smelled now screamed in his nostrils as a river of life streamed slowly down his right biceps from the shoulder wound. Petr hunched forward, trying to rest his right elbow firmly on the command couch armrest. He still needed to manipulate the joystick, but wanted to take as much weight off the shoulder as possible. Eddies of waste heat caressed the hairs on his legs and arms, while sweat drenched him, mingling with his blood, quickening its flow, hastening his eventual death.

Using the foot pedals, he hunkered down a little more in the ravine, hoping the stone contained enough trace metals to throw off Sha's magscan; the humidity might, *might*, soak up enough heat to fool a thermal scan as well . . . provided Sha didn't simply stumble upon his hiding spot.

"Petr," that seductive voice crooned, using his first name for the first time, "why delay? Let us end these Rituals of Combat and we shall both view the final few pairings of the Trial of Bloodright; watch as my Beta warrior takes the Bloodname. A fitting capstone to Beta seizing the Rituals of Combat."

Petr would not be roused by Sha's barbed words. After all, that was what got him into this mess.

Though high in humidity, the day held the quality of emerging from a long darkness into the promise of a new tomorrow. Today spheroids would be out in droves, cleaning their cars and lawns, running errands, visiting friends, making quick plans for picnics and barbecues. The sun danced merry light across lush ground—verdant fields that spoke of a need to be happy, to enjoy the day and all its unspoken promises.

"I know the promise I need fulfilled today," Petr spoke softly, as he brought his *Tiburon* up to a full sprint of almost 120 kilometers an hour. The pounding rhythm of the run felt like the drumming beat of a Marik Jazzilues band he heard the last time they made a port of call, brought a smile to his face, as he began moving at an oblique angle to Sha's oncoming *Sphinx*.

He tapped through several maps to bring up the best topographical of the area, locked his threat assessment screen onto Sha's 'Mech. Unlike most of the 'Mechs participating this day, both the *Sphinx* and his own *Tiburon* mounted medium- to short-range weaponry. As such, they would close to a ridiculously short distance before targeting could be sure and true.

"So, ovKhan Petr, have you come to settle for a tie for Delta Aimag?" The calm of Sha's voice emerged in his neurohelmet. The heat in his chest mimicked the burning within the heart of his *Tiburon*.

"Why should I settle for a mere tie, Sha, when I can win?"

"And how, ovKhan, can that occur? Have you created a new math to go with your recklessness?"

Petr laughed, drenching the airwaves with sarcasm.

The 'Mechs closed rapidly. Though considerably slower than his own ride, Sha's *Sphinx* still held respectable speed. It also mounted massive armor, weighed twice as much as his *Tiburon* and mounted a mind-numbing ten extended-range medium lasers. Of course, that very firepower could be its undoing. It could fire only a fraction of them without overheating; firing them all would generate heat no number of heat sinks could dissipate safely, triggering an automatic shutdown—and Petr would hold the *surat* by the short hairs.

It would come down to superior skill; though the *Tiburon* carried a far superior targeting computer, they both mounted weapons of the same range. Though each warrior angled for terrain, they would let fly their armaments at the same moments. The better hair-trigger finger, the better hand-eye coordination to line up a shot against such rapidly moving targets, would score first.

At the last possible moment, Petr planted the *Tiburon*'s left foot on what he prayed would be firm ground. Stomped down on the left pedal and literally leaned to the left, the whine of the gyro mounted below his feet screaming to a crescendo that sunk into his lower jawbone joint—a painful, sympathetic vibration almost chattering his teeth as the 'Mech wrenched to the left in an amazing display of piloting skill.

At the same moment, his right hand guided the targeting reticule onto the *Sphinx*. It flashed a golden hue and the soft chime of lock rang in his ear; his index finger caressed the trigger, setting off his primary targeting interlock circuit.

A perceptual time dilation washed around him. Petr could practically feel the workings of his 'Mech. Almost became the energy surging through wiring toward the quartet of medium lasers waiting with barely concealed energy to savage a foe of his choosing; became the fusion reactor spiking its power output to compensate for the drain; became the targeting computer as it ran algorithms, plotting numerous solutions, choosing one and unleashing coherent beams of air-shattering strength; became bundles of photons as they slashed into the onrushing *Sphinx* like giant sun swords, carving off almost two tons of armor like a kitchen vibroblade cleaves off meat from a turkey at Sunday dinner.

Reality returned in a rush of victory; the return assault missed completely, sending up multiple sprays of explosive steam as puddles and damp earth flash-heated under the onslaught.

Petr hunched the *Tiburon* slightly and continued the almost breakneck zigzagging; he made his way toward a small copse. He finally responded.

"I *will* win, Sha, because I will beat you." His previous luxurious feeling peaked to a climax as his skills became one with his 'Mech. Repeated counterassault slashes of superheated photons failed to even stroke a touch across armor, much less do real damage.

The small copse covered no more than an eighth of a kilometer on any one side, but it provided plenty of breathing space; that last volley came a little too close. Just like Jesup before him (even more so), one good slap from the *Sphinx* and all of his previous pinpricks against Sha would be for naught.

"How like you," Sha said. Petr hesitated, slowed slightly, struck by the timbre of Sha's voice. Though computer reproduced, the voice managed to retain a quality of . . . what? Sadness? Regret? Suddenly he understood, and his rage seared his insides as though his 'Mech were overheating. *Pity.* Sha pitied him? Him!

Without conscious thought, Petr manipulated the foot pedals and angled the *Tiburon* back around in a arcing sweep, building his speed back up, bringing him back toward Sha.

That Sha would pity him!

"Ah, come back to play, I see," Sha said in his infuriatingly cool voice; he unleashed a sextet of lasers as the *Tiburon* cleared the copse, half of which ripped into the 'Mech's legs like a beast with winter's hunger savaging its first victim of spring. The damage schematic lit up across the bottom of the display—angry red smears that spoke of imminent black.

"Stravag," Petr cursed, riding the storm of damage as armor cascaded off his 'Mech, using the neurohelmet and its feedback keyed to the gyro to keep the *Tiburon* on its feet. Sha goaded him into it.

He closed with the copse and then played me like an instrument. Try as he might, his rage only built—at himself, at the situation.

"You see," Sha continued, as he alternated salvos, filling the air with slicing beams of death; beams Petr barely managed to avoid . . . most of the time, "that is why you will ultimately fail. Yes, you have your successes. Great successes, I will give you that. However, you think only of yourself. You believe you act in the best interests of your Aimag, but you are mistaken. You act in your own interests. I could not goad you to such rash actions if you thought of the honor your Aimag will lose this day because of your defeat. A tie would have been sufficient honor for both Aimags, but you think only of yourself. That is why you will ultimately be brought down. *Any* Sea Fox warrior who shows such selfishness will ultimately, *must* ultimately be brought down."

Petr gritted his teeth as another beam carved a furrow of dripping metal across his 'Mech's torso; she hurt. The strangeness of the conversation almost made the battle surreal: the calm, counseling tone of Sha at odds with the metal-shattering destructive forces being unleashed.

"You know nothing of me, Sha. I have always put my Aimag first." Petr grunted as two of his corkscrewing short-range missiles splashed into the *Sphinx*.

"But I do know you, ovKhan. Are we not taught to know our enemies as ourselves? No matter the battlefield, knowledge of one's enemy is essential, or else how can you defeat him?"

"Am I your enemy?"

"Of course. Are we not fighting? Well, at least one of us is fighting. I am not exactly sure what you are doing."

It shouldn't have, but the goading drove Petr over the edge. To have pity from this *surat*; to be insulted when Petr clearly displayed superior skills; to be called selfish by an ovKhan who rumor held disciplined for the slightest infractions; to be lectured about honor; to have been goaded into the open in the first place— Petr knew it for a goad as well, but could not stop it.

He blanked out.

Hitching his shoulder against the ache, Petr shook his head, felt like he was coming out of a drug-induced haze. Sha's voice continued to drone in his ears, a beehive just outside the cockpit.

"Come, Petr, I am sure it can be marked down as an error. A malfunction. My Aimag will not mention it. I am confident yours will not either," Sha said.

Mention what? He glanced at the damage schematic and his anger kindled once more; in addition to all the other damage, the *Tiburon*'s right arm no longer existed. A vague memory surfaced of blasting away the *Sphinx*'s left arm. ·

"My error?" Petr croaked out, his tongue swollen and dry as sun-bleached coral. "You are the one who violated the training protocols. I destroyed your *Sphinx*'s arm. I claim victory."

A soft pause. "Have you been so wounded, Petr? You obviously need medical attention. I destroyed your arm and you would not relent, destroying mine before I could damage you enough to force you away."

The words came like a sonic echo of events—a blurring effect as they conjured an image that didn't ring true to Petr's own memory.

But it was all so hazy. So hazy.

"That cannot be true, Sha."

"Of course it can. Accept it."

Petr glanced at his own radar and magscan, couldn't see a thing; were they damaged or had he found an effective hiding spot?

"You are fond of that phrase."

"Yes. Accept. Admit. Inevitable. Inexorable. We are Clan warriors. For us such words come naturally, *quiaff?* The Inner Sphere must accept we are superior. We must accept that responsibility, just as inexorable death must be accepted. Life is full of such absolutes. Today has such absolutes and no amount of skill can upset them."

"You talk too much, Sha."

"Is that the best you can do, Petr? After all I have heard about and from you, that is the best you can do? *This* is the best you can do?"

"I may have made an error before, but you will not goad me again, *surat*. Come find me and I will show you my best."

"I already have seen your best, ovKhan Kalasa, and I find it terribly lacking."

A metal grim reaper rising from the bowels of Hell blocked out the sun; the *Sphinx* topped the rise above Petr's hiding place.

Petr immediately tried to swivel the remaining arm to bring lasers to bear.

"Terribly lacking indeed," Sha said as he unleashed the full fury of his 'Mech.

Seven lances of coherent light shafted into the *Tiburon*, boiling away the remaining armor, stabbing deep to destroy innumerable internal systems. One beam flayed the already damaged head; terrible, horrifying heat cascaded across Petr's skin, filling his nostrils with the stench of burning hair and flesh.

I knew I would die with her. . . .

14

The old woman sprawled; her jumble of worn and mismatched treasures heaped around her kept people at bay as much as the filth and stench (especially the stench!). She was covered in a colorless dress that might've been the height of fashion a half century ago; its numerous rips and tears gave anyone peering too close brief flashes of rash-covered skin, itself almost unrecognizable under the glaze of caked dirt and old sweat. For those who looked a little too close, the veritable army of fleas that marched apparently unnoticed across this flesh turned away the most discerning eyes in horror. A giant hat—its ribbons, bows and single feather long since faded and drooping—sat astride her head, a once-proud crest that showed the inexorable march of long decades; it hid her features well in the double shadows of the brim and the parasail (sporting more holes than the dress) propped against an ancient dowry chest and a meaty thigh. The slight rocking and disharmonious singing only increased the size of her personal space; a 'Mech would have had a hard time penetrating the defenses she set up two days after Beta Aimag made landfall.

The security personnel of Beta Aimag assumed the hag to be a permanent fixture of Halifax. After all, she stayed through torrential rains, precipitous cold and brief flashes of wan sunlight. Of course, if they had bothered to ask any local, they would have had that impression quickly corrected. Then again, she expected such Clan arrogance, planned on it.

Shifting beneath the rags she had poached from a burned-out residence some kilometers from Halifax (along with much of the garbage she guarded so jealously), Snow surreptitiously sank her right hand down to scratch at a rash a little too high on her inner thigh; she winced at the idea of it getting much higher.

"This better net me something, or someone's going to pay," Snow murmured

The Sea Fox guards standing some fifteen paces away had quickly grown accustomed to such inaudible mumblings amid the jarring attempts at singing; her mother had told her in no uncertain terms her singing voice could wake the dead and kill them anew. She chuckled (random hilarity when none but you are laughing worked miracles in convincing people you're insane) at how she currently put such voice talent to use.

She gritted her teeth and cackled once more; she could practically feel a new series of bite marks as fleas nibbled flesh. "And I've got plenty to spare, no doubt about it." She hitched her right shoulder, feeling only a slight echo of its usual pain. Hardly turning her head, her eyes roved relentlessly, searching every cranny, examining every event. More important, it allowed her to read the lips of almost anyone in her line of sight, including the Sea Fox guards. And boy, oh boy, were they talkative: no bowl-you-over-this-is-it statement, but enough to keep her there and allowing the insects to snack.

Hadn't expected such loose lips from Clanners—then again, these were Foxes, half-Clanners at best.

Just then a giant of a man trundled around the far corner of the largest semipermanent tent in the compound, made his way toward the two guards. Admiring the mound of muscles and the almost liquid way they swam beneath the one-piece uniform, her eyes dipped low. *Wonder if it's all proportionate.* 'Course she always wondered (as did most Inner Sphere women, she was confident) but had yet to test that theory. *Perhaps this time around.* She cackled wildly.

As the fleshy, 'Mech-sized man drew closer, he hailed the waiting men; she pulled a mound of moldy clothing close and shifted as she always did with a change of the guards (better to see lips moving).

" 'Day, Kota, Sari," the bear of a man said; even at this distance, she could almost feel the timbre of his deep voice vibrate through her; she smiled deliciously. *Yes, he just might do.*

The other two turned toward the elemental, their words lost to distance and angle.

"Acceptable." He laughed loudly, as though enjoying the brief sunshine. "Though I believe I am ready to depart this gravity well."

Sari turned back around, glancing this way and that, but Kota's response remained hidden.

The giant laughed. "If you feel that way, then let us draw a circle and see who is lazy and who is not. I simply prefer the beauty of weightlessness, as do most who have been assigned downside, I would wager."

A pause as the elemental drew next to them, clasped quick hands and stood companionable. He continued after another hidden response. "Yes, the Rituals of Combat do make up for everything else, especially after besting Delta Aimag. That is worth a gravity and a half pressing my frame."

That laugh. Did he always laugh like that? Always bear a smile that revealed enough white to blind her even at this distance?

Kota finally turned to an angle she could read.

"Do you hate them?"

"Who, Delta Aimag? Why in the world would I hate them?"

Kota shrugged, cocked his head, while his eyes still tracked their circuit. Though she gave them kudos for paying constant attention when the residents of this piss-poor backwater world would wet themselves before actually doing something against the Clanners, she noticed his eyes never once acknowledged her. His downfall.

"I do not know, Corin"—so *that* was his name; nice—"just a feeling I get now and then from our Aimag."

"That is called competition. It is healthy. They defeated us last time and we return the favor this time around. No, though the competition might be fierce, especially between our ovKhans"—all three chuckled—"they are still a part of Spina Khanate. They are family."

"Perhaps the feeling, then, is not for Delta Aimag, but for another Aimag outside our Khanate. Or another Khanate."

A semiserious looked twisted Corin's face into an ugly semblance of its normal joviality; she liked him better smiling. And laughing.

"Have you drunk too many fusionnaires so early?"

"Come on, Corin. It is an open secret that ovKhan Clarke has questioned why Spina Khanate continually reaps the greatest honors and glory, then meekly hands them off to other Khanates. To the ilKhanate."

Corin's shrug would've lifted Snow right out of her current bundle of clothing; he wouldn't have noticed.

"Again, healthy competition. Come, we are Clan Sea Fox. We have known for centuries words can be more dangerous than a Star of 'Mechs. ovKhan Clarke is simply pushing for advantages."

Snow cackled to keep from growling, bit at her fingernails (slime, scum and all, she gnawed at them right there); the bastard Kota turned away. Corin's reaction told her she needed to know what Kota just said. Needed to know yesterday.

For just a moment (she couldn't tell for sure, but felt confident Kota missed it), the killer's look tweaked Corin's features: a slight flattening of the brow; a hardening of the eyes; thinning of lips; smoothing of muscles along the throat—for an instant

Corin debated whether to kill the soldiers. And just as quickly discarded the idea: too messy, too public.

An eyeblink later his features settled into their accustomed expression of levity and he laughed long and hard, perhaps a little too long. He finally straightened himself. "That is truly humorous. Have you been taking lessons from Jina? You do not honestly believe that, do you? Especially with the Jade Falcons?"

What about the Jade Falcons? Snow almost asked the question out loud in her frustration.

Kota shrugged, slowly shook his head, turned to look at Sari, but found no support there; she'd been ignoring the conversation.

Corin slapped Kota sharply on the back. Another guffaw. "You are off duty. Go finish that fusionnaire you obviously sipped earlier. Relax. Remember it is all fun and friendly competition. Forget such rumors."

Another shrug and a handshake, and Kota moved away, though he glanced over his shoulder four separate times before he was out of sight. Corin stood and gazed forward, his comrades apparently forgotten; but the set of his shoulders, the placement of his feet: she recognized from her own assassin training that this went beyond a soldier ready to kill for a mission. Kota would be relieved of his life all too soon.

Over what? Snow resettled herself (almost hissed; the rash had indeed gotten higher), slowly began to sing, swayed. She knew all about their Rituals of Combat, but she also felt a strange vibe between these two Aimags during the last several days, a mood she couldn't put her finger on. Not to mention the Clans were known for their waste-not-want-not mentality, especially the tightfisted, advantage-conscious Sea

Fox; she couldn't remember the last time she heard of a Clanner assassinating another. Talk about dishonorable. She chuckled despite herself. When would these Clanners realize honor didn't mean spit when it came to a blade in the dark?

She stopped abruptly, as she remembered the last part of the conversation. How in the world did the Jade Falcons fit in? Were they a factor? Or could she concentrate on maneuvering the Fox Clansmen into interfering with the Marik invasion?

Her eyes slowly tracked through a rent in the hat's brim, rested on the hulking flesh of a man.

Time to uncover some secrets.

15

Overlord-C-*class DropShip* Breaker of Waves
Near Orbit, Adhafera
Prefecture VII, The Republic
15 July 3134

Gacrux and its mining concerns. Ryde and its chemical industry. Konstance and natural gas. More came to mind as easily as letting fly a salvo of missiles.

Sha Clarke floated a hairbreadth above his perch on the wall of the Ritual Chamber. Gazed at the map of the Inner Sphere. Pinpointed worlds on which his Aimag had secured glory for Clan Sea Fox; ignored those where failure had occurred. His cool eyes roved over hundreds of light-years. Tracking, cataloging, evaluating. He knew any ovKhan who looked at the Inner Sphere displayed in the Ritual Chamber did the same, could not help it.

Yet unlike his fellow leaders, in the apparently random position of victories and losses, he saw a pattern a decade and more in the building. A grand design that would benefit Beta Aimag and Spina Khanate—not simply benefit, elevate—them to their rightful place, allow them to bask in the praise and glory they gained, not have it siphoned off to benefit those Khanates that could not carry their own weight.

Sha felt a rumble build within his belly, ignored the familiar ache generated by the day's fasting. He clenched his stomach muscles to disrupt the sound before it carried to the other three occupants of the chamber; it would be . . . unseemly.

Refocusing his eyes on the sides of the chamber deck, he studied the final two Trial of Bloodright contestants. His cold smile barely moved his lips; both were from Beta Aimag. The fourth occupant of the chamber, Jet Sennet, stood on his own platform, but the Oathmaster did not officiate for the final pairing. Petr's absence created a presence all its own.

Sha slowly shook his head, furrowed his brows. Why did Petr have to be so rash? There could be no doubt the man was brilliant. He had taken Delta Aimag from relative obscurity among Spina Khanate's Aimags to a level where it competed regularly with Beta for the most glory. Yet the man who singlehandedly accomplished that task could still be too rash. Still held to antiquated loyalties that bound him, bound them all. If only he could be made to see the possibilities outside such boundaries, Sha knew he and Petr would be unstoppable, a combination that by negotiations or force of arms would shake the Inner Sphere to its core, reshape it to their vision.

The Bloodmaster entered, pulling the senses like blood in the water.

The Bloodmaster stood gracefully just inside a hatch reserved for her entrance alone, her accoutrements strapped with casual familiarity around her person. Though she wore the same single-suit as the others, her features were hidden by a remnant of another age—a ceremonial mask made from the head of a sea fox, its teeth bared and snarling. The mask jutted into the chamber, bringing the essence of their totem to this most sacred ceremony.

Rocking forward onto her toes to break her magnetic slips' hold on the deck, she flexed her leg muscles and took flight toward the center of the dome. As the Bloodmaster reached the central platform, she elegantly grasped a column, slid into the spot previously occupied by the water funnel and tucked her feet under a holding bar. With the ease of long years, she began to assemble the tools of her trade.

Though Sha had witnessed the final pairing of a Trial of Bloodright several times, it never ceased to fascinate him. He found exquisite beauty in the perfection of her craft. Mastering the ritual took most of her life and cost the Bloodmaster her name and identity, but allowed a scientist to reach the vaunted position of officiating to the warriors of Clan Sea Fox. Though she was not a warrior or merchant, Sha gave her his deepest respect by bowing like the Sea Fox as she entered, his suit pulling taunt across the smooth muscles of his body.

Such dedication deserved nothing less.

The Bloodmaster first pulled out a malleable gourd taken from the shores of Doken on Twycross, filled with the waters where the sea fox thrived, and left it hanging in the air, slightly to her right.

Next, from a back pouch she pulled out a clear polymer funnel, a meter and a half long, with the open end less than a half meter and the tapered end just large enough to allow the Bloodright coin to pass through; she set it spinning rapidly directly in front of her.

Finally, she pulled out a half-meter-long opaque beaker, with a large bottom surface and a throat opening slightly larger than that of the funnel end; she set it spinning to her left, opening aligned with the funnel end.

With everything in place the Bloodmaster turned, and a keening voice boomed out across the chamber; the voice of the sea fox calling across the oceans of Twycross; across the oceans of the void; across the oceans of time and distance to demand only the finest, only the worthiest warriors present themselves.

Sha watched with satisfaction as the two Beta Aimag warriors immediately arrowed toward the dome's center. With equal skill and alacrity, they arrived at the platform as one, grasped poles for support and tucked feet under their own holding bars; the three formed a tripod, with the spinning objects in the center.

Another savage cry tore through the chamber, setting off echoes that bounced and soared; no words were spoken here, for these warriors no longer needed to prove their worthiness to occupy their positions—those claims were made plain by their previous four wins. Both warriors extended their arms beneath the spinning funnel, presenting their Bloodright coins.

The Bloodmaster plucked each coin from their exposed palms like a striking viper. Grasping a coin between the thumb and forefinger of each hand, she held them up for all to see—as though showing the universe at large their worthiness—before drawing her hands palm down toward her chest. She then flipped her hands from palm down to up and released the coins. As the coins floated into the large funnel opening, her hands were already moving toward the gourd. The coins entered the funnel and began to strike the sides and ricochet within, and the Bloodmaster squeezed the gourd, at the same time setting it spinning in place.

With a speed and grace only a sea fox might surpass, the Bloodmaster moved without any apparent use of her magnetic slips to stand at the end of the funnel. The water from the gourd shot in a single, pure stream into the funnel, where the coins already had spun down more than a meter within; their movements increased, becoming more frantic as they reached the narrowing end. The stream of water jetted past, snagging both coins, sending them tumbling toward the funnel end. The stream shot out the back of the funnel toward the waiting beaker. At almost the exact instant the water began to enter the beaker, the first coin emerged. In a move Sha likened to the blurred strike of a particle projector cannon, the Bloodmaster snagged the first coin from the stream in her right hand without redirecting a single drop of water; a moment later her left hand snagged the other coin in similar fashion.

As the stream of water from the gourd terminated and the last of it began the journey through the funnel to its ultimate resting place in the beaker, the Bloodmaster turned to the waiting warriors, held their coins out for them to see.

Jard, on the left, immediately spoke up. "I will fight unaugmented, Bloodmaster."

Without any hesitation, Bek responded, "I choose to fight here, now."

Both bowed deeply to the Bloodmaster, who in turn dipped her head in acknowledgment; with the efficiency she'd shown throughout the entire ceremony, she contained the last of the liquid (as far as Sha could tell from this distance, not a drop went uncounted for) and stowed her articles.

With another bow of her head, she grasped the struts of the platform and pushed off, sailing feet first toward her hatch; Sha tore his eyes away from the Bloodmaster as the warriors immediately began maneuvering.

Sha knew Bek would win almost before the Bloodmaster left the chamber. Though Jard, like all Fox Clansmen, knew how to maneuver in microgravity, Bek reveled in it. He immediately clamped both magnetic slips down to the floor, squatted to grasp the holding bar with his right hand and jerked his feet backward, pulling them completely out of his shoes and leaving him barefoot.

Before Jard's face could do more than register his surprise, Bek yanked on the holding bar and shot forward—an eel through water coming for its prey. His outstretched left hand hit like a hammer blow against the side of Jard's face, eliciting a grunt. Yet Jard would not lose so quickly; he let the momentum of the blow push him out and away from the platform with enough energy to reach the wall; as Sha himself discovered early in his microgravity training, no velocity, and no purchase to regain it, meant defeat.

As the two closed on the chamber wall and rebounded back for another pass at each other, Sha's mind was distracted to its previous line of thought. *If only he could change Petr's way of thinking.* No, changing it would not be enough. Sha would need to completely turn it on its ear.

Shifting his gaze away from the unfolding combat (though Jard landed a solid blow of his own, Bek's return thrust sent droplets of blood cascading through the chamber), Sha fixed his eyes once more on the map of the Inner Sphere; on The Republic of the Sphere; on Prefecture VII.

A matter of semantics, perhaps.

Then again, semantics were what divided them from spheroids, kept them from falling back to barbarity and honorlessness. Yes, Petr brought great honor and glory to his Aimag, but only because he worked to bring honor to himself. As he had told Petr during their combat, such thinking would eventually bring a man down, bring down his Aimag and the Clan as a whole. Bringing honor to the Aimag for the sake of the Aimag . . . true honor lay in such currents.

Out of the corner of his eye, Sha saw Bek slice down to the bottom deck, landing on his hands, right by the bulkhead. He used the momentum to somersault into the bulkhead, where he drove off after a half-twist for realignment and vectored back in toward Jard—an aerospace fighter lining up for another blistering pass with charged particle cannons and loaded ballistic weapons. Sha nodded absentminded approval at their silence, despite the hard blows that continued to purple flesh and tear bleeding wounds.

Sha focused on a train of thought only he could drive. It went beyond trying to change Petr's idea of outdated loyalties; it required trying to change the very way in which he lived.

Like this trial, Sha's own trial continued. Yet this new phase would be much more difficult than the last: not simply defeating Petr—that victory could never be in doubt—but defeating his very character.

A genuine smile (as genuine as any for Sha) curved his lips in unaccustomed tautness. Could there be any greater challenge? To change the very essence of another person? Of another warrior?

Sha crouched and hunkered left—the cool metal of the platform a welcome sensation after the heat generated by the combatants—as Jard sailed through the space his head had occupied a moment before, piling into the bulkhead with terrific force. The metal actually vibrated with the force of the impact—the signal the trial was over.

Sha glanced at the body of Jard as it slowly floated away from him, limbs askew and blood bubbling up from the crushed nose.

Of course, defeat was always an option. Yes, if only death would make Petr see, then so it would be, regardless of the lost resource.

16

Beta Aimag Hospice, Near Halifax
Vanderfox, Adhafera
Prefecture VII, The Republic
18 July 3134

His skin did not feel like his own.

Petr swam up through a lake of malaise, his whole body and mind fighting against his indomitable will. Memories, like bubbles, rose to the surface around him. Each exploding in a miniature display of subconscious/conscious pyrotechnics—a sound-and-light kaleidoscope show only seen, only known, only heard by him.

Yet the bubbles did not proceed in any orderly fashion. Percolated by his rage, they swirled into an unknowable pattern, strobing memories from years past with those of recent design.

Petr tried vainly to roll over and crush the spheres

The scent of blood clotting in the nose of an eight-year-old, his first combat lessons begun. The shiv-trainer suspended in the air, a revolving god whose features never changed, never altered, whether handing out praise or a thrashing. The girl, with flashing eyes, short brown hair and heaving chest; triumphant smile; knuckle-scraped left fist, smeared with his blood; defeat, a bitter taste worse than any blow.

though the pain became a living entity when fed

A noble hall on a forgotten world. Strange, slightly noxious scents flooding the room—alien, local food. The viscount preparing it himself, only a loincloth covering his newly shaven body; his loss requiring that no hair be left to mark his manhood. The rump, with tail lashed around several vegetables—apples?—of a local dago, spit fried, served to Petr by the viscount's own hand—victory sweet, supple, hard.

by such movements, yet he needed to

Brown hair grown longer, heaving chest now breasts; a sibkin, a friend. Eyes flashing ecstasy, sweat slicked bodies moving as MechWarrior and 'Mech; becoming one on this battlefield; used and taken, given and gifted. Rhythm building, tongue, teeth and screams. Pain and loss forgotten in an endless flash of primordial need; spent, panting, bodies entwined, an embrace of love . . . of death.

stop the cycle, or fall once more into the abyss of his own

Laser fire punching holes in his armor. Muscles still learning, still straining to manhandle the thirty-ton 'Mech. A cheek two years from stubble slams into the neurohelmet; flotsam and jetsam of his subconscious explode around him, dragging him to defeat. Clenching joysticks, baring teeth, he pushes back, back against the odds. Success on his tongue, not the tang of his own blood sliding back, down, slicing each taste bud with his own mortality.

making.

Bubbles, bubbles, bubbles . . . his bubbles. His life. His memories. His defeats and victories. Petr realized it did not matter that they arose in such disconcerting numbers or such coalescing confusion. They were *his*.

Taking a deep breath, Petr relaxed. Felt the cool sheets under his skin, sunlight across his exposed left leg, the soft, warm breeze redolent with the scent of another monster storm waiting to be unleashed; scents of flora and fauna tickling his nose, still alien though he had been downside for weeks. He sucked in another deep breath until he felt his ribs creak with the pain . . . and pulled his memories within, where they burst like a decompressed chamber.

"And how are you this morning?"

Petr wanted to keep his eyes closed, but realized it would do no good; the witch would know he no longer slept. He cracked his eyelids, felt the not completely unpleasant light fill his vision.

"That is right. I know you are awake. You might as well open them farther." It just did not seem right. Such a soft, comforting voice—not to mention her appealing looks of blue eyes, milk chocolate shoulder-length hair and freckled face—should not belong to the witch; he knew her name, but refused to remember it. The *savashri* simply would not leave him be. Leave him alone. Leave him to wallow in his own pity. Witch!

"What, no words this morning? No cursing or whining?"

"I do not whine," Petr said. Promptly began coughing lightly, his throat still scorched from the fire and heat.

"Ah, so you can speak today."

Petr turned his head away, frustrated. What would a medico know of his disgrace? Of the pain that bit infinitely deeper than any wound or broken bone?

She hummed while checking her monitors; he tried to ignore her, but found it impossible. After his small victory over himself, Petr once more became powerless. He knew full well she strove to raise his spirits, to heal his physical and emotional wounds. Yet she could not know (he would not tell!) that her constant haranguing, her constant pushing to move him out of bed, to flex his muscles and stretch his flesh—his mind—only drove him deeper into himself.

He had suffered the most humiliating defeat possible: he had survived. And now he lay there, nursed back to a gross semblance of life he no longer cared to hold on to. He closed his eyes, but he could almost predict where her footfalls would echo next in the small room, where her ministrations would take her, in a path as surely determined as a hypersonic Gauss round slung from a 'Mech.

"You have a visitor today."

"You can tell Jesup I do not wish to see him."

"Has Jesup ever asked permission to see you?" The tone of disapproval in her voice lightened Petr's mood a crack.

"I suppose not. Then who?"

"ovKhan Sha Clarke."

For a moment Petr could not breathe. Her words were a firebomb that detonated within the small confines of the room, sucking all oxygen to itself, making it impossible to breathe, to talk. He could barely discern the soft beep of the monitoring equipment through the blood pounding in his head; the headache almost surged back. He restrained a gasp—refused to allow her to see such weakness—though he brought his bandaged right arm up to the swaddled portion of his head.

"Are you okay?" Her concern had no effect on his anger, rising hot and viscous as molten lead.

"What do you think?" She never gave him the courtesy of his title—a right he tried to enforce but lost. Another defeat to inferiority. What was he becoming?

"I think you need rest more than company. I will tell ovKhan Clarke to return another day."

Combat ensued within. The cool embrace of silence and the morbidness of his own thoughts, or the contemptuous twist to Sha's mouth at such weakness? After all, the *surat* had already defeated him. What possible additional humiliation could simply allowing the nurse to exert her authority bring? None.

If that was true, why did his rage then burn hotter? It sat like a four-ton broken gyro within him, crushing weight and chaotic tumble bringing vertigo and nausea. He tried hiding, only to see himself reflected in the broken shards of a million spheres within. He *had* to face this. Though he would gladly die at this moment, he would not die in weakness. Not in front of Sha.

He pushed himself up against the inclined bed,

pulled the covers from his swollen and bandaged chest, careful to move his right arm as little as possible.

"What are you doing?" the witch said, a crack in her facade showing real emotion for once. Concern? True concern?

He swung one leg out over the side of the bed and gripped the edge of the mattress with his left hand as bats fluttered wings through his vision. For a moment, he almost gave in, almost dove back to the cool depths of his own void. He suddenly missed the caress of his hair on his shoulders, knew it all had been shaved away after it burned off in the inferno of his cockpit. The right side of his head would never grow hair again.

Cold eyes beckoned, mocked, cajoled. What days of the witch's humming and Jesup's endless, futile banter failed to accomplish, the arrival of Sha's spectral form achieved.

He swung the other leg out and down, until bare toes met unyielding, cold tiles; they talked about wanting you up and around as quickly as possible, yet they made the floor as unwelcoming as possible. The thought quirked his lips in a tiny smile.

"ovKhan, you must stop. Please. You will hurt yourself."

His smile widened; she called him ovKhan. The first time since he arrived. The *first*.

He unclenched fingers to wave away her concerns. Thought about trying for the chair only three steps distant, but it suddenly felt like the gulf between stars, and his Kearny-Fuchida jump drive absolutely remained broken. This would have to do.

"Show my guest in," he said softly. Whether because of the tone of his voice or the expression in his eyes, she immediately withdrew. He allowed himself to show his pain for the first time that day. He closed his eyes, breathed deeply through his nose and tried to forget about his body. To forget about what Sha would see, the leverage he would instantly have, upon entering.

Petr was a mess. The final firefight broke into his cockpit. A residual lance of photons slashed into his right arm, severing muscles and flash-boiling flesh all along the arm and chest, up onto his neck and most of the right side of his skull; his hair caught fire and burned away, further scarring his head.

As ovKhan, he could order the extravagance of new skin to be grown to replace the scarred, puckered mess of his scalp; he could be made new, as though his defeat never occurred. Yet something stayed his hand. Something pulled him out of his delirium long enough to order them not to automatically travel that road. He still couldn't articulate what had happened, but he felt its importance. Something . . .

Sha walked into the room.

No gloating. No sarcastic smile. No satisfaction. Just his endless cool exterior. A face devoid of any emotion—not even a flicker at seeing Petr's condition—and eyes as frigid as the depths of space.

Anything would've been better. Any emotion at all. But this nothing . . . Petr fought to control his rage. Losing control would do no good here, only make him lose more ground.

"You are up?" Sha said, his voice impossibly neutral. Almost inhumanly neutral.

Does he actually practice? "Aff."

Silence. Hot eyes met cold and a silence sharp enough to shatter ferroglass stretched for several long minutes. Neither was willing to speak first. Surprisingly, Sha finally broke the silence with a barely perceptible nod; Petr didn't for a moment believe he'd won anything.

What was the new angle? There had to be an angle.

"It is good to see you up. Clan Sea Fox has need of such warriors. Such leaders."

"Did you not say you would remove such leaders as I, *quiaff*?" Petr flexed his leg and butt muscles to ease his discomfort, kept his shoulder as immobile as possible.

Sha, who stood only a single step inside the room, slowly shook his head; his eyes never once left Petr's.

"*Neg*, ovKhan, those are not my words, but yours in my mouth. I know your body has been ravaged, but we know it will heal. I only hope your mind has not been compromised. I hope it will heal properly as well."

Petr barked in harsh laughter. "My mind has never been better, Sha. Never. Those were the words you spoke. Are you denying them now?"

"I have never needed to deny my own words."

Silence. Fire and ice. The minutes once more stretched and Petr began to suspect Sha's strategy. *Wear me down. Drag the conversation out as long as possible. Force me to show weakness. A very good strategy.* He dug deep, launched his own attack.

" 'That is why you will ultimately be brought down.' Those are your words, *quiaff*?"

Those cool, frosty eyes. *"Aff."*

"Then how could I be putting words in your mouth?"

"Because you assumed I would be the one to do it."

"And you will not?"

"I did not say that either."

"You are not saying a whole lot."

"When important words need to be spoken, they are usually few in number."

Petr barked another laugh, used it to cover while resettling his shoulders, licking his lips against the pain. The dryness. He needed a drink.

"You are starting to sound like a philosopher. Warrior. Merchant. Philosopher. Who knew I would have such guests today?"

"Any great warrior is a philosopher, ovKhan. I would think you of all people would know that truth," Sha replied. "The Founder understood it when he forged us. House Kurita and their bushido code know it. Are their warriors not poets and artisans as well? You can do much worse than be a philosopher. Especially when the philosophy you find leads you down a better path."

"You still did not answer my question, Sha. Are you trying to lead me down a different path? A better path?" Petr smiled very unpleasantly.

"The answer, ovKhan Kalasa, already should have found you. I did not say I personally would remove you. I said that if you persisted in your selfishness, you would be removed. It is inevitable. As inexorable as the pull of gravity. The eventual death of stars. Our eventual demise as well."

"Both? You are not immortal?" The sarcasm practically dripped off the walls.

"I have never entertained such grand thoughts, ov-Khan. I am as much dust as the next warrior. I only hope to leave Spina Khanate with more glory and power than before. Better off."

"Do you not mean Clan Sea Fox?" Petr probed.

'Mechs could shatter against such silence. Fire and ice.

"They are the same, *quiaff*?" Sha finally spoke.

"*Aff*. Yet I do not believe that to be the case for you, Sha. You accuse me of selfishness, yet you are the hypocrite. You are every bit as selfish as you accuse me of being. Clan Sea Fox is the whole, not Spina Khanate. Certainly not Beta Aimag."

For the first time Petr could remember, something moved in the bleak arctic wastes of Sha's eyes. He'd scored somehow.

"You accuse me of not knowing a thing about you, ovKhan." Sha began again; if Petr had scored, it didn't show in his voice. "I would return the sentiment."

"You would destroy Clan leaders. What more is there to know?"

Sha took a single step toward him, the soft soles of his boots whispering on the cool tiles as he stopped again, right hand upraised slightly, as though entreating. Not Sha.

"ovKhan, if I feel you have violated Clan law or traditions, I can call you out in a Trial of Grievance, *quiaff*?"

"*Aff* . . . though not exactly."

"Ah, you see. Not so cut and dried. I can call you out by strict adherence to Clan law, but that is never really the case. Your own subordinates would call you out. And generally, you do not have a cadet calling out too far above his station, or an ovKhan too high above his own."

Petr nodded his head. Why were they having a discussion about something they both knew all too well?

"Not to mention, if I do move too far above my station or too far out of my purview, in all likelihood a newly acquired subordinate will rise to challenge me and I will not survive the sheer numbers, *quiaff*?"

"*Aff*. That is so a warrior cannot challenge his Khan for a decision he simply cannot fathom—it would bog down the Clan in pettiness." Petr explained.

"Exactly. So what do you do when you see that exact situation occurring? Leaders who do not lead all to glory, but sit like fat House Leaders, piling up the glories others reap." Sha's gaze was becoming more intent.

"Are you discussing a hypothetical situation?"

"Whatever way you wish to think about it. Real, hypothetical, I want an answer. If you see such injustice, but know that our traditions actually hold us to certain behaviors in this situation, what do you do?"

"Nothing."

Sha lowered his hand and leaned forward slightly, as though attempting to gaze into Petr's soul; for a moment Petr felt sure a cold breeze scratched his face and made him swallow reflexively with the inability to breathe such cold air.

"You see an injustice you feel cannot be addressed in the standard Clan way and you do nothing?"

"Exactly."

"Then what about our fight? Was that the standard way?"

Anger finally boiled to the surface. He violently

shook his head and winced painfully at the jabs of fire in his shoulder and the pinpricks ignited along his skull. He closed his eyes, felt sweat spring out along his brow and quickly begin to slide down his shaven scalp to his neck.

Wished for a drink of water as he rubbed his tongue, rough as sandpaper, along his lips (refused to ask for a glass; no weakness in front of Sha!) and spoke, slowly, with great deliberation; he could not afford to be angry right now. "I did not fire on you after you took my 'Mech's arm. I took yours."

"If that is the way you wish to remember it, so be it. But I would wager you are lying to yourself. You are not the type to sit back and allow something you do not agree with to occur if you can do something about it."

Petr opened his mouth to voice flat denial and the sound died unborn. If he truly saw injustice, would he do nothing? Would he stand back and say it did not concern him? He hated to admit it, but Sha was right. *Aff.* He would do something.

He tried to not look directly at Sha, but the man knew his thoughts. Oh, he knew, though he kept his *surat* face as impenetrable as 'Mech armor.

"Why did we originally change our name to Clan Diamond Shark?"

Petr's head swirled with such a strange segue. "Um, what?" He hated sounding so stupid; he suddenly couldn't seem to wrangle his thoughts. *Were the meds wearing off?*

"Why did we change our original name, the name the Founder himself chose, to Clan Diamond Shark?"

"Um, every Fox Clansman knows this history. After

the hated Snow Raven Clan introduced a genetically altered shark—"

"Those are just facts," Sha interrupted. "Tidbits of history. Floating pieces of information which do not, cannot, convey what occurred. We changed our name for one reason and one reason only."

Petr began to feel like a student and hated Sha for the feeling. Nevertheless, he fought to think through the haze. *Why did we change our name?* He ran head-long into an endless field of giant cotton balls; nothing hurt, but at every turn something moved into his path, slowing him down, stopping forward movement. Forward thought. Finally, after what felt an eternity, he found an answer. "To survive."

"Exactly," Sha said, with more passion in his voice than Petr could ever remember. "To survive, we adapted to the new situation. When so many Clans lie broken and destroyed along the path of history, Clan Sea Fox has adapted and changed. And now we among all the Clans have one of the most powerful and influential positions in the Inner Sphere." He took another step toward Petr, once again, a look of plead-ing. Or almost pleading. Not in his features, but more in his posture, the slightly upraised arm again. It did not seem possible that Sha would plead. For what?

Sha opened his mouth again but his voice came as though muffled by the endless field of cotton. "Why did we change our name back again?"

Petr thought about this. Time began to trickle one grain of sand at a time through existence's hourglass. Finally found what he needed, though it barely came out as a word: "Sur." The rest lost to mumbling.

"To survive. To adapt. So we morphed into our

current Khanates and Aimags. We have always adapted, Petr. We have never shirked doing what we must. To ensure our survival, we have done what we must. Can you not see?"

Petr found himself lying back on the bed without knowing how he got there. A soft glow smeared everything into a haze of slow-moving shapes and dulled sounds. He tried to concentrate on Sha's words, vaguely saw the nurse talking to Sha, her voice almost strident. Gesturing. To Petr. To the door. She drugged me. The thought should have brought anger, but instead brought only warmth.

His vision began tunneling, but he focused on Sha's face. On his mouth, which suddenly encompassed the universe. Fingers sunk into words to keep him from his own abyss.

"We have always done what we must to survive," Sha continued. "We make the decisions necessary to ensure our survival, regardless of the consequences. Too many Clans have been destroyed because they could not adapt. We adapt. We survive. We must continue to adapt. Petr, we must adapt. You can aid me. What we could not accomplish. . . ."

Existence washed away.

17

Beta Aimag Hospice, Near Halifax
Vanderfox, Adhafera
Prefecture VII, The Republic
22 July 3134

The exercise felt good.

Sweat poured from his body as though from an open faucet. A cleansing feeling, washing away his hurt, his frustration, his darkness; keeping unwanted words at bay. The small exercise room might as well not have existed, its only two other occupants beyond his perception; their own determination to overcome their injuries a pale candle to his own, which burned as bright as a DropShip drive plume in a moonless black night.

Amazing what hating an enemy could do.

Petr redoubled his efforts. Knew the witch would

likely be by soon to scold him. Tell him to slow down. To pace himself. How could he? He felt as though the universe were passing him by. As though great events for his Clan, and possibly for the rest of the Inner Sphere, were in motion and he'd been sidelined. Stuck on the bench.

He could not accept that.

Almost twenty minutes passed; dehydration and exhaustion clawed at him. Finally, satisfied that he had pushed his body and spirit to the very edge, he relented. Stepped off the machine and stood panting, breathing in the stuffy air, breathing in the smell of his own sweat. Slowly, he became aware of another person in the room, realized dimly that she had spoken to him twice already, and he had not responded. He tried to decide what he should feel about that. Shrugged—felt only a dull echo of the pain only three days past—and walked the four steps to his water bottle—a talisman to be grasped only after a straight thirty minutes of work. Such concentration, his ability to simply push away existence in his need to be reborn, should be lauded. A warrior's concentration. An ovKhan's concentration. He nodded his head.

"Merchant saFactor Tia. What news?" She didn't even blink her flashing blue eyes before responding. Didn't show any reaction at all to his new and improved look.

Then again, she probably wore such a look during coupling. Business. Always business and everything else a distraction to ignore.

"The negotiations proceed apace," she began immediately. Blunt as ever. "However, Beta Aimag has made considerable headway, matching our bid point for point. Their interference has dragged out the negotiations interminably, with no end in sight."

"How did this happen? We began negotiations many days before Beta Aimag even arrived. How did they catch up so quickly?"

"Their saFactor is . . . gifted."

Though her face didn't change, Petr understood that to be the highest compliment she'd pay to any other merchant; he'd not drag anything further out of her, even with an assault 'Mech.

"What concessions do we need to make to secure the contract?"

"These merchants are devious. They are playing both ends of the jump drive. Though such a game could lead to an explosive decompression in any other situation, they have recognized the mutual animosity of our Aimags. They believe one side or the other will reach for this contract, regardless of the ludicrous concessions they demand."

Petr stretched his neck carefully, felt the pull of skin healing quickly. Petr had never paid much attention to the medical accomplishments of the scientist caste. Of course, he knew they could grow new limbs from buds and regrow skin. Still, he found it amazing how quickly they could heal skin if the patient didn't mind scars, terrible scars. He felt new respect for their expertise and advancements. For his rapid recovery, though he believed his will (and hate) contributed greatly to his speedy recovery.

"A stiff-necked Falconer could not fail to see our . . . animosity. You did not answer my question. You are my saFactor, Tia. Are you failing me?" He considered what else to say, but knew there were no chinks in her armor that words could penetrate. Someday, he hoped to learn how she achieved such imperviousness.

"*Neg*, ovKhan. I only fail when I do not use all the skills at my disposal. I believe the concessions they ask will make this entire venture cost more than we are willing to pay."

Petr laughed out loud, the sharp bark almost a hammer blow in the small room. "Tia, this venture has already proved more costly than it could possibly be worth."

"*Aff*, ovKhan. This I understand. Nevertheless, I cannot advise you to take any offer other than to concede to Beta Aimag. Regardless of the short-term honor such a victory will gain for Beta, in the long run it will be a drain they cannot sustain. An embarrassment we can capitalize upon, if not steal outright."

"But what of our Aimag's honor now? We did not even place in the top two slots of the Trial of Bloodright. We lost the Rituals of Combat. How can I simply concede the final point without a fight? Can I allow such a blow?"

"*Aff.* Our warriors, our Aimag will survive. Has always survived. We do what we must."

Her words were limned in fire. Stood out like an afterimage of a particle projector cannon beam seen with the naked eye. That her words mirrored Sha's so closely shook him. Disturbed him more than he wanted to admit.

He had worked hard to ignore the specifics of his conversation with Sha. Tried to ignore his own reactions (betrayals) to Sha's words. If he was honest with himself, those words were another reason for his passionate exercises: the physical exertion allowed him to trap Sha's words in a region of his mind he did not have to face.

He must take slow steps. Once step at a time.

He raised the water bottle and drank deeply. Shook his thoughts away like a dog sloughing off water. Concentrated once more on the current situation.

"*Aff.* I know we will survive. But I do not like to admit this defeat by Beta Aimag. There has to be another way."

After a few heartbeats, she said, "Perhaps there is."

He looked at Tia. "Speak."

"Stewart."

"Ah," he responded. Like a contrail, the possibilities unfolded. Long minutes stretched as he gazed at it from several angles.

Of a sudden, Snow came to mind. He realized with a jolt many days had passed since he'd even thought of the repugnant (strangely attractive?) spheroid. The mention of Stewart brought to mind her allegations of a possible invasion by the Marik-Stewart Commonwealth. Then again, he'd been busy, he thought wryly. Invasion or not, Stewart could not be handed off like that.

"No, Tia. We must find some other way. We know Stewart is the biggest prize in this entire region—a fact I cannot believe Beta has not yet discovered." He nodded, giving Tia her due on that point.

"I agree, ovKhan. But distracting Beta Aimag by offering them Stewart is the only option we currently have."

He thought another moment. Felt Sha's words tickling his mind, trying to surge back to the fore.

Could he really have meant what he implied? "We do what we must." Any Clansman, including a Fox Clansman, using such words could mean anything. Could mean they would go to any lengths necessary. And despite Sha's vagueness, Petr knew the rival ovKhan could only be talking about one person.

Khan Hawker.

Could he really mean to move against the ilKhanate and Mori Hawker? A chill wind, as though from Sha's frigid eyes, swept down his skin, wrenching up goose bumps. *Neg*, not even Sha could be so reckless. But eyes of ice burned through his memories to stab holes in these feeble denials.

Aff, he just might.

He realized several minutes had passed. Tia stood waiting, patiently—though she must wonder if his injuries had rattled his mind.

"Tia, delay any resolution to the negotiations. The one thing we have remaining in our favor is time. Delay for weeks if that is what it takes." Her face showed she was unhappy with his decision, but she accepted his order without complaint. Petr could use more subordinates like her, regardless of her bluntness.

"*Aff*, my ovKhan. It shall be as you say." She departed, leaving him alone. No, not alone. He could not seem to escape his thoughts. Sha's words. Petr felt at a loss for how to move forward. This simply went beyond him.

How to proceed?

Moving into his stretching—he refused to do it the first time and regretted it terribly the next morning—his mind continued to follow multiple jump paths. Continued to seek a way forward.

SaKhan Sennet should be at Tania Borealis at this point.

The thought blossomed into his mind as though placed there. He stood up suddenly, heedless of the dizziness that washed over him at the abrupt motion.

SaKhan Sennet. Yes, he would aid him. He would know how to proceed.

18

The rain shielded Snow better than any camouflage. Of course, the driving sheets of water also made it difficult to see. Not to mention uncomfortable, as it plastered her clothing, molding it to her skin, making her uncomfortably aware of her stocky body. She had ample assets (plenty of men said as much), but they were hidden behind a body that refused to yield to slimness, no matter how fanatic her workout regime. For years she dealt with the disappointment of her unattractiveness through work, achieving a level of success that forced her superiors to recognize her prowess, even as they averted their eyes. Her success allowed her to reach a détente with her own body.

Then someone would remind her in the most brutal way possible, and a few too many years of swallowing askance looks and quirked lips would rise like the undead, creating not a hot rage, but a cold fury to scour away mountains and souls.

Or at least to scour away the bastard she stalked.

A particularly strong gust of wind threw a wall of warm water into her face. Most rainstorms she had experienced were cold, and one part of her mind kept wondering why she was taking a shower with her clothes on.

She smiled coldly. Strange the demons we carry. And the demons we must exorcise. Of course, all for duty. All for duty. She tucked away a threatening chuckle for later use.

Coming to the end of the street, she backed up against the wall and did a quick take around the corner as her target passed. Only a handful of people were out this late on an ordinary night; the savage storm kept most reasonable people indoors tonight. However, her target stopped a half dozen paces ahead, apparently deep in conversation with someone she couldn't recognize; the strength of the storm didn't even allow her to identify clothing.

She leaned back. Felt the rough-cut stone press firmly into her back, as runnels of water poured down her neck. Made her shoulder ache slightly, though she was sure it was mostly mended at this point. She began to systematically loosen her muscles, knowing combat loomed.

Though it should be pretty minimal, considering.

Her mind, at that moment, chose to replay this evening's scene. The evening's . . . embarrassment. She hated reliving the pain, yet like a tongue that probes a sore tooth, she couldn't help but worry the wound. Pick the scab.

Anyone got salt?

"Hey, big guy, haven't seen your type around here before," Snow said as she sidled up to the end of the bar next to the Elemental. Corin. Such a nice name to match such a nice body.

The giant slowly raised the fusionnaire to his lips, tossed off the dregs and placed the glass back on the table; he did so with a delicateness she found fascinating. It surprised her such a beast of a man could contain "delicateness." She wondered if those hands were as delicate in other activities.

A vision of endless flesh sparked and warmth blossomed.

The bartender arrived. "Give me vodka, straight up"—she glanced sidewise at her companion—"and my friend here another of whatever he's having." She tossed a five-stone on the bar and swiveled back to Corin. She'd not taken a seat yet, waiting to see how the conversation might unfold.

"Ah, the strong, silent type. I like those kind, too. Though you're not always so silent, right?" In contrast to her body, her eyes and voice were her best assets—instruments her training honed to exquisite sharpness. Instruments that many times allowed her to overcome her body's . . . deficiencies. Yes, that word worked very well.

Corin appeared like a vast tree: unyielding, uncaring, unmoved. His reticence, of course, only ratcheted up her interest. Her heat.

With a smoothness unexpected from her body type, she eased onto the stool, casually leaned back. Let the atmosphere of the place—after the mad dash to avoid being soaked in the downpour—wash around her. Sounds and aromas swirled in a tidepool of friendships and camaraderie.

The bartender came back, slapping down a coaster and slopping the drink in his haste to turn away; she ignored his distaste, her attention focused elsewhere. Saw him make another fusionnaire, and grabbed it out of his hand before he could deliver it.

"Here ya go, big boy," she said, sliding the mug in front of the elemental. *Medication* delivered, with her usual flair and none the wiser.

She watched him pound back this fusionnaire as well and followed suit, tossing off her entire shot of vodka. The liquid splashed frozen-cold through mouth and throat, exploded with nova-hot warmth in her stomach, almost as good as climax. Her eyes watered. She glanced askance at Corin, blinking away tears and imagination. Almost. Yes, this should be very good.

"So you going to introduce yourself, or do I need to do all the talking?" Her voice practically purred, honed by the shot of vodka like fine-grade motor oil to an Avanti V12.

Once more, no response. The tree act again. Did she need to turn up the heat? Singe his whiskers a little? She relished the idea.

Swiveling around on the barstool, she leaned out behind him and called out to no one in particular, "Julia, hey, it's Cindy. Give me a minute and I'll come to your table. Okay." Her voice, despite its volume, carried only a short distance beyond the immediate vicinity, all in the timbre.

Turning back toward the bar, she laid a casual hand on his upper arm (those muscles!), while leaning forward enough to lightly brush her breast up against his forearm, tossing a flash of flesh from her braless, low-cut top up to hungry male eyes.

"That was Julia. Such a sweetheart. We work together." She laughed deeply and kept her touch on him a half heartbeat longer than an accidental touch might have warranted. *Let him try to decide if I did it on purpose or not. Should only increase the tension. The desire.*

As she eased back around, removing her hand from his arm, his head, fully a half meter above her own, swiveled around and tipped down to look her directly in the eyes. Like a flower under the harsh pounding of a desert sun, she slowly wilted. It had been a very long time since she'd faced such loathing.

Without a change of expression, the deep tone she hoped to hear panting her name instead tried to flail flesh from bone. "Do not ever touch me again, filth."

Snow easily discounted such words. She tried to rally, pasted a hurt look on her face. "Hey, sorry. It was an accident." Pushed the look into a sultry pout. "You not into Inner Sphere women? Only Clanners? Don't know what you're missing," she said, trying to parry the emotionless void of his voice and eyes with another glimpse of her ample breasts and a tone that vibrated with sexual tension. She peered up into dead eyes and knew she'd lost this fight already. Time to cut her losses. But his next words slipped under skin, despite her years of training.

"I have sampled such pleasures to my satisfaction. But I prefer my meat fresh and sweet. You are neither. Leave."

From one moment to the next she moved from the warmth of the bar and words that cut more than she cared to admit, to standing in the lukewarm downpour.

Corin. Such a nice name. Too bad it hid such a rotten core, such a void. Now she just wanted to see something in those eyes. Some emotion. Yes, any emotion would be good to see. Squeezed from him slowly and with deliberate care.

Snow shook off the last vestiges of the memory (tongued it one more time for good measure) and peeked around the corner again. She could just see him moving down the street once more—a flicker of movement before the rain washed away his existence.

She casually slipped around the corner, her current jumpsuit the opposite of low-cut and sexy. Of course, sexy came in many forms, and she might still have a chance to prove that to Corin.

She moved to the other side of the street and picked up speed, almost slipping between the droplets of rain. She began to push her senses to the limit, finding ways to blank out the sound and visual obscurants around her. Trying to find and pinpoint the thread of heavy tread—her elusive prey.

Five minutes bled like drops of blood from a shallow wound. She caught up with him almost immediately, but the situation was not yet right. She needed better cover. Better timing. She kept pace, but far enough back to hopefully escape his notice. Finally, the mountain slowed and crossed the street. He almost appeared to be meandering.

He knows I'm here. That someone is here.

She didn't for a moment underestimate him. Regardless of the void at his core, he represented generations of genetic breeding to produce the ultimate hand-to-hand soldier. She could take him, but she needed to be careful. Couldn't relax. Couldn't let her cold fury cloud her judgment. Focus.

With practiced ease she slipped her shoes from her feet, preferring to trust her hard soles on the wet concrete. As he reached the sidewalk on her side of the street, only a half dozen meters separated them; she rushed forward, low, hands out to balance against any move she would make.

At the last possible second the Elemental moved with blinding speed, spinning to the right and following through with a sweep of his left leg, placing himself in a crouch, with right hand firmly planted on the curb.

Snow moved with the sweep, doing a backward flip that briefly touched hands to sidewalk just after his trunk of a leg swept through, before launching herself into a twist, landing facing him, feet already carrying her backward, bleeding off speed. She stopped in her own crouch.

Damn. Hadn't the drugs taken effect yet? He should've been moving at half his current speed, if not less. Chagrined, Snow realized she had not thought to check whether Elementals were naturally resistant to drugs. Still, the dose she'd used could've put a horse to sleep. Almost. Had to have affected him somewhat, right? Enough for her to make it out of this with minimal damage, she hoped.

In the space between two light posts, with the darkness and rain, she could barely make out his face even at two meters; she felt confident he wouldn't know her from a wallflower.

"You have no idea what you have done, *surat*." That deep voice. Even now, she felt a shiver slide up her spine. Something in the timbre. The tone. She chuckled softly. Even now she still wanted him. Still wanted to see what such a mountain of flesh could do.

You're a silly girl. Daydreaming of a romp with a man who insulted you and is about to try to pound you back to the Star League.

She saw him stiffen slightly at her laugh. Snow laughed again, this time with more hilarity at her own fickleness as much as to try to disarm Corin.

"You will soon not have the teeth, much less the jaw, for such laughter, *surat*." Now he talked? Now he couldn't shut up? She smiled and laughed even louder. Could it be this easy to goad him?

He bellowed and rushed forward, low and hands out to try to grab her regardless of which direction she might move.

With a return bark of laughter (a dismissal of his own anger), Snow dove forward in a roll that placed her into a springing crouch as he swept into her. She pounded forward with a triple fist to his crotch as he scrambled to stop his forward movement. Some would be horrified at such an attack, but she'd been taught long ago to set aside such niceties. If she won, who cared how she got there? She didn't and her opponents certainly never did.

Supernova-strength pain blossomed in both shoulders as his 'Mech-sized fists hammered down; she grunted, giving him kudos for sloughing off the pain she had just delivered to his manhood.

"*Stravag*. Time to die."

She flopped backward—marveling he would waste breath right now—and used the momentum to roll herself up and to the side. She planted her left hand and scissored her legs back toward his right leg as he leaned over farther to reach her with those flesh hammers. Though he landed another blow, which momentarily lit off the mother of all bells in her ears, he put himself far enough off center that her blow knocked him to the side and down before he could adjust.

She rolled left several times—felt a jolt as she rolled off the curb and into the street; tasted copper as she bit her tongue—and came up into a crouch, facing him again. She knew he would expect her to pause and assess the damage: such inaction was for the weak. She attacked again, sweeping left toward his blind spot as Corin regained his feet and tried to turn as well.

Planting her left foot firmly (her flesh giving her purchase her shoes would've denied), she swung once again directly into his line of attack. Caught him off guard.

A frenzy of strokes and counterstrokes exploded as she pushed him back by the simple expediency of never letting up. Kept him reacting to her moves. With a feint at her head, Corin backed up against the wall. She moved forward left, slid slightly to the right and took a calculated blow directly to her right chest; she compartmentalized the pain and washed it away like the rain carried away the blood from cuts on her face and her knuckles. In return, she stabbed a flat knife hand directly into his throat.

Years of training allowed her to land the blow with a precision few could match. She felt the crunch of cartilage and knew he now felt the stunning pain of a trachea on the verge of partial collapse; a hairbreadth more pressure would've crushed it, ending his life in gasping, horrified pain. Pain lit his face like fire through old parchment. He grabbed at his throat as he wrenched his head backward in an attempt to ease the pressure . . . and smashed his head into the building wall behind him.

He dropped like a puppet with cut strings.

She breathed shallowly, aware too deep a breath would painfully stretch her right breast; she'd have a 'Mech-sized bruise there come morning. Stretched her right shoulder, surprised the old wound didn't hurt more. She sucked at her knuckles for a moment, then bent to reposition his head to lessen the strain on his trachea—keep it bent too long and it *would* collapse.

She couldn't believe how much he weighed; it took her longer than she could have guessed to move him to his new residence.

Now, with him restrained on the table, she flicked the needle several times to push out the last of the air bubbles and expertly added the drug to the IV line.

Then, with the languid grace of a Holt prairie cat nestling up to its kill to feed, she climbed up on the table, straddled his massive chest (the warmth *still* blossomed; she laughed at her own folly) and placed her face only centimeters from his. She'd not even taken time to dry off, and droplets of water slowly fell from her hair, splashing onto his face, pooling in the corners of his eyes and running down his chiseled features.

Blurry eyes slowly opened. Blank. Not understanding his change of status. She didn't say a word as he struggled to come fully awake—or as awake as she'd allow him to be. Took account of his situation. She smiled slowly, as confusion warred with anger. He couldn't place her.

He tried to speak, but the drugs wouldn't let that happen; she'd upped the dosage after her first mistake. Not yet. Another dozen seconds trickled by before understanding slinked in like a dawn to gray skies. He knew her. She warmed further as something moved behind those vacant eyes.

He'd been so talkative with his fellow Clansmen, and he would be again. She just knew he had *so* much to talk about, after all.

Now the real fun would begin.

19

Clan Sea Fox DropShip **Ocean of Stars**
Nadir Jump Point, Tania Borealis
Prefecture VII, The Republic
10 August 3134

"**W**hat are you hoping to accomplish, oh supreme ovKhan?" Jesup asked, walking onto the observation deck of the *Ocean of Stars* moments before the scheduled termination of deceleration.

Did we not have this conversation a half dozen times since leaving Adhafera? Jesup's sarcasm didn't reduce the irritation this time around. Petr ran his hand over his scarred scalp. Felt the twisted flesh, which would never change. Which would only grow more wrinkled with age. Grimaced at the idea of aging. Felt the twinge in his shoulder—a ghost of remembered pain. He did not answer. Did not feel the question—or Jesup, right about now—worthy of a response.

Just then, the captain cut the drive flare, having bled off most of the velocity in the short trip between the *Voidswimmer* and the ArcShip *Poseidon*. With the loss of the actinic glare of the fusion drive, the *Poseidon*, or at least a portion of her, hove into view. Both men fell silent, marveling at the construct before them.

At what *their* Clan had accomplished.

A *Potemkin*-class WarShip, the *Poseidon*'s original specs pegged her at a hair over 1,500,000 tons displacement and a length of just over 1,500 meters: a giant, round-tipped cylinder, with a slight flaring of her sides near the massive intersystem drive, and a plethora of docking rings dotting her midsection, where she held her twenty-five DropShip capacity like a clutch of possum young on her back.

Now, like a fungus fed to bursting, she'd grown and morphed well beyond the wildest imaginations of the original contractors who put pencil to paper and laid her keel. Though he did not have specifics, Petr felt sure she pushed almost a million tons more, and both her length and width had increased by more than fifty percent.

Beautiful did not come to mind. She had long ago lost her elegant lines to such growth, but the enormity of it still flabbergasted. With a gargantuan capacity of fifty DropShips, dozens of them *Behemoth*s permanently attached and turned into habitats or food repositories, she housed almost a half million inhabitants.

Beautiful did not come to mind. Magnificent did.

"You never answered my question." Irritation

flared, as Jesup's words pulled Petr back from his contemplation of greatness.

"Because we already have had this conversation. Several times, in fact."

"Then what is once more time, *aff*?" His laughter held a brittle quality Petr had never noticed before. He launched for the door.

With his usual grace, he grasped the edge of the hatch—Jesup had not dogged it upon entering—and smoothly twisted through, flinging himself down the long corridor, as though to escape Jesup's words. Why did it so often feel like he fled his aide's words?

"Why will you not answer?" The words came and Petr realized Jesup followed.

"Why will you not stop badgering me?"

"Me, badger you, oh great one? My obsequiousness would never allow it."

Despite everything, Petr smiled slightly, unsure what that meant, but confident Jesup made some point.

"*Neg*, ovKhan, I do not badger. This lowly one simply asks."

"Then ask a different question."

"But a different question would seek the same information."

Petr checked for traffic at a corridor intersection, then passed through. "For all your accusations of obsessiveness on my part, you manage a fair imitation yourself. Why can you not leave this alone?"

"Because you will not let me."

Petr glanced over his shoulder at the slightly strident tone, saw a look of determination hiding behind the light smile Jesup forced on his face. "I will not let you? That makes no sense. Do I force your hand, Jesup? Do I hold a Gauss pistol to your skull?"

"Are you not my ovKhan?"

His words could be taken to mean any number of things. But Petr did not have time to try to untangle the complicated weave of his aide's questioning.

Petr grabbed a stanchion and pulled himself to a stop, causing Jesup to almost overshoot him. "I need to speak with the saKhan about Sha."

Once again, Petr discerned more of Jesup's true emotions than at any time he could remember. *Have you allowed your mask to slip, finally revealing your true face, the clown's paints missing? And what is that truth?*

"ovKhan, can you not let it go?"

"What?" Petr actually averted his eyes, than pulled them back to Jesup, furious at his subconscious attempt to shy away from a simple question.

"Nothing has transpired that you both cannot forgive. Take a surkairede and let your oaths wash away the years of differences."

Petr held himself rigid. His anger was an inferno ready to incinerate Jesup for his audacity. He could not respond, not here. With the confrontation with saKhan Sennet looming and his growing certainty of Sha's guilt, he simply would not have this conversation. Not now.

He turned abruptly and began moving forward again. Like a mantra, Petr responded, "I hope to convince the saKhan that Sha is dangerous."

"How?"

Even more questions! An angry retort aborted on his tongue; his anger centered on himself, not Jesup.

I do not know how I will convince him.

The thought set his scalp itching and the phantom pain in his shoulder surging. As he reached the final intersection and began the descent to the docking station between the *Ocean of Stars* and *Poseidon*, he could not stop the thought from repeating within his head like the hammering of autocannon shells into 'Mech armor.

I do not know.

The thrum of humanity (*his* humanity) felt good after so long downside, among spheroids.

Petr moved with swift grace, swimming along the giant main thoroughfare of the *Poseidon*, parallel to the craft's mammoth K-F drive. Around him skimmed a school of humanity, in a rainbow of colors and shapes. With unobtrusive handholds and lines spaced at easy intervals on almost every available surface of the corridor, Fox Clansmen seemed to dart in and out of the main current, taking side shunts into each perpendicular deck, with amazing speed and grace.

Ahead, what had been Primary Cargo Hold A so many decades ago, Alpha Community Prime now filled to brimming—almost fifty thousand civilians. And four more communities half that size occupied other former cargo holds. Not to mention the dozens of DropShip communities.

Magnificent.

The word once more resonated in his head as he slipped into the hold and beheld the beehive of activity, as literally thousands of people made their way on various errands. Much as he wished to linger and take it all in, he could not delay his own mission.

Surprisingly enough, saKhan Sennet did not command Petr to meet him on his command DropShip, or even his command stateroom. Instead, saKhan Sennet had taken up a secondary residence in Alpha Community Prime (he said it reminded him of his responsibilities to the civilian castes, but Petr believed otherwise), and it was to this secondary residence that Petr now traveled.

Having been on this vessel numerous times, he moved with certainty, reading the jumbling confusion of directions printed in symbols on every corner of every block of residences. Before long he found the appropriate block, moved to the right hatch and rapped smartly, while holding on to one of the bars on either side of the entrance.

Several long seconds passed before the hatch undogged and swung inward; a head came into view and seemed to fill the entire hatchway.

saKhan Mikel Sennet's stature created a legend all its own. A giant brute of a man, he stood 2.4 meters tall, with large, pale features and dirty brown hair and eyes; his opponents whispered his mother must have been an elemental.

Only in a whisper.

"Enter." The deep voice perfectly matched such physical size.

Petr glided through as Mikel moved away from the door and pulled himself down into a seat at a small table. Petr closed the distance to the other chair and sat down as well; the static device in both chairs automatically activated to hold them to the surface. In microgravity, the decorum of waiting to be asked to sit had long since been done away with.

Glancing around, Petr approved of the Spartan accommodations. A place for everything and everything in its place, with little in the way of extraneous accoutrements—a simple, straightforward mind, with greater goals than to collect worthless knickknacks. Focusing on Mikel, he waited for an invitation to speak. Sitting was one thing, talking out of order another thing entirely.

He met the saKhan's intense stare with one of his own. Mikel gave no notice to Petr's disfigurement; he wore his own badges of honor, though none so large, or colorful.

Finally. "How does it progress?"

"Slowly."

He quirked an eyebrow; Petr took the rebuke. Did not respond.

"When can I expect an update?" His tone of voice said there should be only one more time that he'd need to speak with Petr.

"Before the rain's end."

A slight tightening around the eyes betrayed anger—or levity—at such an evasive answer. Petr's instincts said the latter. But mirth only took you so far with saKhan Sennet.

"Why have you come?"

"saKhan Sennet, I felt I needed to bring certain events to your attention."

Petr might as well be talking to a wall. He took a deep breath—always best to be short and direct with the saKhan—and continued. "I believe ovKhan Clarke is attempting to break away Beta Aimag, or even Spina Khanate, from the Clan."

Not a flicker crossed those features. Though he was

trained to spot tells, to use them ruthlessly to acquire any edge in negotiation, to his scrutiny Mikel gave away nothing. Then again, Mikel excelled in such matters as well; he *was* saKhan, after all.

Still, such a statement should have elicited something. Anything. Did he read the situation wrong?

Questions tumbled rapid-fire through his mind as the silence stretched. Petr shifted, once more felt the loss of his braid and squashed the regret as un-Clanlike, felt the hard plastic chair dig uncomfortably into his back and left side. At least it was not on the right.

"Why?" Not a change in tone, simply a question.

He dreaded this part. Even though he had no answers to the inevitable questions, he knew that to speculate on Sha's actions would get him in more trouble. "I do not know."

"How?"

Petr licked his lips, and stopped himself again from speculation. You provided the facts and saKhan Sennet sifted them through his own perception. Not your own. Mikel allowed his ovKhans exceptional latitude, but when you approached him with a problem, you did so on *his* terms.

"I do not know."

"When?"

"I do not know."

"*What*, ovKhan, *do* you know?" The accent fell, stinging—a slapping rebuke.

"I do not have specifics. But my instincts tell me I am right. I have dealt with him for years and he has always had only the best interests of his Aimag at heart."

"Is this not how it should be, *quiaff*?"

"*Neg*, saKhan. Not when it excludes the Clan. Always Clan Sea Fox above everything else." No response. "His current actions on Adhafera, our conversations"—Petr paused, examined his memories and sifted for a final analysis, continued—"I know it. He is moving to try to split Clan Sea Fox. He must be stopped."

"His latest actions?" Mikel said, leaning forward slightly, moving his hand to the smooth blue tabletop; he looked down at it. "Are your new badges attributed to such *actions*?" He looked up once more and the meaning sang clear; Petr's back stiffened.

"If you think I would cast such accusations simply due to my disfigurement," he began hotly, "then—"

saKhan cut him off with a raised hand; the tightening around the eyes recurred. This time Petr felt confident it was mirth. *Laughing at me?* The anger began to mount.

"ovKhan Petr, I would never think such a thing. After all, no ovKhan of mine could possibly be so petty." The tone did not match his words, adding fuel to the growing warmth within. "Or jealous." The last struck like a Gauss slug, shattering firmly held bands around his rage.

"If you believe that, then you must believe that no ovKhan of yours could rise to his position without the instincts to let him know when to seize the deal, when to walk away, when to sweeten the deal and when a Trial is the only way forward. I tell you now, you must keep an eye on Sha. He is dangerous."

For the first time, real emotion transfigured Mikel's face; too late, Petr realized his mistake.

"I must," Mikel said in a soft voice, discordant from such a mound of flesh.

Petr could see the harm had already been done, but nevertheless tried damage control. "saKhan, my choice of words . . . was poor. In my desire to safe-guard our Clan, I overstepped my bounds." That was as close to sucking up as Petr had ever come in his life. Despite the necessity, it made him feel unclean.

"*Aff*. Especially considering your proof." Two slabs of meat lightly smacked the table. "You come to me with nothing. I know your record. I know my ov-Khans, and I trust your instincts. But you cannot ex-pect me to take action based only on your words."

"But the things he has said, about removing those from power who will not be removed by our tradi-tions," Petr replied, desperate to keep the meeting going—a meeting already ended. If Mikel respected his instincts, why did he ignore them? More questions kept falling, one after the other, quicker than he could assimilate. Why?

"We all say things at times we do not mean, *quiaff*?"

Petr stiffened at the reminder of his own mistake committed only moments ago. "I traveled here be-cause I felt I could make a case that a simple message would fail to convey."

Suddenly Mikel leaned across the table, a hard ex-pression falling into place like a sheet of armor moved into position over a 'Mech's chest, ready for welding. "Then you have wasted your time, when you could have finalized the issues on Adhafera. The Khan is nearing this region, and I want it on a platter in front of him." The implied rebuke that Petr also had wasted his time hung between them. Mikel rose from his chair and moved toward the hatch. The meeting was terminated.

But why! I do not understand. He knew saKhan Sennet well enough to know that once he had reached a decision, you might as well try to shift a star's orbit with the thrust from an aerospace fighter.

Confused and angry, Petr slunk toward the hatch. Mikel's voice followed him out. "ovKhan, next time do not be so foolish as to assume I am not aware of what my ovKhans are doing. They are *mine*, after all."

The hatch swung home with a bang, a scrape of metal as it cycled.

What did he mean by that? That he knew I was coming and what I would say? Or that he already knew about the events on Adhafera? With the HPG down, it did not seem likely. But he had learned never to underestimate the crafty saKhan.

As he traveled the corridors back toward his ship, a new thought surfaced, shocking him so that he stopped abruptly and sent a passing civilian careening into the wall.

He knew about Sha. About his plans to try to break away Spina Khanate.

Though he tried to shake the feeling, his instincts sunk their teeth into it and locked their jaws. Not only was he aware of it, but he allowed it to continue.

Why?

He hesitated, felt compelled to return and confront him over this revelation, but knew a trial would be the only result. He would suffer defeat in such a hand-to-hand conflict, especially with Petr still less than one hundred percent.

As he launched himself back into the stream of humanity, his spirits sank further. Not only did he have to stop Sha, but the possibility existed he would have to stop saKhan Sennet as well.

His anger washed away in the cool waters of despair.

20

Beta Aimag Encampment, Halifax
Vanderfox, Adhafera
Prefecture VII, The Republic
15 August 3134

Sha Clarke stared at the hard copies, his eyes unseeing.

Innumerable thoughts tumbled through his head with failed entry trajectories, dead stick and tumbling endlessly, end over end, burning up in the arctic chill of his cerebral atmosphere.

He could not focus, his thoughts too disjointed from the reports in front of him.

To top it off, he only recently learned that Petr lifted off-planet weeks ago. Weeks!

Sha's aide would not make such a mistake again soon. Regardless of how well Delta hid the information, his aide *existed* to provide information. If he could not rely on her to obtain it, especially during such a critical time, then she could *deexist*.

He rubbed his tired face with both hands, blinked several times to moisten his scale-dry eyes and leaned back, throwing a casual arm across his closed eyelids; his subordinates would've been shocked to see such lassitude.

The aromas of this world worked their way under multiple seals and down long corridors, wafted through endless eddies until they moved sluggishly through his office, their scents tickling his nose and bursting images of alien flora and fauna before his closed lids like a holoprojector.

"Java. Java," he spoke slowly. Rhetorically, really, since a half-empty cup steamed on the table. A brewing pot lurked in the corner on the room's only furniture other than the desk and chair, which swallowed the remaining space in dark wood and exquisite whorls of local design.

He leaned forward once more, red eyes open, and picked up the first report again, re-read it for the third time.

<<<*Decript 39A79B454E*
EYES ONLY: ovKhan Sha Clarke
From: Sea Fox Watch, Field Beta, Team Beta
Date: 1 August 3134
My Khan,
    The avians have not been totally successful at Zipper 5-Talon 3, losing many of their number; no additional eggs have been shipped.
    The rest of the flock have begun to gather toward the clouds.
<<<

Sha willed himself not to crumple the paper in frustration. He should have known the Jade Falcons would be his weak link. Should have foreseen they would hood themselves with shortsightedness, as they always did.

A Clan-wide inferiority complex? Centuries later, did their feathers still ruffle and their beaks click despairingly over the Founder's decision to mix his blood with that of Clan Wolf in place of their own?

He snorted mockingly. To be tied to such an event, when every day brought new currents and new opportunities to launch toward glory. They have declawed themselves for so long, they cannot even recognize that their talons no longer can make a lasting impression on their prey, momentarily damaging, leaving the enemy to rise again and destroy them. Or at least drive them back.

He'd read the reports on Kimball II several times. How they could fail to pacify the world boggled the mind. And not having their full forces for Skye?

Sha reached over and tossed back the remains of his Ulan Bator Java, the cooling burned-bean liquid shriveling his tongue, but shaking him awake.

No, they just might fail. Despite their self-declawing, the Falcons could and would hurt their prey in the short term. But Sha had traveled the space lanes of The Republic and the Inner Sphere for too long not to recognize that the Falcons kept their own brand of honor and prowess . . . though theirs was lesser than Clan Sea Fox. *Neg*, when push came to shove, if the Falcons could not bring enough force to bear, Skye might just succeed.

And if they did, then what of his deal with Jade Falcon?

He slapped the paper down and picked up the next sheet, ignoring the stinging in his hand.

<<<Decript 32M45YJ3H5K
To: ovKhan Sha Clarke
From: saKhan Sennet
Date: 30 July 3134
RE: Activities
ovKhan Clarke,
    My ovKhans are given greater latitude than
any other within Clan Sea Fox, but do not
make the mistake of thinking I do not watch.
Your activities are known.
    If you are dedicated to the greater good of
Spina Khanate, then you have nothing to fear.
<<<

Petr leaned back once more and held the report up to the fluorescent light above. Noticed the slightly mottled look all paper showed when held to a strong light source; felt the rough edges and recognized the low quality of indigenous paper stock. Peered steadily, as though trying to find something that did not exist. Some extra meaning hidden within the paper itself; the words remained as opaque as a Nova Cat.

What in the world could the Khan have meant?

His activities here? Trying to deny Delta its prey and subvert Kalasa? Or perhaps his attempts—none of which he'd discussed with the saKhan—to finally crack the Regulan Fiefs?

He didn't for a minute believe saKhan Sennet could be aware of his sojourn to the Falcons. The saKhan had always been a "wait and see" leader, basking in the glory of his subordinates, but stepping aside when failure reared its head, generally too cautious for his own good. Even so, Sha did not believe for a moment the saKhan would condone his actions, if he knew the truth. If he understood the full complexity of the plan.

Then again, saKhan Mikel, despite his station, would miss such a subterfuge, would miss most of Sha's moves, if he did not telegraph them blatantly enough to keep the saKhan and the rest of Spina Khanate's ovKhans focused on his right hand, while his left worked the real deal. Sha's lips tweaked, cold and mirthless.

Of course, so few could understand the glory he worked to bestow upon his Aimag, upon Spina Khanate. The prosperity that would elevate the Khanate to a new level.

A bootheel squeaked outside the door. Sha glanced up sharply, but turned back to his reports when he realized the guard had simply changed his stance; he'd have to remind the man once more about extraneous noise.

With regret, he slowly placed the enigmatic report back onto the glossy wood and retrieved the final report.

   <<<Decript 987DF34L24
   EYES ONLY: ovKhan Sha Clarke
   From: Sea Fox Watch, Field Beta, Team Omega
   Date: 15 July 3134
   My Khan,
     Prey lost.
   <<<

The paper's edge tried vainly to pierce his skin as it trembled under clenching fingers—rigid, steel bands that crushed the sheet to a small, insignificant sphere. Again.

Sha trembled. Had to breathe deeply and relax. For the first time in long years, needed to remind himself anger got you nowhere.

Look at where it got Kalasa.

Sha immediately cooled, his steel fingers turned to flesh once more, though his knuckles ached with the force of his rage, smoothed out the paper as best he could.

All they had to do was follow a slow, ponderous ship.

Unlike the rest of the Khanates and their Aimags, which bid for and fought to acquire the rights in specific regions of space—worlds each Aimag and Khanate would then use to further their revenues, honor and glory for the Clan—the ilKhanate acted as an oversight governing body. Never with a set destination, the Khan and Alpha Clan Council traversed known space, checking in on the activities of the subordinate Khanates and their Aimags, taking their ten percent due. Though it was generally known in which direction the ilKhanate was traveling—as was the case right now, with the ilKhanate known to be heading in their direction—you simply never knew when the *stravag* Khan and his outdated authorities would darken your skies to grasp un-worked-for glories.

And to such a wallowing ArcShip he tasked three tails . . . and still they lost it.

He tried to order his thoughts once more, but felt the weight of the reports pushing at him. Pulling him.

Their combined mass unbalancing the plan. Putting an erratic wobble into its forward motion which, if not corrected immediately would eventually spin it out of control, sending it tumbling to burn up in atmosphere or a stellar mass.

All the more galling, since he could do nothing about any of it immediately. If they lost their prey, he would not find it himself by blundering off; such a hunt would only waste valuable weeks and resources.

He stood slowly, pushing back the roller chair with his knees; it moved with a soft squeal just far enough for him to extricate himself before coming to a stop with a soft bump against the back wall. He gathered the papers slowly together, squared them and smoothed wrinkles.

Nothing to be done about the Falcons. If they have handed the Skye defenders the clippers to snip their own wings . . . nothing to be done. At this point, he simply could not associate with the Falcons in any way; the terse note from saKhan Sennet made it too dangerous. A new thought skewed its way into consciousness.

Disconnect.

He grimaced and moved out from around the desk, toward the java pot. Sha hated that word. Hated its implied weakness. Yet he had not gained such heights without knowing when to pull back. When to disengage. Though secondary plans were in place, with all three of his primary plans in trouble, he must accept the fact he might have to pull back. Might have to wait longer before seizing destiny for Spina Khanate.

Underneath the java pot, a small incinerator waited

for its daily feeding of pulp and information too dangerous to leave in the light of day.

As he fed all three papers into the machine, Sha counted assets in his head. Tallied how many people knew about his encounter with the Jade Falcons. Balanced on scales the needs of his personnel and their future contributions to the welfare of the Aimag against the repercussions of discovery; he had purposely kept the numbers stripped low, not just to minimize leakage, but just in case such actions were needed.

Of course he would still move forward. Of course he would still move to seize the day; not all was yet lost. However, it was important to hedge your bets in every direction.

Time to clean house.

21

Merchant House, Halifax
Vanderfox, Adhafera
Prefecture VII, The Republic
29 August 3134

For once, Petr's disgust at the Merchant House centered on something other than the vile stench still troubling him—especially after so many long weeks in the blissfully clean-scrubbed air of the *Ocean of Stars*.

"What would you have me do?" Tidinic said, his voice pitched to easily cut through the continual hubbub of the giant edifice. The master trader sat across from him; others occupied the large table, but only the two of them mattered. Clean lines to his suit. Well-tailored, but not extravagant. Long, chocolate-colored hair cascaded from a widow's peak to the suit's shoulders. Large eyes hung under craggy, bushy brows like bird eggs hidden from predators just under the cliff's precipice; eyes mimicked such fragility, but Petr saw the raptor within.

Petr shifted, felt the pull of gravity, the pull of the situation. Tried to forget the angry looks from his factors when he returned and thrust himself to the forefront of the negotiations, never mind his right to do so. Tried to forget his weeks of wasted effort with saKhan Sennet.

His failure against Sha. Again.

"Master Trader," he began, layering in respect without drowning it in sycophancy, "I would have us come to some accord. I understand you are hard pressed to meet our demands, as we are yours."

Tidinic nodded his head, though it felt more like a merchant prince accepting pronouncements at his court—decrees he scripted to be read by Petr. Petr kept his temper, banking the hot coals of rage for later use.

"I also understand and appreciate the hardships you and your fellow citizens have suffered following the collapse of the HPG. Nevertheless, it is time to make a decision. You have two offers before you."

They had tried ignoring Beta Aimag, to no avail. Perhaps finally recognizing the competition and actively trying to push the locals to a decision would move them one way or another.

Frustrations gnawing at him, he felt as if he were on an EVA, with low oxygen; no matter how deep he breathed, he could not get enough air (he didn't want *this* air anyway). Felt he needed to make *something* happen.

Though he'd conducted negotiations that took longer, it did not happen often. More important, he'd never carried out such strenuous negotiations as a backdrop against so many other issues swirling around him, creating a mental and physical dervish that threatened to sweep him away.

The image of the pugnacious and repulsive Snow reared its head. He had to deal with that wild card as well. The new data cube, waiting on his desk when he returned, now burned like a hot coal against his leg. Once more she had deposited it where she should not be, and he knew it meant trouble.

As he had stared at the small cube crouching on his desk like a slumbering terror waiting to feast on his mind, he'd realized he had not done a single thing to further investigate her claims of a Marik-Stewart invasion. Though he should not have cared, a surreal feeling crawled across his shorn scalp, prickling scar tissue like a brisk wind. He could not put a finger on it, but he suspected that she could cause him problems. Make his life difficult. Yet if he aided her, her gratitude could be . . . generous. He should've dismissed such musings as stress-induced mania, but he could not. Could not forget the smoky eyes and the gleam within. He'd seen power too many times, despite the unattractive package, not to recognize it.

Aff, she would cause him no end of troubles if he did not find a way to use her in return.

"ovKhan." The sound snapped him back to the present like an emergency safety line wrenching him in from an EVA gone bad. He saw that Tidinic's face held a speculative look, while the other traders at the table variously showed surprise, disgust and outright hostility; he didn't want to see his own Fox Clansmen's expressions at such a lapse.

Petr leaned back, felt the stink of the pens as a physical pressure around him (ignored the lowing, which sat in the lower part of his brain as a vibrating tumor) and steepled his fingers, tried to gain back the initiative he might have just lost. Then again, at this point, he simply wanted resolution on some front, any front. Even if that meant giving something up. At least for now.

He cleared his throat, refused to acknowledge his distraction, continued. "Master Tidinic, you have two offers on the table. Though we wish to aid you, in fact would find great honor in it, The Republic holds numerous worlds in need of our aid as well."

"I'm sure they will all welcome it with open arms, ovKhan Kalasa." Petr sloughed off the sarcasm—oil on water.

"*Aff.* I am confident of that as well, Master Tidinic. However, to bring such aid to those who need it, we need a resolution here. The exportation of your food-stuffs will aid many worlds, not to mention your own. What accord can we reach?"

Almost completely motionless for a half hour, the portly man finally shifted, leaning forward slightly, placing his right hand on the table. "ovKhan Kalasa, I have felt for some time we have been making great progress in reaching a mutually beneficial agreement. I have gone over the respective contracts numerous times and it would appear we are almost of one mind concerning what needs to be given . . . and taken, for an agreement to be signed."

He nodded to one of the myriad trader aides at his side and the man produced a document that he laid carefully upon the table, then slid delicately into the middle. The sudden silence at the table as the papers slowly wisped across wood reminded Petr of religious offering ceremonies he'd seen on several spheroid worlds.

Petr raked his eyes across it for a moment, before glancing back up. "Is this the agreement we have worked on most recently?" he asked, knowing full well it wasn't.

"Not exactly."

"Not exactly? Could you perhaps be a little more specific?" Time to crank up his sarcasm dial.

"There has been a complication."

"Again."

The man shrugged, as though to apologize; the raptor gaze never faltered. "A new JumpShip has entered the system."

Petr barely managed not to glare at his own people for not yet having this information. Petr spoke from a suddenly dry throat. "And what does this have to do with our ongoing negotiation?"

"It seems this ship is also a trading vessel." Again, the insincere shrug. "However, it appears they are not of your Clan, but an Inner Sphere concern." He leaned back once more; Petr felt the man might stretch and snuggle into his chair like a space cat: warm, content and filled with the knowledge he held the upper hand.

"As I would hate to allow this new concern to horn in on a business deal we have all worked so hard to cement, I have suggested two last-minute changes, which I humbly submit for your final review. With your stamp of approval, I can have a contract drafted and on your desk by tomorrow for your signature, days before the JumpShip could possibly set people on the ground to disrupt.''

Petr felt the rage growing, but pushed it aside. Nodded once, thoughtfully, at the adept move.

On my desk, and Sha's as well, waiting to see who bites.

Though angry, he had to give the man his due. He managed to gain information before either Delta or Beta Aimag and made the most of it, holding it over them like a raised 'Mech foot, ready to smash them if they did not acquiesce.

Reaching forward, he picked up the page, and quickly read through it. Just as he thought. An additional half percentage point on gross and a year less on the absolute contract rights. Completely unacceptable.

Opening his mouth to respond, Petr caught movement out of the corner of his eye. Turning, he saw Sha, along with a small Beta cadre, moving toward their table. One look told him they knew of the arriving JumpShip, knew of their current negotiations and had come posthaste.

Though the animosity between the two of them had grown to spectacular levels, they still shared the same Khanate. The same Clan. In the end, though both would chew off their own tongues before admitting as much, they would rather see the other gain victory here than to miss the opportunity entirely, or worse yet, allow a Republic trading concern to sink their greedy talons into it.

The two ovKhans seemed to telegraph their thoughts across the closing distance. In one of the few moments when Sha and Petr absolutely agreed, the time had come for a distinctly Clan resolution to this conundrum.

Returning his attention to Master Tidinic, he allowed a smile to bloom on his face, mirth to widen his eyes. The sudden jerk in his raptor gaze told Petr the man went from total control to doubt in a heartbeat. It only fueled the smile larger.

"Master Tidinic," Petr said, "Beta and Delta Aimags must reach our own resolution to this problem before one of us again sits at this table to discuss your proposal. Please excuse me for a handful of minutes."

Though he tried to hide it, Tidinic floundered; the other traders could not disguise their confusion.

Standing up, Petr turned toward Sha and his own cadre moved away from the table to meet the arriving Betas. He should have been angry at this development, but he actually felt as though a load had been lifted. He stretched his tired back and neck muscles, felt the pull of strong tendons and muscles all across his body, his right shoulder hardly twinging; he breathed in deeply and, for the first time he could remember, didn't mind the stench.

Resolution. If only of one thing, resolution nevertheless.

"ovKhan Kalasa," Sha said, nodding his head slightly.

Though his rival showed no more emotion than usual, Petr thought he detected a look of relief in those too-chill eyes.

He needs this resolution as much as I. For a moment, Petr pondered that thought. *Is it just this deal? Doesn't seem possible. Can his larger plans have problems?* No way of knowing, but Petr smiled larger regardless. Even the possibility buoyed him.

"ovKhan Clarke, I see you are aware of the new arrival."

"*Aff*. And it changes our circumstances. I believe we are of a mind."

"*Aff*, ovKhan. It is time we determine who shall seat themselves again with Master Tidinic and who shall concede defeat."

"*Aff*. I name Bel," he answered, indicating a mammoth elemental, who moved forward with the lethal grace and contained fury of a sphinx raptor.

Petr nodded. "I name Calson." Petr looked over his shoulder as another elemental stepped forward, matching Bel grace for grace. Lethality for lethality. Their eyes met and Petr nodded once. Acknowledgment, blessing.

Petr looked back and at Sha. "Bargained well and done."

"Seyla," the small assembly of warriors spoke. Though short and abbreviated from the usual forms for a Trial of Possession, there was precedence; in the heat of the deal, customs can and will be . . . massaged.

The remaining Clan warriors, including Petr and Sha, immediately began to form a Circle of Equals roughly fifteen meters across, pushing aside spheroids and moving tables. Petr could see the trader group milling about in confusion, while a few chose to try and close the distance. To investigate. Some bovine wranglers moved closer, curiosity overcoming their better sense to stay out of Clan matters.

Petr turned and ignored them all. Down to Clan business now.

Even through his boots, Petr could feel the solid concrete underneath the thin, dirty layer of straw. He tapped his foot twice, felt the smack of his flesh against the unyielding surface even through the soles of his boot.

Hard, very hard. Unyielding. No forgiveness for hard landings here; likely a quick battle.

The two superlative warriors did not waste time with words, nor move into the dance Petr had seen many combatants (especially spheroids) ascribe to. Instead, like two enraged ghost bears, the two launched forward, slamming platter-sized hands at each other's necks and midriffs in a series of blows and counterblows, which looked as though they could dent 'Mech armor.

Neither warrior landed a serious blow or managed to grasp the other in a lasting hold and they broke apart, this time to slouch into lower, more balanced stances as they began to circle each other slowly.

If you do not succeed, try, try again. The spheroid children's fable moral sprang to mind and Petr's smile continued.

A burst of babble slightly behind him and off to his right momentarily pulled his attention; his smile creased his face with deep lines (he'd not smiled so often in long, long weeks) as he saw the fear on the faces of the local merchants. For long weeks the spheroids had blinded themselves to the nature of the traders in their midst, believing them basically the same as themselves.

Now the differences sang among the rafters of the Merchant House and the brutality of it, the *force* of it, sent them running scared. Would make them doubt themselves. Push them back off their guard, when either he or Sha sat down at the table in victory.

He turned back to find Calson in the midst of a stunning flying kick. The man had to be at least 2.5 meters tall and yet he knew the warrior would easily clear his own height.

The shin-high, tight-fitting boot swept through the air occupied a moment before by Bel's head; the impact might have decapitated a lesser man. Bel, however, had no intention of losing his head so quickly. Ducking under the full bulk of Calson, he twisted his body down and back up to the right, latching fingers as strong as manacles on to the legs of his opponent as quick as a cloud cobra strike and continuing to twist. Using the forward momentum and Calson's own mass, Bel further twisted his body and yanked forward, bending and crouching down quickly. With the kicking leg practically lashed over his right shoulder and Calson already committed to the move, the man jackknifed forward, straight into the concrete.

Petr winced at the smacking-meat sound—a little too much like the occasional side of beef that came loose from its hook in the Merchant House during transport from one section to the next. Actually felt the tremble through the ground.

However, genetically engineered warriors could not be removed from the field of battle so easily. Calson had gotten both arms in front of him, and used them to bleed off some of his own velocity; he still smacked his face hard, as straight-arming such a fall would've snapped even elemental arms. Calson rolled four times in rapid succession, tearing lose his leg and putting a little distance between him and Bel. He spun to a low crouch; a shattered nose and pulped lips cascaded blood down his chin and onto his neck and shirt. A slow grin showed loose teeth, but blazed with the attitude prized by any Clansmen.

Pain? Bring it on.

Another flurry of babbles from behind him exploded and Petr grunted in satisfaction, confident they saw the bloody, ghastly grin and trembled. Even if Calson lost, Petr would ensure he would not pay for it with any diminished honor; the fear and confusion gripping the local merchants was sufficient payment for a defeat on Calson's part.

Sliding forward smoothly, Bel feinted left. Then dodged right. Then back one more time, before snapping a knee-capping kick forward, accompanied by an eye-and-chest strike. Calson stood as a malachite statue, unwilling to give into Bel's dance of death, and only moved when the knee-capper flew; sliding backward a half step with that leg, blocking blows with brutal efficiency and then swinging that same leg back up and around with terrible force.

Catching Bel slightly off guard, the thrust slammed the other warrior's legs together, knocking him off balance for a half second.

Which is all a trained killer needs.

Like an aerospace fighter from a launch bay, Calson struck, raining savage blows and side cuts across Bel's head. The elemental windmilled both arms to maintain balance, to drop at the feet of his opponent meant almost certain defeat. As the blows continued, Bel finally got his feet steady once more, but took almost five steps to do it. Near the edge of the Circle, Calson reared back and pounded both fists into Bel's chest, sending the elemental staggering.

Whether through sheer dumb luck, or some preternatural ability that allowed Bel to literally sense the edge of the Circle, he dropped to the ground like a sack of flesh to stop his backward movement.

Breaching the Circle meant defeat.

Sensing victory, Calson launched forward and Petr flinched; perhaps the head slam had affected the elemental more than he knew. This was a classic error.

As Calson launched forward, Bel reached up to lock his hands in a death grip on Calson's arms, forcing his opponent to do the same. Then Bel rocked backward as he planted his feet firmly in Calson's abdomen. Physics did the rest, as Calson sailed out of the Circle and into defeat.

Beta Aimag would be sitting at the table for Adhafera. Once more, the feeling almost unnatural after so long, Petr's lips twisted upwards in a smile.

Beta Aimag wins for today . . . and Master Tidinic will quickly realize he should have taken my previous generous offer.

22

Canopian Pleasure Circus, Halifax
Vanderfox, Adhafera
Prefecture VII, The Republic
30 August 3134

The lascivious mermaid wove her arms and tail suggestively, sickeningly; the bare planks supporting the mud-smeared plasteel looked barely more rotted than her teeth, and her tail had seen better days.

Clan genetics? Petr sniffed in disgust at the stage man's loud cries.

As he stamped past the audience of cast-off males hooting and tossing coins displaying various visages onto the stage, he felt the vileness of the place press in against him.

On the outskirts of Halifax, in a rundown neighborhood—would've seen a Clansman removed in a Trial of Grievance for ineptitude and inability to lead years ago—the so-called Canopian Pleasure Circus squatted like an ancient whore: bruised, sullen and ugly, hiding in the shadows and trying to avoid the notice of the authorities, but still willing to spread her legs for a coin. Any coin.

A putrescence wafted up his nostrils, causing Petr to lurch for a moment and gag before he could master himself. His mood lightened as he realized he had just discovered something that stank more than the Merchant House.

Stepping around a large pile of some unidentifiable offal, he glanced in the direction of the offending stench and beheld a large, blue-and-white-striped tent, perhaps twenty meters on a side; at one point it had been a traveling tent, but the planks of rough-hewn wood around the entire lower exterior and the grass that grew profusely around it attested to the length of its stay. A large, hand-painted sign thrust up from the ground on a small tree in front of the opening, only its branches shorn off, the bark not even removed. On the shoddy sign, a worn, flaking painting of a large feline with a nova burst of poison-barbed mane sprawled, with the words *See the Magnificent, Terrifying Nova Cat from the Clan Homeworlds* emblazoned below.

The terrified and brutalized meowing that emerged from the tent bore no resemblance to the roaring of that magnificent feline; after all, unlike these ground-bound *surats*, he had witnessed a nova cat hunting in the wild in the Irece Prefecture of the Draconis Combine. The difference between the two sounds was like the contrast between the depths of night and a stellar body bursting into reality astern an arriving JumpShip.

The sun poked through tattered clouds for a moment, casting wan light across the entire area: sickly, decrepit, decaying. The words jumbled, raised his ire anew.

He passed the tent with a final, Clan-like epithet: if this miserable excuse for an entertainment establishment actually managed to capture such an animal, Clan Nova Cat would have descended to raze the whole, filthy locale to the ground. Peace or no peace.

I have not even been to the Clan homeworlds. No melancholy, just a statement of reality and acknowledgment of the horrors that had cut off the Inner Sphere Clans from their birthplace, likely forever.

Petr passed into a region filled with stalls and their hawkers, foisting a supposed universe of bounty upon those lucky enough to walk these dirty stalls . . . but *only* for today! Fried branth from Lopez (poison to most human metabolisms); Mycosia pseudoflora from Andalusia (too many buds); real Canopian women for any pleasure (too white-skinned and thin-boned); a Kurita officer's katana from before the Jihad (blade too long, not folded); even a whispered call to view a Word of Blake robe (wrong material and stitching): the entire charade made him ill. The whore putting on her paints and perfumes to blind the customer to her stench, her sham, her total lack of joy.

No Canopian Pleasure Circus here.

In fact, like the Nova Cats, Petr felt confident a real Canopian Circus would use the fusion drive of their DropShips to scour the entire region clean.

Why did Snow pick this location for a meeting?

He closed in on a large, makeshift arena, with stacked and rough-nailed seating; perhaps a thousand people might be able to view the enclosed arena, though he doubted the entire Circus saw that many customers in several weeks, much less a single show.

Moving between the two rows of stacked bleachers, the sour tang of old urine seeped into the pores of his tongue. He swallowed, tried not to gag again. Even after the unbearable reek of the Merchant House, the monstrous-sized smells of this place almost defied description, overpowering olfactory senses bred for shipboard living.

Why?

Petr came to a stop, ignoring the commotion on the arena floor, and immediately scanned the crowd: about fifty people of ages ranging from teenagers to those so long in the tooth they held themselves away from death with their fingernails. He did not immediately spot her and so began to move along the front of the bleachers.

Those who thought to shout at him for blocking their view quickly thought better of their comments at the sight of his uniform and the angry storm raging across his face. Almost immediately, those on the front benches began to move back and up a seat or two as he neared; the killing instinct in his eyes became a glaring torch that strove to burn all before him.

Reaching the end of the occupied seats, he continued on for a half dozen paces, then took three large steps to reach the top row. He rocked the entire section of bleachers as he sat, though no one commented on that, either.

Petr turned hot eyes on the ridiculous spectacle before him.

His thoughts churned sluggishly, as they always did when he could not control himself; he sat unseeing.

Why here? Why now? "You should not trust what you see?" Was the message to look for a deeper meaning? Could not possibly be that. Surely she held enough respect for him she would consider such a message unnecessary. What then?

He shifted slightly and winced as a sliver found its way with a pinprick of agony into his buttocks, probably would need to be disinfected.

Are you jealous?

The words swept toward him like a teleoperated capital-class missile. He suddenly felt like a lumbering *Overlord*-class DropShip attempting to evade the mechanical raptor that swept the void with its electronic eye and zeroed in on its prey, mocking its futile attempts to escape.

Though saKhan Sennet did not say as much, the words resonated within, regardless of his efforts to ignore them.

Are you selfish?

Another ping and another missile dropped into the void from a launch tube, sending out its powerful radar to sweep the emptiness and drive relentless, to run its target to ground.

The roar of a hurt animal from the arena floor did not impinge on the raucous sound between his ears; he tried to shift on the bench again and settled after another white-hot jab from the *stravag* sliver.

He did not wish to face either accusation; the words resonated too closely with those often spoken by Jesup. He trusted himself. Knew himself and did not lie to himself. Such self-deception was for spheroids and Snow Ravens. Not an ovKhan.

And yet . . .

The question hung, balanced over the knife's edge of his self-image. Waiting like the sword of Damocles for him to make one wrong move, contemplate one wrong word that would unleash the blade and cleave his life in twain.

"A stone for your thoughts."

"*Savashri*" slipped out before he could stop it; he flinched, hated himself for it. Not often anyone took him by surprise.

Looking to his left, he gazed into the smoldering depths of smoky gray eyes. For nearly ten seconds he took no notice of his surroundings. The sword within, which felt like the weight of a ArcShip keel, vanished in those depths.

In those stormy currents.

"You know, sweetness, I told you last time what would happen if you kept staring at me like that." She batted her eyes coquettishly, canted her head slightly. "But since I see you went and let someone work you over with the ugly stick, I may just have to reconsider letting you take me to bed."

Petr's tunnel vision collapsed and he could finally take her in completely. Noticed the dirt and caked grime limning her face, spattering down her neck and even onto her clothing, only increasing her unattractiveness. For just a moment, he felt the urge to pull away. Until he realized there was not a hint of repugnance in her gaze at his horribly scarred head.

"Well, I guess I could simply close my eyes, right, sweetness?" Her words, though playful, simply did not match the frank look in her eyes. Those eyes told him she might not be joking.

Though he had banked the coals of his ire since

yesterday's encounter with the merchant traders and the lost trial against Sha, he felt the embers starting to grow dark. For the first time in his memory, someone who should have fired his rage to nova-hot temperatures actually managed to calm him. It was disconcerting, especially when she also managed to aggravate him at every turn.

He didn't stop to contemplate this strange effect she had on him, however, because he wanted to take advantage of it to put her off guard. To score after their last meeting, and to forestall her likely anger at his lack of progress.

He opened his mouth and she smoothly cut him off, pointing to the arena.

"Don't you just love these shows, sweetness? The fun, the thrills. The excitement."

He turned his attention to the floor and noticed it, really noticed it, for the first time. Approximately a hundred meters long and a little under half that wide, the arena was more properly a pit: simply dug straight into the ground about eight meters, with earthen ramps descending on both ends; a series of wooden barricades with small trap doors allowed any to enter, but none to leave except at the sufferance of the arena magister. One look, even at this distance, at the cruel set of his face and large whip—supplemented by an old blazer rifle strapped across his back—told of few returning back through those gates.

Staring hard into the pit (difficult to do, with a good portion of a view of the floor blocked by the steep drop of the side), Petr spotted a small cluster of tall humans, wearing loincloths and with their hair arranged in topknots, using studded tridents to keep at bay a three-meter-tall, four-armed horror. For the first time at this travesty of entertainment, Petr found his interest piqued.

How in the world . . . ?

The living nightmare moved forward at blinding speed, claws and jaws snapping at the human fighters. Petr leaned forward slightly, ignoring a new stab from the sliver, intent on the response of the warriors. With almost practiced precision, they formed a phalanx, the first row dropping to their knees and all thrusting forward to create a double-row wall—with slightly curved ends to keep the creature from flanking—of hard steel. The monster almost pulled a warrior out of place when it stopped abruptly, lashed out, grasped one of the tridents and wrenched it hard to the side. The warrior let go and several tridents lashed forward to draw blood, eliciting a scream of pain and rage.

"Now, sweetness, don't tell me *you* like blood sports, too?" He turned to find Snow avidly watching the unfolding gladiatorial fighting: she had predicted his interest, which would keep him distracted. "I may just propose to you on the spot, and we'll find a place for nuptials under the bleachers."

"It is filled with the stench of urine," he responded. Her lips began curling into her usual sarcastic reply, but he injected his rejoinder first. "Then again, you stink enough now, I probably would not notice."

Snow froze (imperceptible, except that he had been watching for just such a tell), then replied, "Now sweetness, them's loving words. All I'm saying is 'loving words.' "

He allowed himself a small smile, which widened when he caught the brief eye blink. He'd surprised her. And she knew that he knew.

Ah, the games we play in negotiations.

"A Nolan," he said, trying to throw her off her game by switching back to her own bait.

"Yes, they've held it here for some time."

"How? Not even the Sea Fox have managed to keep them alive off Engadine for very long."

"Now how would I know that?" She smirked. "I know lovers like to think their partners are omniscient and all, but *please*."

He watched her attempt to put her hair into some semblance of order and he actually laughed.

"You laughing at me?" Her eyes twinkled with merriment.

He sucked his teeth (wondered for a moment if he would ever get the taste-smell of urine off his tongue), and actually reached out and patted her knee, drawing a startled look. "Of course not, Snow. I'm laughing with you."

"Ah, no talking dirty to me, sweetness. And hands off until the wedding night."

A terrible, gurgling cry interrupted their repartee. They turned their heads in time to see the decapitation of one of the warriors, as one set of arms simply tore the body in two. The Nolan took several gashes from the warriors in return, however, and actually was forced back a step.

With a new understanding, Petr shifted his gaze to the magister and saw the panic on his face, even across such a distance.

The warriors are doing much better than you expected. He just might lose his Nolan.

He nodded thoughtfully at the warriors in acknowledgment of their obvious skills, considered, for just a moment, striking out for the magister in the hopes of ending the match; there would be a good market in Nolans if they could be bred off Engadine and in captivity.

"So, sweetness, about my offer?"

The words brought him back from the potential of a good deal, to the immediacy of a deal in the works.

"Which offer would that be?"

"Don't go all coy after offering to drag me off and have your way with me under the bleachers." Snow shifted and winced; he imagined she'd gotten a sliver in her own ample rump.

Petr maintained his silence until she actually looked put out and broke the silence between them, though her voice dropped several decibels and lost some of its playfulness.

"The invasion of The Republic. Have you decided what use you might make of that information?"

Petr raised his right hand, rubbed the fingers together (ignored the grime transferred from the wood) and looked at them casually; glanced back up. "Perhaps."

She looked at his hand, back into his eyes, her own smoky gaze suddenly burning with renewed intensity.

Fool me once, Snow, shame on me. Fool me twice . . . ? A spheroid saying, but apt nonetheless. This time, he would do the playing.

" 'Perhaps.' That's all you have to say, sweetness?"

That came out between gritted teeth. "You've been doing what for the past few weeks? Not making headway sealing up the beef trade on this sorry-ass planet."

"I have made progress where progress has been needed. And what have you been doing? Sealing up your own deals?"

A look he could not identify came and went on her face. "That, sweetness, is none of your business. Jealous?"

He leaned back and away from her, resting his arm along the short railing that ran across the back of the top bench—a casual gesture that surprised her and would've shocked his own people. "Perhaps."

She swallowed. Once. Twice. Blinked.

"What news have you for me?"

"News. Didn't you read the data cube?"

"I felt the news would smell sweeter coming from you." He sniffed audibly. "Obviously, I was mistaken."

They both ignored another warrior's dying agonies shredding the air, too intent on their own world.

"Now, sweetness, you really are pulling out all the stops. I hope the tales of you trueborns are true, 'cause I got a feeling we're going down under before too long and I got no intention of getting knocked up."

Try as he might, her blatant reference to his actually siring a freeborn child (it could not happen, of course) caused him to flinch with loathing; bile washed up in his throat.

Her knowing look said wonders. Point to her and the battle pulled back more to a neutral ground.

"I told you before, Snow, I will move when and if I feel it is necessary." He spoke in a tone reminiscent of their previous encounter. He would not lose more ground.

Snow gazed at him steadily for several long seconds before she responded, the hubbub of the crowd surging around them, accompanied by the smell of stale sweat and the sickly stench of old age and rot.

"Then it might be of some interest to you to know that I believe someone, or some *ones*, from Beta Aimag recently held a secret rendezvous with elements of Clan Jade Falcon."

Petr straightened up, thunderstruck. "What?"

"Sweetness, do I need to lick out those ears of yours? You heard me."

He reeled, not even registering her comment. They met with elements of Jade Falcon? When, where, how, why? The questions came fast and furious—a fusillade of emerald laser fire, boiling away his calm demeanor.

"I believe the Jade Falcons have invaded The Republic," she said softly, answering his unasked question. She had once more managed to obtain vital information before his own contacts. His own people.

"Sweetness," she began, her voice almost serious, "I'm sure Beta Aimag would have every reason in the world to be in contact with a Jade Falcon force that is right now attacking several worlds in The Republic." She stopped, opened her mouth and tapped her lower lip with her right index finger, as though just now thinking of something. "But, if they have a legitimate reason, why are they keeping the meeting a secret? I mean, considering what a bungled job you've made of negotiations here, you'd think ol' ovKhan Clarke would be crowing the triumph of landing a deal with the Falcons, right? But his own people don't even know about it."

Petr glanced at her sharply at such a statement, read

the knowledge in those words. He also did not for a moment believe she'd *suddenly* thought of this; she had delivered the data exactly as planned. If the information turned out to be correct—he was surprised to realize that, in some strange way, he'd come to trust her—it would change everything.

A new thought blossomed, and a horrifying idea began to coalesce. Something so monstrous and vile he could not suppress the involuntary gasp of his strained lungs.

No. That could not be. Not even Sha would go so far.

As though frozen between one breath and the next, he ran numerous scenarios through his head. Slowly, he realized he needed more information. Had to make his own inquiries among Beta Aimag personnel. And to do so, he must get Sha off-world.

Slowly wrangling his runaway thoughts until they were under control, he looked once more at Snow and stretched a taunt, pain-filled smile across lips abruptly as dry as a godan's scales.

"I believe, Snow, I will be moving to take care of your alleged invasion sooner than I thought.

Her eyes lit up, and she parted her lips, teasing them with her tongue for a moment. "That, sweetness, is what I've been waiting to hear. Anytime you want to drag me under the bleachers, you just let me know."

Still trying to grapple with the sickening possibilities, he looked her full in the face. "Snow, if this information proves as useful as I believe it will, I may just take you up on that offer."

And he meant it.

23

A too-early sun lifted off from the distant tarmac, slowly picking up speed as the ungainly spheroid Drop-Ship gained altitude and velocity. Petr, along with his miserable companion, watched as a second and then a third DropShip lifted: a man-made celestial trinary of fire to prematurely illuminate most of Halifax.

Petr felt warm, though the ships were too distant for him to feel the heat waves of the drives. His warmth came from the glow of misdirection. Of assured victory snatched from the jaws of defeat. Of putting a lesser in his place.

Another handful of minutes slipped by, as the DropShips ascended to the point at which their silver hulls could no longer be seen, only the contrails of smoke and the pinpricks of light that still hurt the eye.

Finally, Petr broke the silence—no sense in salting the wound unnecessarily . . . at least, not *too* unnecessarily. "Master Tidinic, I believe we have some business to conclude. Shall we adjourn inside?

The man nodded slowly. They turned in unison and made the trek to the central negotiation table, past the ubiquitous lowing cattle and shouting workmen, where a handful of both locals and Sea Fox personnel, including Merchant saFactor Tia, were waiting; her averted gaze said she would not soon forgive him for wrenching control of the negotiations away from her when he had been preoccupied and absent for so many weeks.

Deal with it. She had had disappointments before and would have them again.

After everyone was seated, Petr waited; events still pulled at him, but he'd gained some breathing room. Some time to finally, absolutely, close this deal and move on to other things.

Particularly, verifying the truth of Snow's intel.

People shuffled their feet, coughed behind their hands and shifted in their seats as Petr let the silence stretch.

Eyes darting left and right, trying to find an escape that did not exist, Master Tidinic transformed from a raptor to a rabbit. Petr curled his lips at the man's apparent total collapse and finally spoke—time to finish him.

"Master Tidinic, it would appear there has been a reversal. Though ovKhan Clarke won the right to negotiate with you, apparently he is no longer interested in the deal."

"Some of his personnel are still here; I have a meeting with them this afternoon." The words sounded weak, almost petulant.

"*Aff*, that is true. However, I can assure you they are the lowest level of negotiators in Beta Aimag, and can hardly bargain with you without constantly affirming their words with ovKhan Clarke. Something very difficult to do with him out of system."

"They are heading for Stewart," the man said sullenly, accusatorily.

"Really? I wondered at their destination." He managed not to smile at such a blatant lie.

The raptor gaze returned momentarily, as Tidinic knew full well where Beta had gotten its information. "Yes, I'm sure you did. However, whoever let such valuable information slip has to understand the Stewart markets are, to be frank"—he paused, swept his hand around to include the entire beef industry on Adhafera—"much larger. Though we would like to consider ourselves a prize, we are a much smaller catch compared to Stewart. It makes one wonder what value could be placed on our world, which Stewart does not have."

Petr leaned back, ignored the creak of the chair and felt the satisfying pop of his spine adjusting.

Not such a rabbit after all. Good. But I still have you caught in the field, with no cover.

"Master Tidinic, though I am sure I do not know where such information might have come from, I can assure you we also have business of our own that must be attended to." Petr glanced at his chronometer, as though he cared about either the time or the date.

"Both ovKhan Clarke and I answer to higher authority than ourselves, and we have both been delayed too long on this world. A world, at your own admission, which is a small *catch*, did you call it?" Petr quirked the corner of his mouth and watched Tidinic wince at his own error.

Petr raised his hand and a hard copy immediately appeared from the hands of an aide. He settled the paper onto the table, flicked it with the edge of his index finger, sent it shooting across the distance, the stapled pages fluttering like broken wings and spinning askew. *This is how much I care.*

"You will see our new terms, Master Tidinic," Petr said, finally pulling away the glove to reveal the glint of steel beneath. "You have exactly seventy-two hours to respond, before we lift off."

As Petr stood abruptly, turned and moved away with his entire cadre, the shocked looks and uproar that erupted among the local merchants felt very satisfying indeed. Not even the squelch of his boot in a dung pile could dissuade him from his good mood.

A deal ready to seal and Sha out of the way momentarily. Now to find out what he could.

"Jesup," he said, dismissing the rest with a nod, as they walked back into the morning, where the real stellar mass of the system moved behind sullen storm clouds ready to dump their heavy burden.

"ovKhan." His aide attended him as usual, but his voice did not seem normal. Petr glanced at Jesup's face, but could not find anything on which to hang his reaction. Ever since coming to this world, their relationship had become more and more strained. He mentally shrugged.

I will worry about it later. There is too much to do now.

"I need your help. I need information from Beta Aimag, and I cannot get it for myself. It would be difficult, if not impossible, for me to insinuate myself among their personnel even at the local bars they frequent. I take a single step into such a place, and they will clam up tighter than a Lyran fist over C-bills."

Moving to the waiting hoverjeep, Petr pulled himself into the driver's seat while Jesup climbed into the passenger side. He tapped in the start code, and the humming motors sent vibrations up through his body to match the keening pitch from without. Petr spun the small vehicle in a half circle, spitting out a small cloud of detritus, and then poured on the speed as they whipped down the road toward their encampment. The soft-top of the jeep was broken—in the open position—and he wanted to reach the encampment before the potential rain began to fall.

Raising his voice over the chill wind, Petr continued. "I know our personnel mix now and then."

"Really? But we hate each other so."

Petr laughed, the comment *so* Jesup; he was surprised to realize he missed the witty comments of his XO, regardless of their aggravation.

This surprises you because you are selfish.

The words insinuated themselves from the depths of his subconscious. He refused to listen, to deal with it now. If these words were true, there would be time to examine them, to examine his relationships, later. "Regardless of the hatred dividing Sha and me, I know it does not spill down the ranks. You may think I am oblivious to such things, but I am not. I know the lower castes mingle freely, and I am confident the same applies to many of our warriors. I need you to start asking discreet questions."

"And what secret mission, oh great and powerful ovKhan, have you tasked me with?"

The aggravation that rose at Jesup's sarcasm felt familiar and comfortable—almost enjoyable. The voice within him laughed at the thought that he might miss Jesup's attitude if it was taken from him. He swallowed to clear the grit of the road in his mouth.

"I believe ovKhan Sha had a secret rendezvous with the Jade Falcons." A particularly large rut in the road caused the hoverjeep to slew sideways, and Petr missed the flicker of shock that washed Jesup's features.

"Why do we care?" Jesup said. "It would be good to know what deal they might have landed so we can counter it, but why send me? You should be able to get that information just by talking with the lower castes, *quiaff*?"

"*Neg.* The lower castes do not know of it. Most of the warriors do not know of it. Why keep it a secret, especially from his own personnel?" Petr disliked giving Snow her due, but he continued regardless. "Considering how badly we proceeded in our negotiations, would not ovKhan Sha shout a deal with Clan Jade Falcon from the depths of space, *quiaff*?"

"*Aff*," Jesup responded slowly, as though thinking his way through it. Petr flinched as a particularly noxious beetle the size of his hand splattered across the front windshield; it immediately sloughed off the anti-dirt film in rivulets of broken purple shells and almost fluorescent green pulped guts.

"It could be nothing," Jesup finally responded, as Petr moved into the city proper; with so few cars about this early in the morning, he felt reasonably safe in opening up the throttle, shooting the little vehicle down towering mountains of steel (as if local law enforcement would stop them).

"*Aff*. But it could be everything."

"Where are you getting this information?"

"That is not something you need to know." Not even loyal Jesup would likely give Petr the time of day, ovKhan or not, if he knew where such information originated. If Jesup knew of the strange relationship he was developing . . .

"Oh magnificent ovKhan, I apologize if I have offended. This little one is not worth your trouble." The man actually managed to turn and bow several times in the close confines of the hoverjeep. Once more, the words carried humor, and Petr warmed to the friendship.

Perhaps he could allow himself a friendship now, without diving into the deeper questions others had stirred up. Just until he found out what he needed to about everything looming around him.

"Then you will do it?"

"*Aff*, ovKhan."

"Be careful, and discreet."

"I am always careful and discreet, ovKhan."

Petr looked at Jesup and found a wide grin plastered on the other man's face. He was anything but. And they both knew it. As they flashed past the last of the downtown buildings and saw the tops of Delta

DropShips in the distance, Petr knew he did not have a choice.

More important, he knew he could count on Jesup. Had counted on him, without a word of praise or recognition, for years. Though such was the way of the Clans—honor to the Clan for his service—Petr realized now there was another need.

When all of this is done, perhaps I can . . . recognize. The idea trailed out behind him as he raced into a new day.

24

The final deal sat on his desk. Petr enjoyed ignoring it. Master Tidinic surprised him and actually waited the entire allotted time instead of turning it around the same day, which he half expected. Several days now had passed beyond the deadline of when he said he would make a decision and lift off-planet; Petr enjoyed letting the merchants swing in the wind.

Of course, there were other reasons he stayed on planet.

The fleeting pleasure sped away as quickly as it came, and frustration returned to gnaw at him. He had difficulty concentrating and could not bend his mind to what needed doing. Reports and reviews were beginning to stack up. Sickness, downtime, maintenance reports, personnel reviews, lost revenue: he'd be buried under a mountain of paper soon, if he could not regain his efficiency.

The impression of having all the time in the world when he left the Merchant House only days ago departed as quickly as Sha upon learning of the larger, riper markets likely to be found on Stewart. Now the force of time, each tick of each second, seemed to slam into him, rocking him with urgency. He could feel things in motion, great plans put into action outside of his control, and yet he felt nailed to the floor with iron spikes.

"ovKhan," a voice said from outside the small, curtained office in the field tent. Though it managed to keep out most of the pounding rain, noises still easily filtered through.

"Enter." He straightened up. Tried to hide his disappointment when he realized it was not Jesup. The man had reported in once, two days ago, to let him inform him that no leads had surfaced. Nothing since. Where was he? What was happening?

He knew you could not push such things too quickly, but he felt the need for speed.

saFactor Tia bowed into the room, her hair plastered to her delicate scalp, with rivulets cascading down her fully soaked clothing. Though he took a deep breath for a confrontation he had expected some days past, it dawned on him she did not carry the scowl that had tattooed her face for the past week. She actually looked slightly confused.

"saFactor?" He waved a casual hand for her to

make sure the flap sealed tightly, then actually indicated for her to take a seat. "What is it?"

She reached inside her jacket and pulled out a small cube, which she carefully handed over. Confused, but willing to go along, he took the cube, pulled the data reader to the center of the desk, powered it up and slotted the cube.

After a moment's disorientation of a three-dimensional projection spitting snow and hiss, the image of a Fox Clansman (Beta?) materialized: bald head, large ears and eyes and a mouth that wore a perpetual sneer. In a soft voice, the man began to speak.

"saFactor Tia, I regret to inform you I will not be able to make our meeting either this day or any day in the foreseeable future." The man stopped, closed his eyes as though he wished to avoid his next words, then continued after licking his lips. *"There have been several accidents, both within our compound and on the outbound* Cards of Fate, *all resulting in deaths. Though some might believe this simply to be a poor day for avoiding errors, saKhan Clarke is not so sanguine and has ordered all personnel to lift off-planet. He has decreed Adhafera enemy territory and we are to deal with any further security and safety concerns with . . . any needed force."* The man looked positively sick, but finished a last thought before the machine clicked off. *"I hope to see you in the not too distant future, Tia."*

On another day he might have been curious about the relationship of his saFactor (a woman he would not have credited to care about any type of physical relationship that did not impact on the art of the deal) and a Clansman from another Aimag, but the news that all Beta personnel were lifting off-world took his whole attention.

"Stravag!" He slammed his hand down on the table, making the reader leap and tip over, sending the cube tumbling with the same urgency as his thoughts.

How, by the Founder, could he find out anything if they lifted off? He had been handed Sha Stewart, and now he would not get a thing out of it. Unless Jesup had found something. Anything.

"I know, ovKhan. I cannot believe the locals would stoop to this myself. They appear so peaceful and have treated us with respect. It is hard to fathom."

For a moment Petr could not even place her words, he was so wrapped up in his own worries. Then their import bludgeoned through.

The locals. Accidents. He leaned forward and very carefully righted the reader, while reaching across to the edge of the desk where the cube had arrested itself before the sudden drop to the dirt floor below.

Savashri. Now he would lose this deal as well. How many months sitting on this rock and now he might have to lift off without a single card left in his hand?

Could Tidinic or one of his cronies have put this into motion as a last resort to better their end of the deal?

He cradled the tiny cube in his hand, feeling the edges press against his palm, the slick of dampness from its travels here making it cool to the touch. He thought back across those weeks, about everything he had seen. To Master Tidinic's rabbit eyes at the end. Minutes stretched. He knew he should order the liftoff of his own troops. He even considered leaving the trade document unsigned, lonely and bereft on the desk, as punishment for Adhafera turning against his Clan. But his instincts told him something else was afoot.

His mind fastened on that first monstrous possibility that had sprung into existence when he had learned from Snow that Sha may have met the Jade Falcons in secret. If what he believed was true (and he *must* verify his suspicions before going to saKhan Sennet again), then it was a small leap to accept that Sha would cause a few accidents to occur in order to eliminate dangerous loose ends.

Petr himself had occasionally removed an opponent by tearing victory from their grasp right in front of them. But occasionally, he removed his opponent another way.

Regardless of how closely they clung to Clan ways, regardless of their belief that the Clan ways defined them and made them better than their opponents, Petr recognized that Clan Sea Fox had been in the Inner Sphere long enough that "another way" had become an accepted part of the deal. When an enemy could not be removed through the standard trials and rituals of the Clan, other means could and would be used.

Galvanized, he lurched forward, as the idea fully formed. Sha had said the same thing when he visited Petr after their trial; Petr had rejected his words then, as they struck too close to his own history. Yet in retrospect, Sha had plainly told him what he would be willing to do, and Petr had failed to see it. Could not believe it. But now the truth rang like a 'Mech-sized bell hammered with an iron fist.

Sha moved to take down the Khan; he must find proof!

The curtain whipped aside, revealing a haggard and harried-looking Jesup. Tia yelped in surprise and half rose before recognizing the intruder.

Petr almost crushed the cube in his hands as he stared hard at Jesup.

Bitter, ghastly disappointment slid through him at the negative shake of Jesup's head. A panoply of emotions raged across Jesup's face, but Petr focused only on one.

Failure.

Overlord-C *DropShip* Breaker of Waves
Midpoint Turnover, Adhafera

Gravity disappeared in a sickening lurch as the mammoth drive plume cut forward acceleration and the captain initiated a midpoint turnover for the *Overlord-C* DropShip. Several minutes passed as Sha continued to scan the papers he'd been reading (his mind blanked out the four notices that rang the length and breadth of the ship, warning of imminent turnover). Then, with another lurch, which sent the hard copies spinning lazily to fill almost every corner of his office, the drive flare ignited once more, beginning the deceleration burn toward the waiting CargoShip.

A good thing he had not been drinking anything. The thought barely penetrated his bitter mood.

It had to be done.

He kept telling himself that, but the words did not comfort him. His decisions had cost too much, too many personnel. People who could have served the

Aimag, the Khanate, for years to come. People who trusted him to lead, to not throw their lives away without cause. He kept the helm pointed at his target with steady hands, but his heart began to wonder if this truly did lead where he needed to go.

Sha never intended to see so many die, so quickly. Especially at his own hand.

But ovKhan Kalasa was becoming inquisitive, and Sha felt the need to remove his people from Petr's grasp. Especially Elemental Corin, whom he now could not find. And simply removing them off-planet was not enough; they had to be permanently beyond his reach. Sha swallowed dryly and realized he did need a drink. But he needed to destroy most of this paper before an aide could bring it.

He stood up slowly and began to gather the paper. As each report floated in front of him, he glanced at it again. *All I've done for weeks is deal with endless reports.*

Destroy endless reports.

Star Colonel Coleen Nagasawa entered at that moment, unbidden and uninvited. She closed the door slowly. Sha cocked an eyebrow, surprised at her boldness. Then he saw the rage burning in her eyes, in stark contrast to her calm face, and he knew the answer to his question.

Sha casually reached under the desk and pressed a button, which kicked on a white-noise generator. Even among his own Aimag, on his own ship, the words he knew were about to spill did not need to be heard by anyone outside this room.

Enough surgical removal for now. More than enough.

"What have you done?" she demanded quietly.

He nodded slightly at her cool tone; his years of work with her to obtain such objectivity had reached fruition. She had been trained to keep her emotions at bay when making a decision, and she could do that now, regardless of the hate or anguish or despondency that tried to engulf her at this moment.

"What I must."

"What you must. What you must." Her voice rose a pitch and stopped. Her clenched fists popped with tightly wound tendons.

Sha bent and began to pick up the papers, which fell like large, dry snowflakes. Though Coleen knew most of his plans, even she was not privy to the full scope; he needed to destroy some of these before she could become aware and feel compelled to make a decision she would regret.

"What you must. But they were Aimag." The sudden look of confusion that drooped her eyelids and slackened her mouth momentarily pulled at his own emotions, echoed his own thoughts.

He did not answer, but continued to shuffle the hard copies, trying to recapture the order he so carefully had given them earlier. He could then feed them all into the incinerator.

Finally, when Sha refused to repeat himself or elaborate, she took a single step toward him and raised her arm. He would never know what she intended to do, but he simply looked at her.

Though a small man, short and slight of build, Sha possessed a look as cold as the voids of space, which could blast through any defense, harrow a soul, freeze a self-image—ultimately shattering.

He stopped her with a look.

Sha turned back to his papers, finished his reorganization and then, and only then, turned back.

"We have agreed this can be the only way, *quiaff?*"

After a long silence, she finally responded in a low voice. *"Aff."*

"Then we must stay the course, *quiaff?*"

She hesitated another moment before replying, *"Aff."*

At that moment, he experienced an epiphany. Suddenly, he understood her reaction, and though he lost a degree of respect for her, he also felt more confident of her. He understood that now he held the upper hand, not just as her ovKhan, but in every other way. Now he could keep her in line. Keep her from making a foolish error.

"I trust *you* completely," he said. "You need not worry."

She flinched as his words shot straight toward her true concern: her own safety. If it became known that she possessed such an unClanlike characteristic, her position as Star colonel would become . . . uncomfortable. He could feel her anger (read: fear) dissipating as the strings he tied to her wound tight once more.

That she could lack the courage to embrace death yet rise to the rank of Star colonel in spite of it, actually increased his trust in her. His instinct to include her at the beginning was rewarded by the knowledge he could move with more freedom with her at his back.

She is more spheroid than Clan.

He could see her self-loathing. His new understanding of her weakness should have made him sick. Instead, he smiled gently.

230 Randall N. Bills

She turned her face away, though her shoulders lost some of their slump. *Give acceptance with one hand. Take away self-respect with the other.*

Everything is a compromise, Coleen. Everything.

But Sha knew she'd known that much longer than he. Reminded now, he firmed his resolve.

He felt more committed than ever.

25

Halifax DropPort, Halifax
Vanderfox, Adhafera
Prefecture VII, The Republic
10 September 3134

Petr tried to decide if the torrential rains were preferable to this soupy mist. Because moisture was not actually falling, you believed you would not get wet; but in the brisk walk between buildings or vehicles on the hard tarmac of the DropPort, the dampness built up until you were covered in a fine layer of water. Most of the drops maintained their cohesion for a certain period, then suddenly soaked your head, and everything else.

He was not sure his mood could be more foul.

"ovKhan," Jesup said, coming up from behind him as he stepped into the Command HQ vehicle, which sat almost three hundred meters from the closest of Delta's DropShips.

He noticed that Jesup somehow managed to keep mostly dry and cursed under his breath. "What?"

"Most personnel have reported in. We have an exercise running out beyond Tumbled Heights, but word has gone out to all troops."

"About time. What has happened to our discipline? How did we grow so lax?" He moved around inside the main briefing room and squelched into a seat at the holotable, disregarding the water saturating the seat and now soaking through his pants; he waved a hand at his aide to take a seat as well.

"Sha lifted off in, what, less than six hours? We should have done the same."

"He did not take all of his forces with him."

"*Aff*, but I wager he could have if he intended to. We have been here too long."

"Then why would he wait to leave until the sabotage by Adhafera terrorists? I disagree. He could not have lifted off so quickly."

The musk of their warm, damp bodies quickly pervaded the interior, mixing with the stale sweat of years of use, creating a miasma he'd almost gotten used to. He shivered.

Aff, a sure sign he'd been downside too long.

He ignored Jesup's insistent belief in the Adhafera terrorists. Petr had broached the topic at least a half dozen times with the man, and he refused to acknowledge any other possible explanation. Considering what they had seen together over the years and the impossibilities made truth before their eyes, Petr was infuriated by his obstinate refusal to even entertain an alternative. It confused him, made him wonder, briefly, if Jesup *needed* to believe in the terrorists for some reason.

In fact, it dawned on him that his aide's usual sarcastic mockery no longer echoed in his every word. It was as though something had stripped away, or at least blocked, his capacity for looking at the world with cynicism.

The cacophony of a thousand autocannons burst across the tarmac and drove all such thoughts from his mind. He jumped for the door, ignoring the rain; Jesup followed.

Outside, the first of the DropShips began to lift off, illuminating the late-night darkness.

"About time," he said again, aggravated by his reaction to the liftoff. He had ordered it, and the captain had informed him it would occur soon, so he should have expected it. He was jumpy. Upset.

After a moment, Jesup said glumly, "I hate gravity. I cannot bear to think about how horrible two gravities will be. *Stravag* Sha for pushing his DropShips to such extremes."

"He must believe we would pursue him as soon as we knew he had secured the Stewart information." *Does he have a clue about the rest of what I know— what I suspect? Is that why he ran so fast?*

But he must know I will follow him to Stewart. I have to wring information from him I can present to Sennet. Or is Stewart a diversion and he flees elsewhere?

He shook his head, moved back inside and sat down, turning on the holographic table, which sputtered to life, showing the entire Adhafera system with the estimated whereabouts of Beta's ships; both the first group with Sha himself, as well as the smaller group that departed later. He ran some numbers and realized Sha's JumpShip transport must be available to depart the system immediately upon his DropShip reaching the nadir jump point, leaving a second ship to depart with the second group; he hoped—vainly he was sure—that Sha would not be able to remove all of the forces from the system for another two days.

It would take Petr ten days, perhaps a day less, to intercept Sha, but pushing at two gravities for the entire haul. Petr rubbed his hands together, almost wincing at the aching tendons and joints that would result from such punishment, especially for a Clan used to long years of microgravity.

A small price to pay to stop Sha's plans. To stop him from shattering Clan Sea Fox.

"What are you going to do once we catch him?" Jesup asked in a small, deadly serious voice.

Gazing up into his aide's serious eyes, Petr wondered the same thing himself. Had been wondering since he made the decision to lift all available forces off world and head out after Sha.

He felt pulled. He was reacting to events as they unfolded rather than controlling the situation; he had felt this way for weeks. He hated that sensation and knew such strategies always lost. If he hoped to find victory, hoped to do something beyond following Sha around as though led by the nose, failing utterly to stop him, he must seize the initiative again.

But how? *That* question did not yet have an answer.

He opened his mouth to reply and blackness

stepped into the doorway, as though detaching from the night itself.

Jesup glanced over his shoulder to find the source of the absurd look on Petr's face and immediately threw himself out of his seat toward the back of the room, spun into a low crouch and sized up the situation.

Clothed in a pitch-black sneak suit with night-vision goggles dangling around the neck, totally drenched (probably why none of the area's IR sensors squawked), the short, stocky intruder moved with lethal grace. The Shredder heavy needler pistol swung in perfect arcs, one-two-three, checking the room, placing targets, before sliding back on straps to a hoisted position under the right arm, easily pulled into position if needed. Though the gun almost looked too large for the intruder's stature, Petr didn't doubt for a moment the efficiency with which this person could use such a weapon. Every action, every muscle movement radiated competence and lethality.

Death dressed to kill.

Though the intruder's eyes were difficult to see in the shadows playing across the doorway, they were visible.

Smoky eyes.

"*Savashri,*" Petr breathed, unable to restrain himself. He had known all along, though he never admitted it, what she likely must be. But her profile, the body that did not fit her movements, all allowed for easy denial. Allowed him to lead himself astray.

Now, however, the strange emotions he had felt at their last meeting coalesced into something more, something he could not ignore. Respect? Admiration? Esteem?

Aff. And more.

Though the traditional Clan warrior within warred with the vision of the obvious special forces persona before him (such dishonorable tactics!), the tough merchant-warrior respected any acumen, under any circumstances.

And acumen she held in abundance.

"I see you recognize me, sweetness." Her sultry, almost naughty tone and the breathless chuckle that came with it, so incongruous with the walking assassin standing in the doorway, pulled a return chuckle from him before he could stop himself.

She looked pointedly toward Jesup.

Petr stood, turned to look at Jesup and watched a war between confusion and horror on his face.

What in the Founder's name is going on? Jesup's unasked question practically rang out in the silence.

The implications of Jesup's response crashed down on Petr like a tsunami. Sharing a coquettish chuckle with an obvious spheroid special forces intel agent? A dishonorable assassin? *Aff*, that would go over very well indeed with his Aimag. If Jesup was having a hard time buying it, he shuddered at the thought of the rest of them swallowing such behavior.

But he'd come this far, trusted this much. Events were moving too quickly for regrets. Like a true Clansman, he simply moved to seize the moment. Perhaps her sudden appearance heralded the ability to act, not just react.

He turned back to her. "Why have you come, Snow?"

She casually stripped off her mask, her wet locks framing her face, those amazing eyes. A grunt from behind brought Petr's head around again to see the look of extreme distaste Jesup wore.

Petr slowly turned away from Jesup and his mind illuminated with an epiphany. Much to his astonishment, at some point, he had stopped seeing her as he did at their first encounter. Though this was only the third time they had met—their banter, her obvious intelligence and military abilities—they all stacked up to change his perception. She was not, could never be, beautiful, or even pretty. But she had transformed from his initial impression of ugly to . . . striking.

Those smoky eyes.

Her gentle smile told him she had read his emotions on his face. And with no Clansman able to see his face, he did not care; he returned the smile for a moment.

A shared promise for a future they both knew could never be.

The rumble started low and then built to a crescendo, rocking the vehicle gently, an illumination briefly flaring outside, before fading. The second DropShip lifting off brought them both back to the reality of their situation. Of the here and now and the responsibilities they could not ignore.

"What have you brought for me?"

"Oh, a fine wedding present, sweetness. A mighty fine present. You just wait a moment and I'll be back." She slipped into the night as though parting shadows. The sudden silence in the vehicle felt louder than the burn of the DropShip.

"That"—Jesup broke the silence after only a handful of breaths—"is where you have been getting your information." "Sweetness" hung suspended in the air between them as though carved from 'Mech armor.

Petr had never heard Jesup speak in such a deadpan voice, as though his emotions had been stripped and painfully flayed from within. Petr did not turn, not wanting to face it. Responded softly.

"You have trusted me through honor and disgrace, across a dozen worlds and more. You must trust me now." Years of taking this companion, this friend, for granted yawned before him.

He felt he might shatter from the stillness. He should have brought Jesup in from the beginning. Should have done so many things, which had escaped him.

Which he took for granted.

Sha's face rose before him. Though he still emphatically believed Sha to be heading down an irredeemable path, some of his words held truth. Petr *was* lying to himself. Placing his desire above that of his people. Above his Aimag.

Above his friends.

For a moment, he embraced the ache that blossomed and threatened to overwhelm him. He luxuriated in the pain, finally understood the depth of the redemption he would have to undertake. Then he took the ache and wrapped it around and back down, spiraling it, sending it down into the depths, to be dealt with another day.

A day when the fate of his entire Clan did not hang in the balance.

Just then the darkness split asunder and Snow returned, moving fully into the vehicle. Behind her, wearing nothing but short briefs, an elemental stepped up and into the HQ, rocking the vehicle as much as did the DropShip. He bent over considerably to fit through the door. Though his head would have brushed the ceiling if he stood straight, the man bowed himself, as though his mental spine (his self image) were shorn away, torn from him. Slack lips formed a perpetual "O" of surprise, and his eyes darted this way and that, like Tidinic's, trying desperately to escape, but with the full, horrifying knowledge none existed.

Petr looked in dismayed revulsion at a Clan elemental, bearing few physical marks, reduced to such a state. Snow snapped her fingers and the elemental immediately went to both knees, cradling something in his hands. Jesup's grunt of disgust echoed his own.

He looked at the smug expression on Snow's face and once again found himself torn between two emotions. He felt awe for her ability to break an elemental, and revulsion at seeing the epitome of the Clan eugenics program brought low by a spheroid.

Smoky eyes.

If he thought about those conflicting emotions too long, he knew which side he would come down on. The rest of his Aimag would never understand.

"What . . . is . . . this?" The slow, drawn-out words from Jesup scraped across the room, heightening the tension. Petr could almost feel Jesup's hands reaching toward Snow's neck with delusions of snapping it; there could only be one outcome to such a gesture, and Petr would hate to lose a friend he only recently came to appreciate.

A chair scraped loudly across metal as Snow pulled

it out from under the vehicle's holotable, placed a booted foot on it. "*This* is the proof you have so desperately been seeking." She raised her chin, a clear challenge to Jesup.

He did not rise to it, though Petr swore he could hear Jesup's teeth grinding.

"Snow," Petr said, trying to refocus the moment, "what is it?" In all their eyes, the elemental had lost his human status.

"This is Corin," she said, caressing his head as though petting a favorite dog. "He and I have had many long, long talks. You Clanners are so stoic, but once I get to know you, you can't shut up." She batted her eyes in his direction. "Right, sweetness?"

Petr cleared his throat, actually uncomfortable. Could she make it any worse? "Please, Snow, get to the point."

"Oh, the point," she began. "Well, that would be the fact that this here fine specimen happened to accompany ol' man Sha on his sabbatical to the Falcons."

"What!" both men cried simultaneously. With avid hunger, Petr appraised the elemental in a new light. Proof! The proof he needed.

Then he contemplated saKhan Sennet's reactions. His probing questions. *Any answer can be dragged out through torture.*

Snow smiled a look of pure triumph, which transformed her face. Victory made anything, anyone, beautiful. She gently tapped him on the head, and the elemental opened up his hands, raising what he held. The dim lighting of the flickering holotable revealed a small, mechanical plug-in, like a small noteputer memory cartridge. It took a moment for them to recognize what they were seeing.

"Savashri!" Petr growled, triumph washing over his face. He looked at Snow again and once more they shared a fleeting moment, her blazing eyes matching his, their emotions raging across the short distance between. Though the storm still blew in, they just might have found the shield to ride it out.

A battle armor ROM memory core—the elemental had worn his armor during the meeting.

26

Location Unknown
12 September 3134

The uniforms gleamed in the sun, royal garments for the homecoming ceremony.

Two DropShips were already aloft; the third loaded the final 'Mechs and vehicles, battened down hatches, performed final systems checks and secured vehicles into their bays in preparation for liftoff.

The forces had gathered from across dozens of light-years to this rendezvous point: an out-of-the-way world, with no working HPG, the only inhabitants subsistence farmers on the northern continent who would not know a landing DropShip from a falling star, much less an ascending one.

Secrecy.

The commander hated it, yet understood the need. She wanted to crow to the stars that, after long decades, the return had begun. Wanted to shout about the successes achieved so far. Could feel the need churning, the desire to challenge someone, anyone.

Soon, soon enough.

The men and women chosen for this mission shared her desire: the snap of eyes, quick movements, lips firm with resolve. Knowing the prize they reached to grasp, fully aware of the difficulty of the challenge.

But victory, oh, victory would be sweet.

Would teach the renegades a lesson they would not soon forget.

After decades of enforced peace—a peace that benefited only the despotic and the moneylovers—the time had come to challenge, to grasp the fruit from the forbidden tree.

Time to seize destiny. Time to shake the universe. Time to reclaim the honor lost.

Time for war.

27

Clan Sea Fox CargoShip **Voidswimmer**
Nadir Jump Point, Adhafera
Prefecture VII, The Republic
21 September 3134

Warning Klaxons blared down the length of the
CargoShip, strident, demanding instant action to avoid
catastrophe. The tone and frequency of the bursts sent
personnel running in every direction. Some took up
emergency stations with practiced calm, others fum-
bled in confusion; aside from drills, such a warning
had not been heard in the lifetime of most of those
aboard.

Incoming JumpShip . . . Voidswimmer *within the
projected KF-drive emergence bubble.*

"What in the Founder's name is happening? How
is this possible?" Petr bellowed from the bridge of
the CargoShip, forgetting the impropriety of such an

outburst on Star Commodore Konner's vessel. His status as ovKhan did not excuse his behavior.

The bridge personnel ignored him. Unlike so many of the civilians on board the vessel and in the pod communities on the attached DropShips, they knew their jobs by rote and responded with instant action.

In a pendulum counterpoint to Petr's bellow, Konner's voice remained calm, cut through the bridge hubbub and the siren like a diamond through glass—a sound that could not be ignored. "Full thrust on my mark."

The collective indrawn breath of those present filled the bridge with the pummeling heartbeat of the entire Clan Sea Fox *Voidswimmer* community. In an instant, the tens of thousands on board his community paraded before Petr's mind's eye; their scramble to prepare for impact or thrust would not be enough. Regardless of shipboard discipline, such an event simply had not occurred in too many years and people had no time to take the correct precautions. Things would not be completely stowed. Individuals would be unable to sufficiently secure all items, including themselves.

There would be damage.

Numerous injuries.

Fatalities.

"Three, two, one. Engage, maximum thrust." As though driven by the vocal synapses of Konner's voice, the pilot's arm responded instantly, cascading across a series of switches and buttons, before initiating a full burn: maximum power.

Like a beast suddenly thrown into heat, the entire ship thrummed, shook; vibrations undulated the length of the keel, sending secondary reverberations out along the main struts on each deck, the shockwaves whipping out into the skin, which oscillated well beyond allowable stress levels.

Small breaches on two decks occurred immediately.

As the mammoth interplanetary drives pummeled the ship forward under gravities not experienced in decades, three more small breaches occurred, while power failures plunged several decks into darkness.

The mass of the CargoShip made the move seem almost miraculous. Petr imagined he could see the fabric of space splitting along the bow of the ship: a snarling swirl of raging space water, torn from its placid calm and thrust into a maelstrom that arced around the ship and into violent vortices in the ship's wake.

Seconds ticked by as the behemoth vessel tried to slough off the chains of gravity and inertia and launch itself into motion.

At a command from Konner, the main viewscreen split into two sections: the left side showing forward, the right showing rearward toward the incoming JumpShip, toward their potential doom.

Petr's hands clenched the edge of his jumpseat. Though he was the ultimate leader of the community, in such crises the ship's commander took absolute authority. Petr hated feeling helpless.

Though the crew attacked their tasks relentlessly, with Konner issuing numerous commands sending personnel toward hull breaches and power failures, all eyes stayed glued on the rear viewscreen.

Not enough thrust. Petr ground his teeth, his muscles aching after so many days at double gravity to reach the jump point quickly.

For the first time, he regretted downgrading the *Voidswimmer*'s massive drives, now striving through old grit and disuse to push out a paltry two gravities; the disharmonic pings and odd thumps reaching his ears reminded him (as if the bucking of the vessel itself did not) that the *Voidswimmer* might not survive such abuse. Slowly, achingly, she picked up forward momentum.

Sweat beaded across his face and fell toward the back of his head.

The seconds ticked into minutes and then long minutes. Velocity increased. Though wretched, horrible sounds still spanned the length of the CargoShip, Petr could feel it acclimatizing to the punishment, adjusting to the pounding rhythm of the fusion drives.

As Petr's mental clock reached fifteen minutes, a wretched smile stretched his face. When the tortured time dilation tipped the scale at twenty minutes, he began to laugh out loud a wheezing of tormented air. Though he knew his laughter was raising hackles around the room, he could not stop; his was the laughter of the damned.

Delicious irony. The man I am most desperate to see arrives days ahead of schedule and might just kill us all in the process.

His frenzied laughter reached a crescendo, filling the bridge as the universe vomited an ArcShip from its belly, tearing at its only reality, spewing forth an emergence wave of pain, suffering, anguish, before sealing its wounded shell and vanishing once more from human perception.

Delta Community (the *Celestial Thirst*, an aging *Behemoth*-class DropShip attached to the *Voidswim-*

mer for long decades) took the brunt of the damage. Most of the casualties occurred there and the docking ring, regardless of its carbon-carbon reinforced struts, crumbled and partially tore, shifting the entire ship during the mad forward thrust. Then, as the incoming emergence energy shattered atoms all along the front of the wave, the ship actually lurched forward, for a brief burst obtaining a velocity it never achieved even before its transformation. Though the hard work of Fox Clansmen engineers in decades past kept the ship from completely tearing away, it listed radically, throwing objects and personnel from their stowed positions. These became projectiles fired as though from a gun, causing massive damage inside the old ship and hundreds of casualties. Though the other DropShip communities and the *Voidswimmer* itself sustained some damage, of the four hundred and thirteen injuries, more than three hundred of them occurred in Delta Community; of the twenty-seven deaths, nineteen.

They all got off lucky.

For the second time within as many months, Petr moved along the corridors of the *Poseidon*. Blind to the humanity around him, he swam with the relentlessness of the hunter. Ignored the sights and smells in which he usually took such pleasure.

The *almost* death of a good portion of his Aimag opened his eyes.

As with the epiphany concerning Jesup, Petr's eyes were opened to the uncompromising truth of his own hypocrisy. For so long Petr had believed himself to be doing the best for his Aimag.

When in reality, he worked for himself.

That Delta Aimag truly prospered under such leadership meant nothing. Such thinking by Sha was how they arrived at this day, this hour. This moment in time.

The ends justify the means. Or in this case, my *means justify the ends.*

Stripped of every charade and rationalization by such a close brush with the annihilation of most of Delta Aimag, he could not avert his eyes from his own selfishness. From the way he took his own people for granted. Their cares, their worries and fears, their honor and contributions to the Clan: all cast aside and ignored. By him. The ovKhan!

Now, as he pushed off one last stanchion and sailed toward the saKhan's main office on the *Poseidon,* he did not ignore the people around him because their regard was nothing more than his due, but because of a duty to fulfill, a mission to accomplish.

A fine line, but one that made all the difference in the world.

Petr rapped sharply on the hatch, which swung in almost immediately. A haggard face greeted him; he'd never see saKhan Sennet look so terrible.

"ovKhan Petr, what occurred," he began, holding up a hand as though to stay a strike of condemnation. He paused, continued. "I cannot begin—"

"saKhan," Petr cut him off. "What almost occurred was a mistake . . . but it is the past. We must now move quickly to the future. We must move, or our Clan may be sundered beyond redemption."

He risked much with his words; one did not cut off saKhan Sennet midsentence without good reason—

accidental near-annihilation of Delta Aimag or not. His rage visible in his eyes, saKhan Sennet angrily demanded, "What are you talking about?"

"ovKhan Sha, saKhan. He lifted from Adhafera a week and more past, and we are giving chase. He must be stopped." Petr stood just inside the hatch, his strained muscles pounded by multiple gravities for endless days calling out for rest. For sleep.

Disgust swam out from deep eyes to envelop the man's face; a giant hand flicked, as though to cast away an unseen filth. "Not this again," he began, the scorn in his voice a mirror of his visage. "You risked what you did on a whim? On your own assumptions of ineptitude? I have never made such an error before, but with you . . . a Trial of Grievance, here and now, is the only way you might survive this disaster." Though the volume did not change, his voice hardened like endomorphic steel extruded from one of their many orbital factories; worlds might shatter against such a force of will.

Petr took the verbal whipping without a wince and walked past saKhan Sennet, his magnetic boots clanging softly, to the other man's desk. Reaching into a hip satchel, he pulled out the battle armor ROM memory core along with a small reader. He placed the machine on the desk, where it audibly clicked with suction. Fitting in the core, he flicked the switch and took one step back. He did not turn toward the saKhan, unwilling to watch his reaction, his surprise.

Hopefully, surprise.

Petr tried not to think of the ramifications if this were not a surprise. Of the quick and brutal death at the other man's hands if he guessed wrong.

The scene played out. He had only been able to bear to watch it one time before this. The art of it, a thrust to the midsection.

Audacious. Brilliant. Brutal. Terrific, and terrifying. Sha's plan encapsulated all a Clan Sea Fox merchant aspired to accomplish. To be. A hundred generations of teaching and refinement led to this. The sheer genius of it all simply took the breath away.

Yet, ultimately, it was traitorous. Destructive. The breaking of what made Clan Sea Fox . . . Sea Fox.

As the feed clicked off and the machine autoterminated its power, Petr slowly turned toward saKhan Sennet; for just an instant, the back of his neck itched, as though he waited to feel a hand descending in a strike to send him into ultimate oblivion.

Horror illuminated Mikel Sennet's features in harsh lines. Petr let out a breath he had held unknowing. Though Fox Clansmen, as with any merchants, knew when to hide their hand, Petr did not think such emotion feigned. It was too primal; Sennet was truly stricken.

Eyes locked onto Petr's like laser-guided landing lights. In those depths, the stunned disbelief read like a holofax in fifty-point type, able to be read from across the room. The man actually staggered slightly, tried to right himself and managed to unlatch himself from the floor. He swept his arms and legs back and forth futilely; a clumsiness embarrassing under any other circumstances went unremarked as his brain consumed what he'd just seen, unable to devote energy to fine motor control.

After a pregnant pause, full of strained anger and incredulity, Petr broke the silence. "My saKhan," he began, as formal an address as he ever gave Khan Sennet, "there can be only one course of action. We must find the Khan. We must mobilize the fleet we have at hand and begin to move from system to system along the path he is likely to take."

Licking his lips, Sennet began to nod slowly: a child coming out of the darkness with the realization he can turn on the light. He can act.

Petr felt like pushing forward, yet realized he might go too far too fast. He must allow Sennet to come to grips with this. To see the urgency himself and make a decision.

After what felt an eternity, Sennet responded, "*Aff.* Yes. We must move to protect the Khan." Regaining his feet, he mastered himself, bringing his emotions under control and superimposing the ubiquitous Fox merchant caste mask.

"And what of Sha?" he asked, his voice once more as hard as a ferrous-nickel Gauss round, with eyes to match.

Petr's eyes mirrored the savagery; his voice was a sentence of annihilation. "One *Scout* JumpShip. My personal Trinary.

"Leave him to me."

28

A new world. New possibilities.

ovKhan Sha Clarke felt more confident than he had in days. Gazing out from the top of the off-loading ramp of the grounded DropShip *Breaker of Waves*, he could see the cityscape spread out before him, moving away from the DropPort into the distance: a surrealistic matte painting.

A twisting skein of metal, ferrocrete and high-strength polymers: man-made stalagmites rupturing the planet's crust; spreading scintillating, serrated bones to the lapis lazuli sphere swathing Stewart.

In his years as a trader, Sha had beheld many cityscape vistas. Many that eclipsed New Edinburgh in

size, or height, or population, or any number of parameters. But the jagged, strange design of the city's
largest buildings and its odd, twisting streets, set
against such a magnificent dome of a sky, with literally
not a single puff of white to pull at the eye (a *stravag*
relief after the endless cloud cover of Adhafera), ge-
stalted into a striking beauty all its own.

A light breeze—a touch harsh—carrying the dry
aroma of desert sage and the ubiquitous reek of petro-
chemicals found in any city in the human sphere, caressed his nostrils.

Familiar, yet alien. Comforting.

Yes. This must be a sign. A change. A move to the
future. Here deals would once again be quickly struck.
Here his plan would reach fruition. Here mistakes
could be put at a distance. Forgotten.

No, never forgotten: you learned from your mistakes. No, they could be put into . . . perspective.

"ovKhan," Coleen said, coming to a stop slightly
behind him.

He did not respond immediately, still drinking in the
sights and aromas like a man deprived of sensation.

Finally, forever-cool eyes swiveled to take her in,
his voice a chill wind in counterpoint to the warmth
of the breeze. "Any news?"

"From the planet, ovKhan?" She had always
avoided using his first name, but after Sha had learned
her secret, Coleen retreated completely from him,
wrapping formality around her like armor.

*If that is what she must do in order to not fail, then
so be it.*

"*Neg.* I already reviewed all three messages from

Earl Stewart, as well as one terse message from the legate. Other news."

"*Aff*, there is news."

He waited, but she held her peace for several long seconds. *She still attempts to kick against the manacles.* His eyes narrowed.

Petty. Perhaps he would have to deal with her after all. A pity.

Finally, she responded, "We picked up a transmission that was broadcast into the clear by a tramp freighter that jumped in-system a few hours ago. They came from the Adhafera system."

"The ship that precipitated our Trial of Possession?"

"I do not know, but it is conceivable."

"It does not matter." He looked away and shifted his stance, feeling the solid thud of his boots against the metal deck—the pull of a large gravity well. "The transmission."

"What by their description can only be an ArcShip jumped in-system at Adhafera, where a collision nearly occurred. The Delta Aimag DropShips burned toward the jump point with undue haste after our departure. They were in the process of maneuvering to jump when the ArcShip arrived."

"An accident."

"*Aff.* It is difficult to discern from their barbaric descriptions, but it would seem the *Voidjumper* managed to escape serious damage to all but one of its DropShip communities."

"Is that so?" They could have been discussing the price of beef, or the transfer of personnel between ships, instead of the potential death of tens of thousands of Sea Fox personnel.

The death of ovKhan Kalasa.

Gazing into the sky, searching to pinpoint the location where the Adhafera jump point would be visible from his position were it night, Sha could not help the sigh that escaped his lips, a small, soft decompression of resignation.

A loss to the Khanate, but it might have been best in the end.

He swiveled back. "And?" He could tell she held back more.

"Shortly thereafter, a frenzy of DropShip transfers took place between the waiting JumpShips and CargoShips, then a spasm of jumping. The *Voidjumper*, despite her damage, jumped." She paused a moment, swallowed.

Afraid to say it? He knew her next words.

"Before the tramp freighter jumped, all that remained were the ArcShip and a *Scout*-class JumpShip." She finally turned toward him and several seconds passed as unasked questions fired like synapses, quick, decisive, angry.

His turn to hold out, despite the obvious question burning her lips; she grew visibly agitated. Finally broke the silence, though to her credit she kept her tone level.

"You know what this means, *quiaff*?"

"Perhaps."

She tried to stare him down for such a response, but could not. She blinked, spoke. "*Aff*, ovKhan. *Aff*. You know what this means. They know. They have discovered the plan and are scrambling even now."

He shrugged lightly, dismissed all of Kalasa's efforts in one brief muscular twitch. "We cannot undo what has been written. Only deal with what might be, or what is coming. I am still not convinced they have the whole plan." For once, however, Sha did not even believe himself. Such activity rarely occurred and after their own quick departure. . . . No, it did not bode well.

"And if they come here?"

"Then they come."

She closed her eyes momentarily, as though marshaling strength to forge ahead. Spoke again without even opening them. "They will fight us." She did not see the look of disgust that washed his features.

"We have fought them before," he replied, abruptly moving down the ramp as though that ended the discussion.

"ovKhan," Coleen called out, her voice rising. Massive vibrations ran through the ramp, sending shocks up into his groin and standing the hair on his neck on end; for an instant he imagined them coming from the tread of Coleen. From the questions she would not give up. From Kalasa's footsteps, thudding through the cosmos, looking for him.

He squinted, angry at such fantasies, and continued down the ramp. He heard the servo whine of the first 'Mech unlimbering in preparation for patrol duty around the grounded DropShip fleet.

"ovKhan," Coleen said again, her voice urgent. She pulled abreast just as they reached the hard tarmac of the spaceport and kept pace with Sha, who was walking briskly toward the command vehicle, debarked almost as soon as the fusion drives were extinguished. "They will fight and this time will be different. This will not be a Trial of Possession or Grievance or even a Ritual of Combat. They know and they will come to annihilate. A Trial of Annihilation!" Fear coated the word with desperation.

He stopped abruptly, rounded on her and raised his voice fractionally—the equivalent of a shout for anyone else. "Then . . . we . . . fight." She stopped as though poleaxed by a 'Mech fist, her mouth dropping open, eyes wide, wild.

Sha hardened his gaze until he could have carved his words into lamellar ferro-carbide armor, his voice a tornado to shred any resistance. "I have told you, what we do comes with risk. Great risk. And if they come to fight, then so be it. I have bested Petr and will do so again. In the end," he finished, unable to refrain, "you are Clan. A battle should be relished, *quiaff*?"

"But they will come with overwhelming force," she managed to mewl. He didn't expect a real answer, but Sha felt disappointed despite his expectations. Her fear diminished her ability to think. Dangerous in one who knew so much.

"No, they will not. The *Scout* ship is for us. The rest will be hunting for the Khan, trying to stop the inevitable. No, Petr will come alone, and with a smaller force than what we wield." He slowed his breathing, brought his emotions back under control, leashed his blue eyes and the power of his personality. Coleen sagged after the onslaught, as though an arm pinning her in place had been jerked away.

"If you think clearly for a moment, you will remember that any merchant worth his salt has plans within plans. My cards have not yet all been revealed." She looked up at that, and then turned as a technician rushed toward them from the command vehicle.

Sha turned to follow her gaze, and frowned at the unseemly haste. Petr could not be here this quickly. What else could be happening? Nothing that required such a state of frenzy. Sha was on the verge of opening his mouth for a reprimand, but the man's words robbed him of any such desire.

"ovKhan, DropShips inbound as we speak, orbital insertion already begun."

"What!"

"We have multiple contacts, verified. Cocoons already in interface, with numerous DropShips in stages of descent."

"I told you," Coleen said vehemently, the note of victory in her voice warring extravagantly with her panic.

He hardly heard, concentrating on the hard copy the breathless tech thrust into his hand.

"How were they undetected?"

"We do not know, ovKhan. A pirate point. Disguised as local traffic. Either might explain it. A tap on the legate's channel confirms agitated voices; we have not yet broken their encryption, though one would assume they are as surprised as we."

Perhaps he had truly underestimated Petr after all.

The words seemed to echo in Sha's brain, reminding him too much of his flight of fancy a moment ago. Frost practically cracked his lips as he smiled cruelly, suddenly relishing the fight to come. He did not notice the tech blanch at the killer's look that filled his eyes.

Let Petr come!

29

A skein wove slowly, intricately through the stars—a net to capture the elusive prize.

Starting at Adhafera, the first strands jumped to the Savannah system, where those ships with lithium-fusion batteries immediately jumped again to the Bordon system; a lone ship jumped to the Dieudonne system, where rumor said a lone Sea Fox JumpShip held station.

Those that did not immediately rejump unfurled kilometer-wide sails and began to drink in the universe's life energy. Yet they could not wait the one hundred seventy-three hours for a standard recharge. Instead, tight-lipped commands were issued. Nervous technician castemen massaged controls; sweat-slicked palms eased safety parameters. The onboard fusion reactors spiked as the energy draw siphoned off into the Kearny-Fuchida hyperdrive. Each ship sought to shave some sixty percent off the normal charge times, but the forced quick charge might be catastrophic. A drive damaged by the force-feeding of such mammoth energies might blow during jump initiation or discharge violently upon arrival; either would strand a JumpShip for long weeks, if not months (averted eyes spoke volumes of the simple disappearance into hyperspace such measures might precipitate).

The skein continued to grow as sister ships met in transit were immediately tasked with the great hunt. Tendrils stretching out blindly, hunting, covering every possible location, avoiding the thought of a dead system jump.

The horrific beauty of the Castor trinary system, with its mammoth red giant and its evilly, brilliantly white twin sisters.

Blazing-hot Zosma, with its sparse system and monthlong intrasystem travel to a habitable planet.

The Dubhe binary: a cool orange giant and its lonely, pale yellow main sequence companion, orbiting a scant twenty-three AU.

Each system felt the pinprick of quantum mechanics and human ingenuity shred reality for a strained heartbeat, before the materialization of a JumpShip, the infinitesimal alteration in each system's solar winds as sails rapidly deployed.

Each future day sluicing into today's frothing rapids, flowing into the flatlands of the past and soon to be history saw Sea Fox JumpShips hitting additional systems.

A web interconnecting each world in a frenzy of need.

Birthed on Adhafera, it grew into an unfolding weave that flowed into an ever-widening cone, moving through most of Prefecture VII, into the interior of Prefecture VIII and sweeping relentlessly into Prefecture X.

The ilKhanate had to be found, the ilArcShip located.

The Khan saved.

30

Clan Sea Fox DropShip Ocean of Stars
Near Orbit, Stewart
Prefecture VII, The Republic
26 September 3134

"**W**hy again are we holding station?" Jesup asked; the strain in his voice transmitted as a shout, yet Petr did not look up.

Jesup stood restlessly across from Petr in the main cargo hold of the converted *Overlord-C* DropShip. Originally designed to carry an entire Cluster of 'Mechs (Petr shivered to contemplate such a force of BattleMechs at his disposal), it now transported mostly cargo, with only a mixed Trinary of units left— a skeleton compared to the glory of years gone by.

Petr ignored Jesup for the moment—the echoes of focused activity as that small military force readied for action falling away as well—and continued studying the small holographic table between them.

Tapping the controls lightly, Petr zoomed through several regions of Stewart, what they were able to tap from the satellite comms. Enough to show the wicked battle raging in at least two different areas around New Edinburgh. Petr coughed, tasted the snotty phlegm coating his tongue and grimaced.

Am I getting a cold? The fate of Clan Sea Fox hangs in the balance and I'm getting a cold? He frowned in frustration, ignored his own vulgarity in his anger.

Jesup's anxiety—he practically hopped from one foot to the other like a warrior ready for his first Trial of Position: a warrior who would lose with such impatience—peeled away Petr's concentration layer by layer. Forced him to glance up, regardless of his wish to ignore the question.

Petr finally sighed, turned off the machine, which immediately folded back into the wall, straightened to a ripping crack of vertebrae. "You seem to be questioning all my actions of late. Demanding answers when I have already made my reasons clear."

Jesup leaned toward him, as though to keep the words between them. "I would not need to ask for such clarifications if your decisions made sense."

Petr stiffened. Felt the rage he had almost lost across the last week flare up, bringing a familiar warmth. "In case you have forgotten, *Jesup*, I am ov-Khan. I need not explain my actions to you. You follow my orders." He bit off the last words as though taking a mouthful of Jesup's hide. He knew the rejoinder before the words emerged from the other man's lips.

"*Neg*, ovKhan. Your great and powerful person *does* need to explain itself to me. Or I, like any of those under you, may decide to call a Trial of Grievance, *quiaff*?" Though the words came coated with his usual sarcasm, Petr noted, to his chagrin, that nothing touched his eyes.

Have I estranged him so much? Has our friendship gone so far afield? Petr closed his eyes for a moment, wished he knew how to undo enough of the damage to satisfy his aide until there was time to truly repair their relationship. To implement the changes he finally understood were needed. Yes, Jesup should serve the Clan and serve his ovKhan, but Petr had come to realize that by taking such for granted . . . he might as well be a spheroid.

But the time was not now; later, (had been saying that too much of late) he would fix it later.

He opened his eyes, and his shoulders slumped slightly at the admission. "*Aff*, Jesup. *Aff.* We stay in orbit because we do not have sufficient forces to defeat what we will face on-planet. We hold station until the forces on-planet have been weakened enough that we can make a difference."

Jesup cocked his head to the side, confirmation and disgust warring for dominance on his face. "You hide," he said.

Petr jerked as though slapped. Words of denial flooded his mouth, but he choked them off by refusing to open his lips. He refused to add lies to a situation that already sickened him. Already forced him to question everything he believed about being Clan.

Clan Sea Fox knew the trials, rituals and traditions of the Clans were flexible—guidelines to be bent and twisted when needed in order to further their goals. But this went beyond twisting, or bending, or winding . . . this stank of shattering.

"We have no choice," Petr finally responded.

"There is always a choice, *quiaff*? Have you not told me that again and again?" His strident tone changed to that of a pupil reciting rote text. "A Sea Fox merchant makes choices every day. And none are trivial or insignificant. Each has a consequence that will unfold for the benefit or detriment of the Clan. It is you who must decide."

Petr sniffed, felt the *savashri* phlegm at the back of his throat, focused on not gagging for a moment (subconsciously knew the gagging reflex stemmed from his current decisions as much as his cold), nodded his head. "*Aff*, Jesup. But there are times when both choices lead to detriment, and only by measuring the degrees can you know which is the lesser of two evils."

"You sound like a spheroid." A momentary lull in the general noise of the cargo hold allowed the words to be heard by innocent ears; stunned faces turned to watch the scene unfolding in the far corner.

Petr's rage burned hot and bright, filling his eyes with a fire he directed first at Jesup and then swept the large cargo hold, sending personnel scurrying about their business. His ire, though directed at Jesup for allowing their heated discussion to spill to the lower castes and the rest of the warriors, found equal target in himself; Jesup's words mirrored Petr's own thoughts too closely for comfort.

He took two steps toward Jesup, his heavy magnetic boots dragging at him like the load of current events strapped around his neck. "Then what would *you* do, Jesup?"

"Attack. Now. That is the Clan way."

"And if Sha defeats us? Or if we are caught between them and the Marik forces? We would be crushed."

"Then so be it. Such is the way of the Clan. This hiding"—he swallowed, licked his lips as his eyes darted, trying to find a target—"I cannot abide it."

"Then Sha escapes."

"Others will hunt him. He may hide, but others will find him, will hunt the deep currents and run him to ground."

Petr had to get through to him. Must make him see. The time for justice was now, not later. "What happened when the Bears made such a decision? When Clan Ghost Bear let those most deserving of Clan justice escape?"

Jesup reared back, his jaw falling open at such a comparison. At the memory of the Not-Named Clan and the total annihilation they escaped . . . the havoc they wrought.

"Would you let such happen again? Look at what he has done right under our noses. Imagine what he might accomplish hidden from view. Imagine what he might unleash against our Clan. *Mark my words*, Jesup," Petr said, trying to infuse each word with the hellish energy of a particle cannon, tried to ram it past the other man's doubts and fears. "He will not be satisfied until he sees the Clan shattered for destroying his dreams of rebellion." *Me shattered.*

Jesup looked like a cornered animal. "He would not do that," he finally said.

Petr's eyes went wide. "You defend him? After all that he has done!"

"You consider it misguided, but he has done what he felt best for the Clan. What every Sea Fox Clansman has done for centuries. He has made decisions."

"Yet you're the one saying each leader must answer to his superiors."

"Do not throw such vulgarity at me," Jesup said, straightening, regaining some of the spine Petr thought knocked out of him.

Stravag. "Each leader must answer. Now I am coming to give him his Trial of Grievance over the decisions he has made."

The two eyed each other across some gulf that Petr could not see. Finally, as though losing the will to continue such a battle of words, Jesup turned away. "So be it. In a Circle the rightness of his decisions will be decided."

Petr felt unsure how to answer; he was further distracted by the harsh stench of spilled diesel. "Then you understand the need to wait. To even attempt such a Trial of Grievance, their force must be brought closer to the strength of ours." Though he hated himself for it, Petr wanted Jesup's approval. An understanding of the path he chose.

"Aff." The tone carried a half dozen flavors. Could be taken any way Petr wished.

Dissatisfied by the answer, but realizing none other would be forthcoming, he sighed, coughed again, sniffed hard and felt bands of light pain bind his forehead. "Tomorrow, Jesup," he said softly, moving toward the small medstation. *Must find something for this* savashri *cold.*

"We shall move tomorrow at dawn. And then it will be done."

Petr did not know if the words were for Jesup. Or himself.

31

Near Stewart DropPort, New Edinburgh
Lothian, Stewart
Prefecture VII, The Republic
27 September 3134

With the invading forces of the Marik-Stewart Commonwealth running headlong into the unforeseen presence of most of Beta Aimag, and the on-world militia splitting along lines of loyalty to The Republic (led by the legate) and loyalty to the old House Marik—forces determined to fight alongside the invaders (led by the earl)—the battle for the world of Stewart devolved into utter chaos within hours, as the multisided conflict spilled heavy blood on all sides before the sun set on the first day.

With careful planning, Petr unleashed his mixed-force Trinary in the early dawn hours several days later, the sun just peeling back the veil of night, piercing curtains and wooded thickets with equal diligence. Weather reports from satellites—and mean temperature averages gleaned from a quick stab of the electronic finger into planetary weather databases—showed a bright, crisp morning in the offing. Hoping to catch the combatants tired and worn-out, and using the dawn attack—a classic tactic since the beginning of warfare millennia in the past—Petr set down near the largest remaining concentration of Beta Aimag personnel, prepared for a quick and decisive victory . . .

. . . and all hell broke loose.

"I have contact, sector 3A, twenty-two by four. Approximately eight hundred meters. Coming fast." The disembodied voice seemed to materialize within the confines of his cockpit—a spectral entity to accompany the snow-thick fog that layered the entire region so thoroughly that Petr felt as though his *Tiburon* was pushing handfuls of the stuff aside just to move.

"I copy, Garo. Do not engage unless they leave you no choice."

"*Aff*, ovKhan." The voice carried about as much confidence as that felt by a Knight left by the disorganized Republic to face a Capellan onslaught.

No plan survives contact with the enemy. The aphorism did not help in the slightest.

Petr felt the drag of the cables behind the neurohelmet momentarily as he leaned forward slightly to toggle from magscan to radar on his secondary screen. He shook his head and swallowed roughly; phlegm caught for a moment, and he swallowed it with a grimace. Looked at the jumble of markers staining his screen like toys randomly thrown from a child's hand, clenched his jaw to open a secondary channel.

"Jesup, where are you?" The commline remained silent, his call on their private channel dead as well. He opened up the general frequency and called again.

The world strobed to brilliance, as sun-hot energy flared within the fog, washing his forward viewscreen into total whiteout; even protected by the polarization of the viewscreen and his neurohelmet, he blinked several times to clear his vision. Afterimages of a particle projector cannon-stream roping through the air, crackling with savage energy, left his eyes aching. It missed by scant centimeters.

Petr cursed loudly, stomping down on pedals (left, right, left, right) as he threw the throttle full-forward; the whine of the gyro setting into the base of his skull like an angry hornet as the *Tiburon* jinked wildly to his commands.

"Where the hell did that come from?" he raged, turning a quick eye to his radar, trying to determine why his attacker didn't show up. With casual ease, even considering his hastiness, Petr raised the 'Mech's right arm and flashed off twin heavy medium lasers in the general direction from which the shot came. The fog almost rolled back from the hellish orange energy streams as they tore through the air, hopefully backing off the opponent he'd not yet identified.

He ground his teeth. With the mangled confusion of the assault broken up by multiple sides and the heavy fog, the computer's IFF tags refused to accept the input that Beta Aimag personnel were the enemy.

Sudden shapes loomed: spectral corpses rising from the ground, reaching out toward him with large skeletal claws to rend and tear. Startled, he had both 'Mech's arms up and blazing away before the small copse of trees fully registered in his forebrain. As he unclenched his fist, cursing himself for a fool, he watch as several trees collapsed, sections cleanly, surgically removed, while others remained afire.

The abrupt tone of incoming fire pierced his skull and years of training sent the 'Mech swiveling one hundred eighty degrees and dropping to a low crouch, the giant left hand digging deep furrows into the loam for balance as a quartet of missiles spiraled down, finding him unerringly regardless of his preternatural move. Armor detonated into shrapnel and debris as the streak missiles found ample targets across the *Tiburon*'s chest and its left arm.

This time, however, through the shifting sheets of cottony white, Petr glimpsed a shadowy shape backing away and to the left of his current position. Without conscious thought, frustrated by his inability to find his tormentor, Petr launched forward from the crouched position—a sprinter flying off the stops, almost gaining air before the heavy treads tore into the ground, gaining purchase and sending the 'Mech careening toward its target.

A quick left-right flick of the targeting reticule sent a brace of missiles to either side of where Petr saw the ghostly 'Mech-shaped opponent; he hoped to corral the enemy and keep it off guard. A sudden dip in the terrain dropped his stomach, causing his gorge to rise (the phlegm slick did not help) as he actually rose slightly out of his seat, only kept in place by his five-point harness. The *Tiburon* slammed down into the depression with bone-shattering force, then continued on.

Petr cursed at the pain of having bitten his tongue,

cursed again as he just managed to miss a large boulder that he swore sprouted from the ground like a giant toadstool. Readying another curse, he instead clamped down hard on a threatening cough and felt satisfaction as his elusive prey finally presented itself: a *Panther* tried to imitate the boulder recently left behind, springing up from a low-lying position, weapons blazing.

Through luck or good maneuvering, the *Panther*'s most devastating weapon swung wide, its arcing energies reaving an arc of death past his head. The missiles, however, proved more accurate, with an avalanche peppering his 'Mech. Weathering the storm of metal, Petr brought his own weapons to bear, firing off quad short-range missiles and an equal number of heavy medium lasers. With the accuracy that had landed him a command slot right out of his Trial of Position, three of the four lasers found their mark, carving a scar of runnels over the right torso; they burst past the outer armor and savaged the interior as the missiles followed up with their own explosions.

A bright light blossomed within the gaping wound, seeking to escape. The top of the *Panther*'s head blew away, the command couch rocketing to safety as the streak missile ammo detonated, carving the 'Mech cleanly in half. Bringing his dangerous mad dash to a more manageable level, Petr closed his jaw, which hung open in stunned shock.

Already well damaged. The fighting must have been truly intense.

He passed the burning wreckage, trying not to think about the parafoil even now deploying and bringing a Sea Fox Clansman down to the ground. His Clan. His

Khanate. No Rituals of Combat, but battle to the death.

Neg. He must avoid such thoughts at all cost.

Unclenching his right hand, almost rigid with stress and pain, from around the targeting joystick, he pumped several fists and rotated the wrist; popping tendons told of still too little strength in his right arm. As with his thoughts, he ignored the dull pain throbbing through his right shoulder. It would live, as would he.

"Jesup, where are you?" he called once more, trying to locate his XO, bringing the *Tiburon* to a full stop as he concentrated on his secondary display.

They had set their DropShip down scant kilometers from the DropPort. With air cover nonexistent and the fighting winding down, Petr felt the risk worth the prize: a quick victory. But in the chaos of a three-sided (and sometimes four-, whenever some of the on-planet militia decided they wanted to change allegiance) conflict and the *savashri* fog, they'd been splintered, lost.

From some of the others he could accept such ineptitude, but not from Jesup. Regardless of his faults and impatience, the man held real tactical sense. Should not have become so lost.

"Jesup, do you copy?" he said again, opening the commline to the general frequency once more, regardless of how insecure it might make the rest of his troops feel. He must locate his aide and then begin to pull his forces back together. Back together, to move against Sha.

"ovKhan Kalasa, so nice of you to drop in uninvited." The voice blossomed in his ears with its usual coldness, a clamminess that fit the austere, fog-wrapped landscape like a Kuritan fit his blade. "Then again, I did drop in uninvited on you last time, so I guess it is only fair you return the favor, *quiaff*?"

Though his left fist clenched immediately on the throttle, eyes scanning the radar screen and magscan as he toggled back and forth, Petr realized he simply could not untangle the mess of smeared images across the screen; Sha could be any of them.

Unclenching an aching jaw, he finally responded, "But, Sha, you did invite me."

"Oh, how so?"

The hint of levity sent Petr's vision red. "By your actions. By your desire to sunder Clan Sea Fox, you invited me."

"And what actions would those be, ovKhan Kalasa?"

"Your collusion with the Jade Falcons to murder our Khan." The words rushed out of him, as though too large for his body to hold any longer. They took on a life of their own, growing until Petr felt they rose over the battlefield, almost over the entire world of Stewart, screaming to the universe of Sha's horrible perfidy.

Silence stretched long, leaving Petr alone, enclosed within his own tomb of white. After some time, a chuckle sounded across the line; he stiffened. The affront simply proved everything. Sha did not try to deny the words. Did not try to rationalize or convince Petr of his actions. He simply laughed. For a moment the rage welled up and he shook, felt as though he would tear the joysticks from their mounts.

"Petr," Sha said. The familiar form of address only

strengthened his anger. "I am surprised at you. Such a spheroid term. If I shot him in the back, then you could accuse me of such an act. But my actions? I simply arranged for a test. A Trial of Grievance, if you will, against our *beloved* Khan. If he passes, so be it. I am proved wrong. But if he does not—and I for one, believe he will fail—then I am proved right.

"Is that not, ovKhan, the essence of the Clans? Might makes right."

Petr felt his nose itch, wriggled his face and sniffed hard, grimaced again at the slickness sliding down his throat, coughed.

"Are we getting a cold, ovKhan? Not very warriorlike, eh, Petr?"

"You twist the ways of the Clan," he began, ignoring the snide remark. "Such trials are for within a Clan. You do not, in secret, contact someone outside of the Clan to enact a trial you yourself do not dare declare. You cannot—"

"And what if I had, Petr?" Sha broke in, raising his voice slightly, catching Petr off guard. "I told you the day you lay in bed after your defeat at my hands, the Khan would have ignored my requested trial. saKhan Sennet would not have moved, no matter how much convincing I might be able to do. I have heard of your constant spouting of 'choices,' ovKhan. Well, I have made mine."

"Then you have made them to your own defeat."

"And who will defeat me? You? Have I not already defeated you?"

"*Aff*," Petr said, slowly beginning to move his 'Mech forward once more, pinpointed Sha's location on his radar. "You did defeat me, which should make your acceptance of this Trial of Grievance easy for you."

"And if I wish to simply continue battling? Regardless of the interruption of the Marik forces, I still have superior numbers. And, ovKhan, a wonderful move, that. Just wonderful. Worthy of myself."

The chuckle felt like a tossed gauntlet, hard and unyielding as it slapped his face.

"Then you would be as selfish as you have accused me of being." Petr swallowed, closed his eyes momentarily and realized he must make the admission. Must goad him into single combat. To resolve this, so the rift could be healed. Much more of this brutal fighting and the remnants of Beta Aimag might never be fully integrated back into the water's embrace.

"And, Sha, regardless of your misguided efforts, I must thank you. You were right. I have been selfish. My actions have been geared toward my own glory and not that of Clan Sea Fox. Not that of my people. For that, I will make sure your memory lives on . . . for me."

Another lengthy pause swallowed the moment, while the whine of gyros and the thudding of 'Mech footfalls accompanied the *Tiburon* through the fog.

You are right there. Petr kept his eyes alternating between the graphic display of the radar and his forward viewscreen. Light flared ahead, sunlight streaming in, as though eating away the fog like a virulent pathogen consuming flesh.

"I never thought to hear such an admission from you," Sha responded, his voice subdued almost to a whisper.

"We can all learn from our errors. I certainly have learned from mine. Will you learn from yours?"

"Ah, reverse psychology." The chuckle once more, cold and unfeeling. "But *aff*, ovKhan. I will accept your rebuke and your conditions. I will end this here and now. All my hopes and plans placed in the balance of might makes right. The Clan way, *quiaff*?"

"*Aff.*" As he responded, the *Tiburon* stepped from the edge of the fog as though it were sheered away by a glacier: one moment darkness, and the next, not a hint of cloud in a lapis lazuli vaulting sky and a sun reaching zenith, pounding down with brutal brightness, sparking tears despite the polarization in his viewscreen. Some five hundred meters before him, as though they knew exactly where he would appear, a handful of 'Mechs and vehicles waited, Sha's *Sphinx* in front.

And slightly to the left, the unmistakable outline of Jesup's *Thor*.

32

Though his boots smacked the damp ground with firm reality (water vapor steaming from the ground in every direction under the merciless onslaught of noon), Petr felt his head no longer attached fully to his body. Instead, it became a balloon, tied to a ten-meter cord, bounced, jounced and jangled in a stiff gale, as he slowly began walking toward the gathering of Beta Aimag personnel.

Though most Sea Fox trials involved hand-to-hand combat—a result of so much time aboard starfaring vessels—Petr particularly felt the burning need to face down Sha, to look the man in the eyes as he defeated him. Still, it had surprised Petr for a moment when

Sha actually agreed, until he remembered his wounded arm.

No surprise at all, an excellent tactical move.

Tears coursed unfelt down his cheeks at the too-bright light. Eyes too used to the playfulness of Adhafera, whose sun beamed momentarily from behind an endless slate comforter before quickly hiding its face—a toddler laughing mischievously, hiding until the next moment to take someone unawares with its brightness.

The smells of the new world could not dent the numbness wadded around him. Not even his anger, which should have been white-hot and searing, could penetrate the depths of his malaise.

Jesup.

Petr's feet followed a course presented by his subconscious brain while he continued to float, to spin lazily, to withdraw in denial.

Not the treachery, anger.

Not the seemingly unClanlike behavior, bitter disappointment.

His detachment hid a deeper emotion, one he could not bear to face. He had finally, painfully come to grips with his failings, had finally recognized how much his aide—his friend—was a part of the fabric of his life. Now, to have that foundation destroyed, to have the source of his pain flaunted in front of him by the man who sought to destroy his Clan . . . hiding was the only option.

The last distance passed as a dream. One moment Petr crossed the distance, and in another eyeblink he stood before Sha and his confidants. Those who tied themselves to his plan and to the ultimate consequences. Unblinking, he gazed at the crowd, his brain automatically editing the image: a human-shaped black outline in their midst cut out by his own eyesight.

With the words he wanted to say damned up tight, Petr stood motionless, unblinking, unfeeling, uncaring.

He once told someone he would do whatever it took to stop Sha. Whatever it took.

Now, standing in the bright sunshine, he had no shade for relief, no shadows for protection from the harsh consequences of his actions, from the recognition of the true cost of the butcher's bill laid upon the scales. Despite his smothering numbness, the cold, analytical merchant brain summed up the columns of debts paid and owed and came up with a balance sheet in the black. Every individual in front of him would cease to exist, paying for their crimes of treachery with their life . . . and against the continued existence of the Clan, there could be no comparison. No compromise.

Yet the personal price . . .

"Is something wrong, ovKhan Kalasa?" Sha finally broke the tableau, his cool features quirked into the semblance of a smile—a predator toying with its prey. "Has your cold gotten the better of you?"

Petr opened his mouth to speak, but nothing emerged; moths of despair had eaten their fill and fled.

"Well, I believe that flu has him under the weather. Perhaps he is not nearly as strong after our last encounter as he believed. *Quiaff*, Jesup?"

"*Aff*," came a muffled, soft reply.

Petr quivered for a moment as though in a palsy, before stillness returned. He did not wish to hear that name, hear that voice. Simply to the fight and be done with it.

"A Trial of Annihilation," Petr spit his challenge through frozen lips. "Now." A gasp from a woman to Sha's right caused Petr to transfer his gaze momentarily, before returning his concentration to the only opponent who mattered.

Sha's eyebrows rose and his thin-lipped smile stretched into a ghastly grin. "Annihilation," he said, as though tasting the word for its weight, its power. "And I thought we were simply here for grievances between friends."

"It cannot be any other way." His shoulder ached with a hint of the pain to come; as with all else, Petr ignored it. "There can be no other way."

"There are always other ways, other choices. Jesup has told me often of the choices you have made. Of your prattle *about* choices. *Quiaff?* You make a choice. I make a choice. We all make a choice. There are always other ways." Sha glanced back over his shoulder, focusing on the person Petr fought desperately to ignore, turned back and began moving toward him. "Jesup made a choice some time ago. Saw what I and so many others have known for so long. Saw you using all around you without a care for their potential beyond numbers on a balance sheet." He stepped into the large circle quickly inscribed into the ground. "Amazing what a hand in friendship can do."

The crushing weight of that statement slammed through all the defenses he had carefully erected. Cutting straight, a saber thrust true to the heart.

Petr slowly swiveled his head (felt like the ratchety

swivel of a worn gun turret zoning in to target) toward Jesup. The other tried to avoid his eyes, then seemed to suck in a breath and stare at him across the distance. Petr tried to find something within those depths to explain what happened, but he already knew. Knew and did not want to face it, any more than he wanted to face Jesup's betrayal and the ultimate cost of that choice.

A memory from what seemed a lifetime ago surfaced. He had finally found Jesup without words; the *wallowing* almost broke him.

I did this. His callous arrogance would kill a valuable asset to the Clan: a valuable asset to him, a friend.

He stepped into the circle.

"Trial of Annihilation," Petr said again. The words carved themselves in fire in the afternoon sky, unretractable, unforgiving, unrelenting. If Sha lost this battle, all those who stood with him would die, as would any sibkos carrying their genes. Every ounce of blood, every splice of gene that carried their tainted code would be spilled, expunged from the Clan's genetic repositories and breeding programs. A surgeon's practiced slice to remove the malignant tumor.

Such, after all, was the way of the Clans.

Such would be the way all would perish, the way Jesup would perish.

Sha nodded once, finally; a moan from amid the onlookers was the only sound.

Petr simply walked slowly toward Sha, who dropped into a low, stable stance, hands outstretched.

"You still do not look well," Sha said. "Should we call a break first, have some fusionnaires to deaden the pain in your arm?"

Petr hesitated, confused. This talking did not fit Sha.

Several scenarios rolled around in his head, but none could find purchase to materialize. Too much cotton still left, too much numbing and distance. He shrugged slowly, moved again, uncaring of the quick darts left and right made by Sha.

Almost within arm's reach, Sha took a quick step forward and jabbed three times in succession at different parts of Petr's body. Hammer right, chop left, thrust straight.

Petr countered each with a smooth deflection of hand and forearm, though a hair slower than Sha. Although Sha had a slim frame, his muscles were whipcords of strength and speed.

Taking a half step back, Petr tried to better gauge Sha, but felt hampered by his mind's continued lack of interest. Of simple curiosity. It had utterly shut down upon learning of Jesup's betrayal, was not yet recovered. He simply didn't care. Yes, he would do his duty; he would save the Clan. But how he got from here to there no longer held interest for him.

Whether *he* got there, he cared not at all.

As though sensing easy prey caught in the shallows, Sha slinked left, trying to place himself into Petr's right quarter and the weakened arm. Petr, still slack faced and unemotional, made no move to counter the tactic. With a twist kick and spin, Sha hammered a blow in toward Petr's midsection, which his years of training deflected with a raised inward right leg and swung right arm; the dull ache spiked alive, a dragon awaking from slumber, unsheathing claw and tooth.

The two moved smoothly back and forth, trading blow for blow, with Sha landing more often, all concentrated on the weakened right side.

Through Petr's disconnected haze, the shocks felt distant, delivered to a body viewed at arm's length, outside of himself. Blood ran down a face not his own from a roundhouse splitting open skin under his left eye, right hand curled in three broken fingers he did not feel, torn ligaments in the right shoulder an outcry for a different face and name.

Three times he fell and each time rose.

The look on Sha's face waxed and waned, from confidence, to arrogance, to frustration and now verged on something Petr could not put his finger on. Regardless, the fists and feet moved with preternatural speed, continued their incessant attempts to knock him down. To keep him down.

Though Petr delivered his own set of badges in return, he fell behind the damage delivered with gusto by Sha.

A particularly savage uppercut slipped past Petr's ineffectual right-hand guard, connecting with his jaw and lifting him clean into the air before dropping him like a 'Mech with a destroyed gyro, splayed, to the ground.

Head ringing, fireworks exploding in eyes wide with anguish, Petr responded as his mind immediately rolled its disconnected body enough to the side that it could gain a purchase and began to lever itself back up.

"Stay down, *surat*!" Sha panted, standing at a kick's distance. "Admit your defeat."

Petr slowly swiveled swollen eyes in his direction, briefly felt the sting of sweat in the corners of his eyes, the copper hint of blood from broken teeth and torn gums.

Tried to understand the look on Sha's face. Surprise. No. Fear? (Not a hint.) Disbelief. No, more. Awe.

Slowly maneuvered himself back to his feet, stood swaying for a moment; not even his mind's indomitable will could ignore the massive trauma to his body indefinitely. Loss of blood and pain brought blackness that threatened to sweep away his cares.

Deep within the confines of such uncaring, a spark of Petr remained. The spark that cared. The spark that knew he had already paid the ultimate price for stopping Sha, for his own arrogance. Knew the price of his body a small notation on the balance sheet in an already giant column.

Clumsily moved forward.

"Stop," Sha said again, grunting with his own pain and effort. "Admit defeat!" he thundered; Petr stopped in stunned disbelief at the completely out-of-character outburst. Another note entered Sha's voice, something Petr could not place right away. Through the shrouds of pain that lay across his brain like a veil, it slowly surfaced: a cork popping up from too much pressure.

Respect. Honest, true respect. A warrior acknowledging the valor of another.

Creasing split lips, spitting out blood and a tooth, he gazed at Sha. Switched the gaze momentarily to Jesup, who stood impassively watching on the sidelines; dual epiphanies sprang into existence, grew and intertwined with verdant, desperate need. With understanding.

Nothing he could do would change the pain of Jesup's betrayal. You could not expect someone, not even a Clansman, to serve for nothing; yet he made a choice as well.

Petr had already defeated Sha, shown him and those who followed him that whether Petr lived or died, regardless of the distances grown between the Khanates, the spirit of the Sea Fox Clan could not be broken, would never be sundered, not by forces without and certainly not by forces within. Realized that this strength flowed in him, could be tapped when all else failed.

Straightening, smiling, without anger, without pain or bitterness for the first time in long weeks, Petr responded, "*I* am Clan Sea Fox."

Dragging in a deep breath to lungs starved of life, he launched one final assault.

Epilogue

The data cube fit in the palm of his hand.

Petr arrived at his command cabin from Delta Community—assessing the ongoing repairs, pleased with the speed of recovery—where the passage of Fox Clansmen still flowed around him, but the distance no longer ensured he would never be touched; nor, if jostled, would there be abject horror and obsequiousness.

Nor did he take such as his due, now truly conscious of those around him. Of their moods, their desires, likes and dislikes. Of how he might make a difference. Wanted to reach out to grasp a shoulder here, an arm there, shake a hand or two. To ask how they fared.

How their lives progressed. Were they acclimatizing to the changes?

But too much, too soon. They might retreat into past attitudes and customs. No, he must take it slowly, as he must take the recovery of his body, having pushed it to the brink.

Sitting in the familiar chair with its quirks and creaks, he clenched his fist, felt the cube bite. Yes, times for speed and times for sedateness. All just a matter of degrees. And right now, all aspects could use a little slowing down.

He peeled his fingers from the cube one at a time, a fruit revealing its luscious pulp. A heavy sense of déjà vu swept him and he expected the door to open to reveal a smiling and sarcastic Jesup informing him of the repairs to the *Starmoth.*

Petr felt an ache. Knew neither those smiling eyes nor even a genetic legacy would ever lighten someone's countenance again. Knew that, unlike the pain in the muscles and ligaments of his ruptured shoulder, that ache would never truly heal. That scar he would carry a lifetime, a reminder of his own failings.

To keep him from making the same mistakes again.

Petr moved the data reader in front of him and placed it atop the report he received yesterday from the ilKhanate. A summons to the Khan's presence. Whether for good or ill, he simply did not care. He did his duty for the Clan and he wished for no reward or special treatment. In fact, he almost hoped for a punishment. For the lives he squandered, the resources lost to the Clan.

The lost friends.

With a weary sigh, growing more nostalgic and less

bitter every day, he slotted the cube into the reader, the warm hum setting the hairs on his right hand on end; ozone sat heavily on his tongue momentarily as the machine buzzed and sparked before the image clarified, springing into view.

Maintenance lying down on the job? He smiled before the familiar ache of his rage could even echo. *Or did I forget to submit a service work chit?*

Smoky eyes swallowed him, while a throaty voice carried him away.

"Hey, sweetness, you sure do give mixed signals. One day we're talking wedding and dreaming about the night after and the next you leave me at the altar? Now what's a girl to think?"

Petr chuckled, gently (lest the recently unwrapped ribs protest too much), realized the view centered only on her face, showing nothing below her neck. Different from her previous communiqués.

"Now I think you just got cold feet, sweetness, and deep down you just can't live without me." She actually brought up her right-hand index finger—the chewed nail exquisitely detailed at this scale—and tapped her pursed lips. "As such, I guess I'm willing to forgive you. There's more than a ghost of a chance we'll meet again, sweetness. And don't forget the flowers and chocolates. I love chocolate."

She winked and his smile grew wider.

"Now let's stop beating around the bush and get down to some serious stuff." Though she tried to rearrange her features to be serious, Petr could see the amusement of the whole affair sparkling in her eyes like distant nebulas viewed from the observation deck. "It would seem you managed to stop the Marik invasion cold, though to be honest, it seemed they really didn't put their heart into it. Makes you wonder if this was a litmus test."

He'd thought the exact same thing.

" 'Course, your Khanate paid the price for stopping it. Then again, I guess you stopped ol' Sha from taking your Clan apart from the inside out. So you did yourself a favor more than you did The Republic one."

The thoughtful look, as though she actually contemplated going back on her word, might have worked for someone else. Though their time together had been short, he knew her. Knew her in a way he never thought to know a spheroid. She simply liked to play; it was her way.

She smiled brilliantly, and once more the striking gray eyes glowed, outshining the holoprojector itself. "No, I suppose I'll keep my word to you. If you need aid from The Republic—if you need *me*—just put a call out to Snow through your contacts . . . and you'll find a data cube waiting for you when you least expect it." She turned her head away slightly, then back, glanced down momentarily as though truly trying to decide if she would speak again. Finally, looked back up at the camera and slowly licked her lips before continuing.

"You know, sweetness, you sure were hot to trot to know who I worked for, but then you simply let it drop. I don't know about your Clanner girls, but us spheroid females, we like to keep our secrets . . . but we like you to keep asking, regardless of how many times we tell you no." She paused, smiled that wicked grin that never failed to raise his hackles. "And I just might be naked. Right now. Just thought I'd give you something to dream about until the wedding night. Bye, sweetness." Her smile grew to fill his world and suddenly the message ended, her face dematerializing, dropping away into his past as surely as Jesup, Sha and the events of the last months.

His jaw dropped open momentarily; just when he thought he'd taken her measure and knew what to expect, she could take his breath away *that* easy. Petr slowly lowered his head to the desk. Slipped both hands back across his bald pate; the one side filled with scars, the other surgically altered so no hair would grow. Visible scars for the ones underneath, prices paid for his choices.

On the verge of sighing, he suddenly laughed out loud, the good-natured sound bouncing and echoing in the small room, the first such sound from him in too long; his world filled with smoky eyes.

Somehow, Petr knew she did not belong just in his past. After all, she made her choices as well. Made them boldly and clearly for those with eyes to see.

About the Author

Randall N. Bills began his writing career in the adventure gaming industry, where he has worked full-time for the last eight years. His hobbies include music, gaming (from electronic to RPGs to miniatures to all those wonderful German board games), reading (of course) and, when he can, traveling; he has visited numerous locations both for leisure and for his job, including moving from Phoenix to Chicago to Seattle, numerous trips to Europe, as well as an LDS mission to Guatemala.

He currently lives in the Pacific Northwest, where he continues to work full-time (and then some) in the adventure gaming industry while pursuing his writing career. Randall has published four novels and two *Star Trek* novellas; this is his fifth novel.

He lives with his best friend and wife, Tara Suzanne; their precocious son, Bryn Kevin; their utterly adorable daughter, Ryana Nikol; their wonderful new son, Kenyon Aleksandr; and an eight-foot red-tailed boa called Jak o' the Shadows; not to mention George the Sneaky, the mouse that didn't get eaten.

MECHWARRIOR: DARK AGE

A BATTLETECH® SERIES